THRAXAS
and the
ELVISH ISLES

By Martin Scott

THRAXAS
THRAXAS AND THE WARRIOR MONKS
THRAXAS AT THE RACES
THRAXAS AND THE ELVISH ISLES
THRAXAS AND THE SORCERERS

THRAXAS
and the
ELVISH
ISLES

Martin Scott

www.orbitbooks.co.uk

An *Orbit* Book

First published in Great Britain by Orbit 2000

Reprinted 2001

A CIP catalogue record for this book
is available from the British Library.

ISBN 1 84149 002 4

Typeset by Solidus (Bristol) Ltd, Bristol
Printed and bound in Great Britain by
Mackays of Chatham plc, Chatham, Kent

Orbit
A Division of
Little, Brown and Company (UK)
Brettenham House
Lancaster Place
London WC2E 7EN

CHAPTER
ONE

It's well past midnight and the air in the tavern is thick with thazis smoke. In front of me the table is groaning from the weight of money in the pot. Every week the Avenging Axe plays host to a game of rak, but there's rarely been this much money riding on a single hand. There are six of us left in and Captain Rallee is next to bet. He stares at his cards for a long time.

'I reckon Thraxas is bluffing,' he says, and pushes forward his fifty gurans.

Next to him is Old Grax the wine merchant. Grax is a wily card player. He once won a thousand gurans off General Acarius, and General Acarius is universally acknowledged to be the finest gambler in the Turanian army. It's never easy to read Old Grax's intentions. From the confident way he slides his money into the centre of the table you might think he's got one hell of a hand. I'm not so sure. I'm guessing he hasn't.

Outside the streets are dark and silent. The front door of the Avenging Axe is locked. Light from the fire and the torches on the walls flickers over the faces of the dozen or so spectators. They nurse their drinks in silence, caught up in the tension as the game nears its climax.

'I'm out,' says Ravenius, a young guy from uptown who joins us most weeks. He's a big loser on the night and looks disappointed, but he's the son of a wealthy Senator so he'll be back next week with another bag of money.

Gurd the landlord is still in the game, and next to bet. The heat from the fire brings sweat to his brow. He pushes back some strands of grey hair from his face and stares at his cards, which are dwarfed by his great hands. Gurd is a Barbarian from the north. In our younger days we fought all over the world together as mercenaries. We also played rak. Gurd's a shrewd gambler. He thinks he knows everything there is to know about my technique at the card table. He doesn't.

'I'm in,' he grunts, pushing his money forward with his brawny arm.

Captain Rallee raises his flagon and sips his ale. Two of his men, Civil Guards still in uniform with their swords at their hips, sit close to him, their interest fixed on the game. Tanrose, the tavern's cook, has abandoned her position at the bar and edges closer to peer at the players.

Last person to bet is Casax, head of the local chapter of the Brotherhood, the powerful criminal gang that runs the southern half of the city of Turai. It's not often you'll see Captain Rallee at the same table as a Brotherhood boss. Unlike most of our city officials, the Captain is way too honest to socialise with figures from the underworld. But the Captain loves to gamble at rak so he makes an exception for our weekly meeting.

Nor would Casax normally be sitting down with me. Brotherhood bosses don't take kindly to Private Investigators. More than once Casax has threatened to have me killed. Karlox, his oxlike henchman, who sits by his shoulder, would like nothing better than to gut me with his sword. He'll have to wait. There is never any violence at this table, which is why it attracts such diverse people as rich wine merchants and Senators' sons down to Twelve Seas, a rough part of town they'd normally work hard to avoid.

Casax glares round at us. He tugs at his earrings. Might be a sign of tension. Might not be. Casax is a very hard man to read. We wait for him to make his move. We wait a long time, in silence.

'I'll cover,' he grunts, eventually. 'And raise.'

Casax reaches out a hand and Karlox drops a fat purse into his palm. Casax rips it open and counts rapidly.

'Your fifty gurans and another two hundred.'

The onlookers whisper in excitement. Two hundred gurans. It takes an honest citizen a long time to earn that amount. It takes me a long time to earn it, and I'm not that honest.

Makri appears with a tray of drinks. Ravenius studies her with interest. She's worth studying if you're a young man with the energy for that sort of thing. Strong, beautiful, and possibly the only person in the West to have Orc, Elf and Human blood in her veins, Makri is quite a sight. She wears a tiny chainmail bikini at work for the sole purpose of earning tips and as Makri has the sort of figure men dream about when they're far from home, and maybe dream about even more when they're actually at home, she earns a lot of tips.

My five cards lie face down on the table in front of me. I don't bother looking at them again. I don't react to Casax's raise too slowly or too quickly. Two hundred gurans on a single hand might be getting out of my league in the normal course of things, but last month I walked out of the Turas Memorial Chariot Race with an extremely handsome profit, thanks to some very astute gambling on my part. I still have most of my winnings. I can cover Casax's bet. I take a beer from Makri's tray and edge my chair back an inch to give my belly a little more room. I take my purse from my lap and count out two hundred gurans and I push it into the centre of the table.

The tavern is completely silent apart from the spitting of the fire. Makri stares at me. She's one of my very few friends in the city. I can tell from her expression she thinks I'm a fool who's about to be parted from his money.

The betting has gone too far for Captain Rallee. That'll teach him to be honest. To compete at this level he ought to be taking a bribe every now and then. He hands in his cards with a look of disgust.

Old Grax is next. Despite the heat he's still wearing the dark green cloak with the fur collar that denotes his high ranking in the Honourable Association of Merchants. He's a wealthy man – he should be, with the amount of wine drunk in Turai – but he doesn't seem so keen on risking two hundred gurans on the card he holds.

I guessed right. He folds, his face betraying neither anger nor disappointment. He motions to Makri for some wine. I motion for another beer. I'm not the sort of man who needs to stay entirely sober at the card table. So I like to believe anyway.

Gurd sighs deeply. He's already a loser on the night and another two hundred gurans would make a substantial hole in his tavern's profits. Gurd had a lot of expense rebuilding after the city-wide riots last year and maybe this influences him. He hands in his cards, reluctantly.

I notice Tanrose smiling. She doesn't like to see him lose. Tanrose is sweet on the old Barbarian. Also, he pays her wages.

Makri hands me my beer and stands next to me. Here in the Avenging Axe everyone is more or less used to her by now, but in much of the city her appearance still draws a lot of attention. It's not just her looks and figure. The reddish hue of her skin and her pointed ears reveal her Orc blood and anyone with Orc blood is regarded as cursed, a social outcast, and totally unwelcome in Turai. Everyone hates Orcs, even though we're at peace with them just now. Makri's only a quarter Orc, but that's more than enough to get you into trouble in many places.

Casax has a glass of water in front of him. No alcohol has passed his lips since he sat down at the table almost six hours ago. His eyes are deepest black and in the torch-light they shine with malevolent intelligence. He snaps his fingers. Karlox the enforcer digs deep into his robe, producing a larger bag of money.

'Count me out a thousand,' says Casax, casually, as if betting a thousand gurans on a hand of cards is an everyday occurrence.

The spectators can't help showing surprise and there are excited whispers as they crane their necks to see the action.

Karlox counts. Casax looks me straight in the eye. I stare straight back at him and I don't allow the slightest flicker of expression to show on my face. I don't think the Brotherhood boss is bluffing. He has a good hand. That's fine with me. I have a good hand too. I have four black dragons. Four black dragons is practically unbeatable at rak. The only thing higher would be a full royal mansion, and if Casax turns up with a full royal mansion at the same time as I have four black dragons I'm liable to suspect that things have not been entirely above board, and to start asking a few questions with my sword.

I calmly sip some beer, and make ready to clean out the gangster. While my face is devoid of expression, inside I'm feeling pretty damn good. I've fought all over the world, I've seen Orcs, Elves and dragons, I've been employed at the Imperial Palace and I've been down and out in the gutters. I've talked, drunk and gambled with Kings, Princes, Sorcerers and beggars. And now I'm about to walk off with the largest pot of winnings ever seen in Twelve Seas. I've been waiting for this moment all my life.

'One thousand,' mutters Karlox, and hands the money over to his boss. Casax gets ready to make his bet.

'You mind if I sit down on the edge of your chair?' says Makri to me, breaking the silence. 'I'm feeling a bit weary. I've got a heavy blood flow this month.'

I blink at her. 'What?'

'My period. You know, it can make a woman tired.'

For a split second a profound, awestricken hush descends in the room, followed immediately by the most God-awful racket as people rise from their chairs in a panic. To my certain knowledge no women has ever said such words in public in Turai before. Menstruation is high up the list of taboo subjects in this city and in the assembled company of gamblers and drinkers the words fall like a fiery blast from a war dragon. Casax freezes. He might have once killed a lion with his bare hands but he's not up to this sort of thing. Beside him Gurd's face assumes a look of terror the like of which I've not seen since we were tramping through the Macian Hills and a large and venomous snake suddenly reared up and bit him on the leg.

Chairs crash as people start heading for the exits. Young Pontifex Derlex, the local Priest, shrieks as he runs out the tavern.

'I'll open the church for immediate purification,' he yells over his shoulder, and bursts out through the door to safety.

'You filthy whore!' yells Karlox, helping his boss to his feet. Casax is looking shaky and has to be led away. His other companions scoop up his money before they depart, taking not only his thousand but the other money he's already put into the pot.

'You can't do that!' I yell, rising to my feet and fumbling for my sword, but they've already got their blades out. From the way Captain Rallee is buttoning up his cloak I can tell he's not going to hang around to help me out. Gurd, my trusty companion in adversity, is disappearing into the back room muttering that if this sort of behaviour continues he's going to close the tavern and move back north.

About thirty seconds after Makri's grim utterance I'm staring at a scene of total desolation. Everyone has fled, either to the safety of their homes or straight to church for ritual purification. I stare at Makri. I try to shout at her but nothing comes out. I'm too shocked even to yell. Makri is looking puzzled.

'What just happened?' she asks.

My arms are shaking. It takes me a while to get my tankard up to my mouth. The ale revives me a little, enough to get some words out.

'You . . . you . . . you . . .'

'Come on, Thraxas. It's not like you to splutter. What's going on? Did I say something wrong?'

'*Something wrong!*' I bellow, my voice finally returning in fury. 'Something wrong? "Can I sit down because I've got a heavy blood flow?" Are you completely insane? Have you no shame?'

'I don't see what all the fuss is about.'

'It's completely taboo to mention . . . to mention . . .' Somehow I can't say the word.

'Menstruation?' says Makri, helpfully.

'Stop saying that!' I scream. 'Look what you did! I was about to rake in a thousand gurans from Casax and you scared him away!'

I'm livid. Strange emotions well up inside me. I'm forty-three years old. As far as I can remember I haven't cried since I was eight, when my father caught me raiding his beer cellar and chased me round the city walls with a sword in his hand. But at the thought of Casax's thousand gurans, rightfully mine but now disappearing into the depths of Twelve Seas, I'm pretty close to tears. I consider attacking Makri. She might be a lethal swordswoman but I'm the best street fighter in town and I figure I could take her low down with a surprise kick.

'Don't try it,' says Makri, taking a step backwards towards the bar, where she keeps her sword hidden during working hours.

I advance towards her. 'I'll kill you, you pointy-eared freak!' I yell, and get ready to charge. Makri grabs for her sword and I draw mine swiftly from its scabbard.

Tanrose appears and plants herself between us. 'Stop this at once!' she demands. 'I'm surprised at you, Thraxas, drawing your sword against your friend Makri.'

'That pointy-eared Orc freak is no friend of mine. She just cost me a thousand gurans.'

'How dare you call me a pointy-eared Orc freak,' screams Makri, and advances towards me, blade in hand.

'Desist!' yells Tanrose. 'Thraxas, put that sword away or I promise I will never cook you a venison pie again. I mean it. And Makri, put your weapon down or I'll have Gurd get you to clean out the stables and sweep the yard. I'm surprised at you both.'

I hesitate. It shames me to admit it, but I do more or less depend on Tanrose's venison pies. My life would be far poorer without them.

'It's not Makri's fault if she didn't know she shouldn't say that. After all, she grew up in an Orcish gladiator slave pit.'

'Quite right,' says Makri. 'We couldn't mess around with social taboos. We were too busy fighting. Just get a towel in place and chop up the next enemy. When you've got four Trolls with clubs trying to knock your head off, no one worries about whether you're menstruating or not.'

I can't take any more. I swear that when Makri says this Tanrose actually smiles. I begin to suspect that these women are conspiring against me. I am now madder than a mad dragon, and maybe a little more.

'Makri,' I say with dignity. 'For the first time in my life, I find myself in complete agreement with Karlox. You are a filthy whore and you have the manners of an Orcish dog. No, Orcish dogs have many social graces which you lack. I am now going upstairs to my room. Kindly never talk to me again. And in future please keep your disgusting revelations about your bodily functions to yourself.

Here in the civilised world we prefer not to know what goes on between the legs of the Orcish half-breeds who sometimes see fit to infest our city.'

Somewhere in the middle of this speech Makri explodes in fury and tries to rush forward and sink her sword in my guts, but fortunately Gurd has re-emerged from the back room and places his brawny arms around her shoulders to restrain her. As I mount the stairs, still with dignity, I hear her screaming that she looks forward to the day when her sword pierces my heart.

'If it can make it through all that blubber, that is,' she adds, quite unnecessarily referring to my excess weight.

I place a locking spell on both my doors, grab a bottle of beer, drink it down, then slump on my couch. I hate this stinking city. Always have. Nothing goes right for a man in this place.

CHAPTER
TWO

Next morning I'm woken up by the shrill voice of a street vendor outside, eager to sell her wares in the last week of autumn before the evil winter takes hold of the city. It doesn't improve my mood.

Winter in Turai is grim: bitter cold, howling gales, freezing rain and enough snow to bury the homeless beggars that huddle miserably in the streets of Twelve Seas. Back in the days when I was a Senior Investigator at the Imperial Palace, winter didn't trouble me. I hardly even saw it, just remained within the comfortable confines of the Palace walls, where a combination of engineering skill and sorcery prevented the inhabitants from feeling any discomfort. If any investigating needed doing, I sent a subordinate. Since I was booted out by my boss, Rittius, my life has changed considerably for the worse. I'm a Private Investigator in a dangerous part of town where there is plenty of crime to be investigated but precious little money to pay me for the investigating. I'm reduced to living in two rooms above a tavern, eking out my existence by risking my life against the sort of violent criminals who'll happily gut a man for a few gurans or a small dose of dwa.

The sign outside my door says *Sorcerous Investigator* but that is somewhat misleading. A more accurate version would say *Investigator Who Once Did Study Sorcery But Now Has Only The Feeblest Of Magical Powers. And Works Cheap.*

I sigh. It's true that my winnings at the chariot races will enable me to make it through the winter in more comfort than I otherwise might have. But if I'd taken that huge pot at rak last night I'd have been a good way towards moving out of this dump. I've had my fill of the slums. I don't have the energy for it any more.

I need some beer for breakfast but that means going downstairs and facing Makri. She will be out for vengeance. The woman – I use the term loosely – has in the past refused to speak to me after far less wounding accusations. What she'll do after the things I said last night, God only knows. Attack me, probably. Let her. I'm feeling angry enough to attack her right back. I tuck my sword in its scabbard and am on the point of marching right downstairs to confront Makri with her many crimes when there's a knock on my outside door and a voice I recognise calls out my name.

I banish the minor locking spell from the door and haul it open.

'Vas-ar-Methet! What are you doing in the city? Come right in!'

Vas-ar-Methet walks in, dumps his green cloak on the floor, and embraces me warmly. I embrace him back, equally warmly. I haven't seen him in fifteen years but you don't forget an Elf who once saved your life during the last great Orc War.

I saved his life too. And we both saved Gurd. The last Orc War was grim. There were plenty of occasions when lives needed saving.

Like all Elves, Vas-ar-Methet is tall and fair, with golden eyes, but even among the upright Elvish Folk Vas-ar-Methet stands out as a distinguished figure. He's a healer, an Elf of great skill, and well respected among his folk.

'Would you like some klee?'

Klee is the local spirit, distilled in the hills. Elves in general are not given to strong drink, but I seem to remember that Vas, after the months we spent together fighting, was not averse to something to keep the circulation going.

'I see you haven't changed,' he laughs.

Vas always laughed easily. He's rather more emotional than your average Elf. He's some years older than me but, as is the way with Elves, shows little sign of advancing age. If he's reached fifty, which he probably has, you'd be hard pushed to guess.

He brings out a small packet from within his green tunic. 'I thought you might like these.'

'Lesada leaves? Thank you. I just finished my last one!'

I'm grateful. Lesada leaves grow only on the Elvish Isles and they're hard to acquire in Turai. They're used as a cure for many things and have a great purifying effect on the body. I use them for hangovers, and can personally state that there is no finer remedy.

The memory of where I obtained my last supply of lesada leaves causes me to frown.

'Did you hear about the two Elves I encountered last year?' I ask.

Vas-ar-Methet nods. They'd arrived at my door claiming to be friends of his and hired me under false pretences to work for them. As it turned out, they were Elves of the criminal variety – rare, but not unheard of – who had been using me for their own ends. It got them killed

in the end, though not by me, and I've worried slightly
since then that they might really have been friends of Vas.

He reassures me. 'No, not friends, nor relatives. We
heard the full tale on the islands eventually. They used
my name and the name of my Lord only to gain influence with you, Thraxas. It is I who should apologise to
you.'

We beam at each other. I clap him heartily on the
back, break open the klee, and tell him to fill me in on the
last fifteen years.

'How's life on the Elvish Isles? Still paradise on Earth?'

'Much the same as when you visited, Thraxas. Apart
from . . .' He frowns and breaks off.

My Investigator's intuition lumbers into action. In
the excitement of seeing old Vas again it had temporarily
switched off, but now, looking at his troubled face, I can
tell that something is wrong.

'Is this a professional visit, Vas? Do you need my help?'

'I am afraid so. And if you can forgive my rudeness, I
must explain my business quickly, though I would far
rather talk with you a while of old times. Is Gurd still
alive?'

'Still alive? He certainly is. He owns this dump. I'm his
tenant.'

Vas guffaws at the thought of Gurd turning into a
businessman. And when Vas-ar-Methet guffaws, he really
lets it out. He's pretty unrestrained for an Elf. Not the sort
to sit around in a tree all night, watching the stars. I always
liked him.

'What's the rush?'

'I am here as part of the retinue of Lord Kalith-ar-Yil.
We sailed in early this morning, earlier than expected.

Lord Kalith has been keen to complete the voyage as he is anticipating bad weather on the return journey.'

I'd heard that Lord Kalith-ar-Yil was due in Turai. He's the ruler of Avula, one of the Elvish Isles to the south, and a friend and ally of our city. Some of our Turanian officials are going down to visit as guests of the Elves for the Avulan festival, which is held every five years, I believe. The invitation was sent up by way of Lord Lisith-ar-Moh, another Elvish ally, who visited Turai recently. Lisith-ar-Moh is the ruler of Ven, an island close to Avula.

'I heard you were of some service to Lord Lisith,' says Vas.

'I was. I helped make sure the great chariot race actually happened, though that involved helping the Orcs' entrant as well, which I could have done without. A man doesn't want too much of a reputation as an Orc helper. So you're here to pick up our Prince and take him to the Avulan festival?'

'We are. And as we are earlier than expected, and Lord Kalith wishes to sail tonight, I imagine there is some amount of panic at the Imperial Palace. I myself have much to do and can't spend long here.'

'Well, tell me the trouble, Vas. We can reminisce another time.'

Elves can be a little wordy. I heard Lord Lisith when he proffered the Avulans' invitation to their festival, and to be honest it dragged a little. We all like Elves in this city, and we're pleased they've invited our young Prince to the island of Avula, but we don't necessarily want to hear endless speeches about it. Fortunately Vas is more direct than an Elf Lord.

'Two months ago our Hesuni Tree was damaged by fire.'

My eyes widen in surprise. Every Elvish island is inhabited by one clan of Elves and every clan has its Hesuni Tree. It's said to record the history of the clan. In some ways it's their soul. I've never heard of one catching fire.

'It never has happened before. And it was not completely burned, though it suffered considerable damage. The tree-tenders of our tribe have saved it, though it will be some time before it is strong again. This is not public knowledge. I know that Lord Kalith will have informed your Royal Family of the occurrence, but we would not wish for people to know the true state of affairs.'

I light up a thazis stick. Vas frowns.

'These narcotic substances are bad for a man, Thraxas.'

I shrug this off. Thazis is a very mild drug, calms the nerves, nothing more. Compared to the plague of dwa that has recently gripped the city, its effects are negligible. Since dwa started flooding in from the south, Turai has advanced several giant steps on its way to hell, damnation and destruction. Crime has mushroomed on all fronts, which is good for my business, I suppose.

'Tell me about the Tree.'

'Someone attacked it with an axe, and then with fire. It took the greatest efforts of our tribe to save it.'

He pauses to sip some klee.

'No Elvish tribe has ever suffered such an attack. The Hesuni Tree of the Uratha Clan was struck by lightning and killed three hundred years ago, and this calamity has ever since plagued the Uratha. That, however, was an act of God. It is without precedent for a Hesuni Tree to be attacked. You have been among the Elves, Thraxas;

you may have some idea of what the Hesuni means to the clan.'

I nod. I know enough to realise the seeming impossibility of any Elf harming it.

'Coming before our Festival it is particularly unfortunate. Many Elves from the neighbouring islands visit Avula and it has cast a shadow over the occasion.'

'Who was responsible? Has Orcish sorcery extended its arm so far south?'

Vas's eyes mist over. 'My daughter stands accused of the crime.'

Unexpectedly, a tear rolls down the face of Vas-ar-Methet.

I see too much misery on the streets every day to be much affected by it, but I'm greatly touched by the sight of my old companion-in-arms reduced to tears.

He tells me that his daughter is currently under lock and key on the island, accused of the terrible and unprecedented crime.

'I swear she is innocent, Thraxas. My daughter is not capable of such a terrible act. I need someone to help her but there is no one on the islands who can do what you do. No one has any experience of investigating . . . we have no crime to investigate . . . till this . . .'

I finish off my klee and bang my fist on the table in a reassuring manner. 'Don't worry, Vas. I'll sort it out. When do we sail?'

You can trust me in a crisis. Thraxas will always come to your aid. What's more, it will get me away from the terrible Turanian winter, which is all to the good.

'We sail with the evening tide. The winter storms will soon be here and we must be well clear of your coast before then.'

The thought of winter storms makes me wonder if I might have leaped in too hastily here. I've sailed enough to take another long voyage in my stride, but even under the fine seamanship of Lord Kalith and his Elvish crew I don't relish the prospect of battling though the icy winter gales. Vas reassures me: Avula is one of the closest of the Elvish Isles, about three or four weeks' journey due south, and we should be able to pass through the most dangerous waters before they become too troubled.

'I appreciate this more than I can say, Thraxas. It is no light thing for a man to drop everything at a moment's notice to travel far, even in answer to a call from help from an old friend.'

'Think nothing of it, Vas. I owe you. Anyway, who wants to sit through another Turanian winter? You ever been here in winter? It's hell. Last year I had to spend three weeks at the harbour sorting out some shipping fraud. I was colder than a frozen pixie and you couldn't move without tripping over some poor beggar's corpse. Anyway, I've a little personal trouble at the moment I wouldn't mind being far away from.'

'Personal trouble? What sort of . . .'

An almighty crash comes at my inside door. It's still protected by my locking spell but this minor incantation isn't going to hold out for long against such a determined assault.

'An angry woman,' I grunt. 'If you can call her that.'

I grab my sword and bark a few ancient words at the door, removing the spell. It bursts open and Makri practically flies into the room. She has an axe in one hand and is trying to fend off Gurd with the other. She makes good progress towards me before Gurd manages to get his arms round her and bring her to a grinding halt.

'Let go of me, damn you,' yells Makri. 'I don't care what you say, I'm going to kill him.'

Gurd hangs on, using his extra body weight to his advantage. Makri struggles furiously. Normally in this sort of situation she would produce a dagger from somewhere around her body and stab whoever was unwise enough to be hanging on to her but she has the disadvantage of not actually wishing to kill Gurd, who is her employer and has always treated her rather kindly.

Vas has stood up in astonishment at the sight of Makri and Gurd struggling at the door. Like any Elf, he can sense Orc blood, and Elves hate Orcs even more than Humans do. But of course he can also sense Makri's Elf blood. Elves are always confused by Makri, while Makri herself finds relating to Elves troubling, so troubling that, at the sight of the dignified presence of the healer, she stops struggling and eyes him coldly.

'Who the hell are you?' she demands, in fluent Elvish.

'A friend of Thraxas,' replies Vas.

'Well you better say your goodbyes,' grunts Makri. 'I'm about to send him to hell. No one calls me a pointy-eared Orc bitch and lives.'

Vas walks up to her, bows politely, then looks her in the eye. 'I have rarely heard our language spoken so gracefully by someone not born on the islands,' he says. 'You speak it quite beautifully.'

Makri is not placated. She spits out an Orcish curse at him. I wince. I myself am fluent in the Common Elvish tongue and since Makri arrived my Orcish has greatly improved. I can't believe that she just said that to a well-bred Elf. I hope he didn't understand. It's about the rudest thing you can do to an Elf to speak Orcish in front of him.

Vas does the last thing I'm expecting, which is to put his head back and laugh heartily.

'You speak Orcish very well also. I picked up quite a lot during the war. Please tell me, young lady, who are you that you live here in a tavern in Twelve Seas and have such command of three languages?'

'Four,' says Makri. 'I've been learning the Royal Elvish language as well.'

'Really? That is unheard of. You must be a person of unusual intelligence.'

Makri has now stopped struggling. Having this cultured Elf compliment her on her high intelligence puts her in a quandary. Makri is not short of compliments on her looks, her figure, her spectacular hair. She hardly notices them any more, unless they are accompanied by a hefty tip. The main reason she stays around here is to attend the Guild College. Makri is a budding intellectual of a serious nature and an Elf complimenting her intelligence can't fail to have some effect.

'Well, I've been reading the scrolls at the library . . . you know . . .'

'Have you read the tale of Queen Leeuven?'

'Yes,' replies Makri. 'I loved it.'

Vas is delighted. 'Our finest epic. So fine that it has never been translated from the Royal language for fear of spoiling its beauty. You know it originated on Avula, my island? It is one of the glories of my tribe. I am indeed pleased to meet you.'

He bows to her again. Makri bows back. Gurd lets her

go. Makri frowns, realising that she can't really hit me with her axe. It would completely spoil the good impression she just made.

'Calmed down now?' says Gurd.

'No,' grunts Makri. 'But I'll save it for later.'

Tanrose calls from downstairs, something about a man arriving with a load of fresh venison, and Gurd hurries off. Makri is about to turn and leave when Vas calls her back.

'I am pleased to have met you. I sail on tonight's tide and may not see you again. But the Elves of my island will be pleased to learn of the person in Turai who respects our tale of Queen Leeuven.'

It's struck me before as peculiar the way Makri can make all sorts of people like her. Every time she comes across some well-bred or high-up member of society, the sort of person who would, not without reason, regard her as an ignorant Barbarian not worthy of notice, she always seems to end up creating a good impression. Cicerius, our Deputy Consul, was practically eating out of her hand the last time I worked for him. And now my friend Vas, an Elf of the highest repute, who quite possibly has never so much as spoken a word to any creature with a speck of Orc blood in them, is chatting away to her when really we should be discussing business. Any moment now they'll be reciting poetry together.

Just because Makri and Vas have hit it off in a big way doesn't mean I'm keen to spend time with the woman. I'm still mad as hell about the money she cost me.

'How long till we sail?' I say, muscling into the conversation.

'About eight hours.'

'Where are you going?' asks Makri, immediately interested.

'To Avula,' I reply. 'Far away from you. Vas, I'll need to make preparations. I'm going out to buy a few things. There will be plenty of time to fill me in on the details while we're sailing.'

'I want to come,' says Makri.

I laugh. 'No chance. As the well-known saying goes, you'd be as welcome as an Orc at an Elvish wedding.'

'It's the Avulan festival, isn't it?' says Makri. 'I've read about it. Three staged versions of the tale of Queen Leeuven and competitions in choral singing, dance and poetry. I want to come.'

'Well you can't,' I say. 'The Avulan festival is not open to everyone. It's strictly an Elf-only affair, plus a few honoured guests. Like me, for instance. I'll see you on board, Vas. If you wish to stay here and discuss poetry with this barmaid, I must warn you that she is not fully trained in the ways of civilisation.'

And with that I depart. As I head down the stairs I can feel the air getting colder. The voyage may well be chilly till we reach the warmer waters of the south. I'll need a warm, waterproof cloak for the journey and maybe a new pair of boots. And some beer. I'll get Gurd to load a barrel on to a wagon for me when I get back. The Elves have fine wine but it wouldn't surprise me if there was no beer at all on board their ship, and that's a chance I'm not prepared to take.

CHAPTER
THREE

Around seven and a half hours later I'm ready to sail. I arrive at the harbour on a wagon and load my belongings on board. The Turanian soldiers on guard duty look at me suspiciously as I roll up with a small bag of provisions and a large barrel of beer, but as the Elves are expecting me they let me past. The Elvish crew assume that as I am a guest of Vas-ar-Methet I'm probably part of the official Turanian party heading south for the festival, and I don't bother to correct them.

This festival is held every five years and, as far as I know, is mainly attended by Elves from the three neighbouring islands of Avula, Ven and Corinthal. There are several distinct great tribal groupings of Elves on the Southern Islands, and all the Elves from these three islands, while forming separate nations, belong to the great Ossuni tribe. Whether Elves from further afield will be in attendance I'm not sure, but there will certainly be few Humans there. It is regarded as a great honour in Turai that our representatives have been invited, a mark of the continuing friendship between our nations.

Turai needs this friendship. We have declined in importance in the last fifty years or so, mainly as a result of the internal strife within the League of City-States. It is now pretty much politically impotent. When the

League was strong Turai could speak with a powerful voice. Now we're weak. Despite this we are still high among the nations who are regarded as friends of the Elves. They saved us during the last great Orc War and if the Orc nations ever unite again and start heading west over the Wastelands, which is more than likely, we'll be relying on the Elves again. Hence the importance of this invitation. Prince Dees-Akan won't just be attending a festival, he'll be cementing our diplomatic ties.

Turai is sending the young Prince, second in line to the throne, and Deputy Consul Cicerius, the city's second highest official, along with a few other minor dignitaries, a couple of Sorcerers and various royal body-guards and attendants, a party of twenty or so, which is why the Elves sent up such a large ship. It's a bireme with twin banks of oars along each side, although it's unlikely that these will be much in use. Elves don't enjoy rowing any more than they have to and they'll be planning on running with the wind for most of the journey.

It's against the law for the city's highest official, the Consul, to leave the state during his term of office, which is why our government will be represented by his Deputy, Cicerius. I've worked for Cicerius on several occasions, and he's been satisfied with my achievements, but I couldn't claim to be friends. I know he has neither forgiven nor forgotten the time I was carried drunk into the Palace, singing songs. I'm not under any illusions that he'll be pleased to have me along.

I expect that the Elves have proffered other invitations to Humans. Turai was not the only city to fight alongside Lord Lisith-ar-Moh and Lord Kalith-ar-Yil. Important politicians from other sea-going nations will be gathered on Avula. Maybe I can pick up some business.

As I'm lugging my travelling bag up the gangplank I notice Lanius Suncatcher striding nimbly on board, followed by his apprentice struggling with the heavy baggage. Lanius is wrapped in his rainbow cloak, denoting him as a member of the Sorcerers Guild. I used to know him back in the days when I was a Senior Investigator at the Palace. A nice young guy, as I remember. He's been recently promoted to a senior spot in Palace Security because of several unfortunate deaths among our more experienced Sorcerers.

He greets me as I reach the deck. 'Thraxas. Wasn't expecting to see you here. Are you back in favour with the Palace?'

'Afraid not. Still pounding the streets in a private capacity. I'm not part of the official party, just here as a guest of the Elves.'

I congratulate the young Sorcerer on his promotion. 'You've come a long way. Last time I saw you, you were still running errands for Old Hasius the Brilliant.'

'The way our Sorcerers have been handing in their togas recently has been good for my career,' he admits. 'I'm Chief Sorcerer at Palace Security these days, promoted after Mirius Eagle Rider got himself killed. It would be just fine if it wasn't for Rittius.'

He makes a face. So do I. Rittius, head of Palace Security, is not a popular man with his staff. He was the man responsible for my sacking and any time our paths cross there is trouble.

'He's not part of the delegation, is he?'

'Fortunately not. Cicerius refused to sanction his

coming. You're not going to Avula to work, are you?' asks Lanius Suncatcher, suddenly suspicious.

'Work? Of course not. No call for an Investigator in those parts. Purely a social visit.'

Lanius might be an old acquaintance, but I'm not in the habit of sharing my business secrets with Palace officials. I wonder how powerful his sorcery is these days. As often happens when I encounter a young Sorcerer on the way up, I grow suddenly depressed at the sad decline in my powers. I admit I was never the most powerful Sorcerer on the block, but I used to be able to perform a trick or two. These days I'm lucky if I can put an opponent to sleep, or temporarily blind him with flashing lights, and even these small spells wear me out. It's a long time since I've been able to carry around more than two spells in my head. A powerful Sorcerer can carry four or five.

I sigh. Too much drinking and high living. But I've had bad luck as well. I never did get the breaks I deserved. As a man who fought loyally for his city, I shouldn't be having to scratch a living in Twelve Seas, declining powers or not.

Harmon Half-Elf, another of our important Sorcerers, arrives on deck. He greets me with a nod before going off with Lanius Suncatcher, discussing the probability of their needing to calm the ocean on the way. The harbour at Twelve Seas is well protected and the ship is lying calmly on the water, but already the open seas are rough. It's not unusual for the winter storms to descend early, though on an Elvish ship, with extra Sorcerers in attendance, I figure I'm safe enough.

I hunt for Vas-ar-Methet, taking care not to run into

any Turanian official who might not be delighted to find me aboard. Vas has reserved for me a tiny cabin where I dump my stuff, haul my boots off, drink some beer and wait for us to sail. Vas arrives and I tell him that an unexpected voyage to the Elvish Isles is just what a man needs after his idiot companion has cost him a thousand gurans at cards.

Vas still seems impressed by my idiot companion. 'After you departed she told me of her studies at the Guild College. I just cannot believe that any woman with Orc blood should be so civilised and intelligent.'

'What do you mean, civilised? The first time you saw her she was trying to plant an axe in my head.'

'Well, Thraxas, you had grossly insulted her. She also told me about the card game.'

'Oh yes? Did she tell you about the outrage she caused by wilfully offending public decency?'

Vas laughs. 'She did. And I can understand why it caused such a disturbance. The subject is calanith among Elves also.'

'Calanith' roughly translates as 'taboo'. The Ossuni Elves have a lot of them.

'Often during my healing it has caused awkwardness. But the young woman was surely unaware of the offence it would cause. I feel you must make allowances for her. Had you not abused her so virulently at the time, she would quite probably have apologised for the loss she caused you.'

I snort in derision. Makri would probably leap from the highest part of the city walls rather than apologise. Stubborn, that's what she is. It's a very bad trait and one she would do well to overcome. But Elves are always keen to see the positive side.

'Try living in a tavern with her. Then you'd see how likely she is to apologise. And anyway, what good is an apology to a man who's just been cheated out of a thousand gurans? I tell you, Vas, I'm desperate to get out of Twelve Seas. If I don't raise enough money soon for a villa in Thamlin, you're going to find me swimming south looking for a permanent residence in your tree. Any chance of a game of rak down on your island?'

This makes Vas smile, troubled though he is. He shakes his head. 'Elves are not fond of cards as a rule. We play niarit though. I remember you used to be keen on that.'

'Still am,' I inform him. 'Local champion in fact. I'm hell at the niarit board.'

Niarit is a complicated board game involving two armies of Hoplites, Trolls and Cavalry along with assorted other pieces – Harpers, Sorcerers, Plague Carriers and such like. The aim is to defeat your opponent's army and storm his castle. I brought my board with me, thinking that it might while away a few idle hours on the long voyage. When it comes to niarit I'm sharp as an Elf's ear and undefeated champion of Twelve Seas. Since I taught Makri how to play she's never come close to beating me, for all her much vaunted intellect. Drives her crazy. Whether or not I find a game of rak or niarit anywhere along the way, at least Makri will not be along to ruin it, and that's a bonus.

'Well, if you find yourself on the wrong side of Lord Kalith,' says Vas-ar-Methet, 'try challenging him to a game of niarit. He's the finest player on Avula, and can't resist a game.'

'That's good to know. I could do with a little practice.' I break open another beer. I've brought as many bottles as I could carry and a barrel for when they run out. I'm still sketchy on the details of the case I'm being asked to investigate. All I really know is that Vas's daughter Elith is currently imprisoned on a charge of attempting to kill the Hesuni Tree. I'm about to ask Vas-ar-Methet to fill me in, but before I can he is called away. Vas is not only Lord Kalith's chief healer, he is close enough to him to be his trusted adviser as well, and this makes him a busy man. Well, there will be plenty of opportunity to learn the full facts of the case before I arrive on Avula. And once I'm in command of the facts, I'm confident I'll be able to sort it out. When it comes to investigating, I'm number one chariot, and no one can deny it.

Lord Kalith is insisting that we must sail with the next tide and urgent last-minute preparations are underway. I settle back on my bunk. My mood mellows. No winter in Turai for me. No pounding my way to Minarixa's bakery through the frozen streets for a few pastries to keep me going. No hunting through snow-bound streets for debtors, robbers, murderers and assorted other degenerates. No murderous gangs carving out their dwa territory. No filth, squalor and general misery. Just a pleasant visit to the Elvish Isles where I shall no doubt clear Vas's daughter without breaking sweat and spend the rest of the time lying under a tree in the warm sunshine drinking beer, listening to Elvish choirs and swapping war stories with some of the more experienced Elves. I can't wait.

We cast off and start to manoeuvre our way out of the harbour. I've decided to keep my head down till we are well at sea for fear that Deputy Consul Cicerius or some other official might start beefing about my presence here and try sending me back, but all of a sudden a commotion breaks out on deck. I never can ignore a commotion – I'm just too nosy. It's a problem I've always had. I hurry out of my cabin and up the stairs to the deck. All along one side of the ship the Elvish crew are gathered, talking and pointing with excitement at something that's going on back on the pier.

I use my body weight to force my way through. What I see leaves me gaping. Makri is pounding down the dock with a sword in one hand, a bag in the other and around thirty armed men in close pursuit. Makri's well in front but she's running out of room. They've chased her to the end of the pier and there's nothing in front of her but the sea. Even at this distance I can identify her pursuers. The mob comprises a large part of the local chapter of the Brotherhood. I'm astonished. I've only been gone five minutes and already Makri is waging war with the deadliest gang in the neighbourhood.

Makri reaches the end of the quay and whirls to face her attackers, drawing her second sword as she does so. The first two assailants to come near her fall beneath her blades but the others fan out and surround her, then close in with their weapons at the ready. I look on helplessly as we sail slowly away. There are cries of concern from the Elves alongside me at the sight of a lone woman up against such murderous odds, but we are powerless to help. Even if Lord Kalith turned the ship, by the time we made it back it would be far too late.

'Jump,' I scream at Makri.

I can't understand why she doesn't leap into the sea. At least there she would have some chance of escape. Instead Makri stands fighting against hopeless odds.

Supreme swordswoman or not, she can't fight off that number of well-armed men attacking from all sides. A pile of bodies lies prostrate at her feet but any second now one of the multiple blades facing her will find its target.

'Jump into the sea!' I scream again, but we are now more than eighty yards distant and my voice probably doesn't carry over the noise of the battle, and the waves, and the seabirds that soar over the harbour.

Finally Makri seems to realise that there is no way she's walking away from this one without getting wet. She spins on her heel, rams her swords into the scabbards that form a cross on her back, and leaps from the quay into the water below. By this time I'm already lowering a boat from the side of the ship with the aid of several young Elves. They don't know Makri, but the sight of her battling such enormous odds has enraged their sense of fair play.

The boat hits the water with a mighty splash and I swarm down a rope into it, looking all the while for Makri's head to appear above water. Meanwhile the thugs on the dock are peering over the waters, hunting for their prey. As I start to row another body clatters into the boat. It's Vas. He wastes no energy in talking but grabs the second set of oars and starts to pull. We make our way against the tide, back towards the mouth of the harbour.

'Where is she?' I cry, alarmed.

'She must be swimming underwater to safety.'

I'm dubious. Makri has been under for a very long time. We're almost at the spot where she went in and there is no sign of her. Perhaps she took a wound in the fight and is unable to swim. Perhaps she has already drowned.

'Goddammit,' I growl, and stand up in the boat, scanning the waters for any sign of her. Suddenly I spot something – a dark mass like seaweed on the water. Makri's hair. Makri's head appears, twenty yards or so from our boat. Before I can yell for her to swim to us she goes under again, in a manner that suggests she won't be coming back up.

Without hesitation I strip off my cloak and plunge into the sea. I've always been a strong swimmer and it takes me very little time to reach the spot and dive under the surface. The waters are cold and grey, impossible to see through for more than a few yards. I sink deeper and deeper, hunting desperately for sight of Makri, and the thought flashes through my head that if I was any sort of Sorcerer I'd have some spell ready to help me. But I've no spell for this, nothing to help me except a grim determination that I'm not going to see Makri drown.

My lungs are bursting. I can't stay under any longer. I keep swimming. Finally I see Makri rising slowly in front of me. I kick towards her, grab her arm and head for the surface. We arrive there spluttering, coughing up water, but still alive. Makri seems in a bad way.

'Thraxas,' she mutters.

I start swimming for the boat, dragging her along behind me. Vas rows towards us and soon he is helping us on board. I think I hear some cheering from the Elves' ship, and maybe some howls of anger from the dockside.

Makri retches over the side of the boat, and suddenly looks more alive.

'Nice escape,' I say to her. 'But it would have been better if you'd actually swum somewhere. Sinking like a stone was never going to work.'

'I can't swim,' says Makri.

'What?'

'I can't swim. You think I'd have hung around on the pier so long if I knew how to swim?'

'Well, maybe. You like fighting. I figured you were just enjoying yourself.'

Vas brings us alongside the ship and we are helped aboard.

The Elves are full of congratulations for me at my fine rescue and there are words of admiration too for Makri for the fighting spirit she showed on the pier. Their praise dries up as the Elves suddenly notice that Makri is not the standard-issue woman they took her for.

'Orc blood!' whispers one young member of the crew, quite distinctly.

Deputy Consul Cicerius, resplendent in his best gold-rimmed toga, strides over to us.

'Investigator Thraxas!' he rasps. 'What are you doing here?'

'My guest,' explains Vas-ar-Methet, which surprises the Deputy Consul but doesn't prevent him from rounding on Makri.

'You cannot remain on this ship.'

'Well, I can't go back there,' points out Makri, quite reasonably. The dock, now receding into the distance, is still lined with armed men.

'Lord Kalith,' says Cicerius, as the Elvish Captain strides along the deck towards us. 'You must turn this ship around.'

At this moment the wind blowing us from the harbour suddenly strengthens and the sails bulge as the ship spurts forward. Lord Kalith frowns.

'Impossible. We cannot miss this tide. To do so would make us lose a day's voyage and quite probably run into the first winter storm.'

He stares at Makri. For him this is something of a dilemma. He doesn't want to turn the ship around, but there is no inhabited land between us and Avula. If he lets her stay he's going to be the first Elf Lord to arrive back home with an Orc in tow. He doesn't look thrilled at the prospect.

I'm none too pleased myself. I didn't want Makri to drown but that doesn't mean I want her along spoiling things for my visit to Avula. No Elf is going to want to talk to a man who's brought his mixed-blood friend along for a visit. The Deputy Consul is all for sending Makri back in the boat but the shore is already fading in the distance and it is just not practical.

'We'll decide what to do with you later,' Kalith tells Makri. 'Meanwhile, stay out of sight.'

'Fantastic,' says Makri, brightly. 'I've always wanted to go to the Elvish Isles. How long till we get there?'

Lord Kalith doesn't reply. As he departs to the bridge he's not looking pleased at this turn of events. He orders his crew back to their posts, and his voice is harsh.

I scowl at Makri. 'Is there no end to these outrages? First you ruin my card game and now you've muscled your way on board my ship.'

'Well, thanks for saving my life,' says Makri. 'I forgive you for the insults you heaped on my head. Could you get me something dry to wear?'

Makri tugs at the man's tunic she's wearing. In common with all of Makri's clothes, it fails to cover nearly enough of her. I hurry her off in case she commits some further outrage, such as taking it off in front of the crew. I notice that the young sailor who first commented on Makri's Orc blood has not actually departed back to his post but stands staring at Makri with some fascination. I scowl at him, then notice it isn't a him but a her, a young Elvish maid, along on the voyage for some reason. A fairly scrawny-looking specimen, not blooming with health like your standard Elvish female.

We make for my cabin. Small though it is, I will now have to share it with Makri for the voyage. I continue to complain.

'Couldn't you just let me sail in peace? What the hell were you doing fighting the Brotherhood anyway? Did you arrange the whole thing just so you could come to the festival?'

'Certainly not,' replies Makri. 'Although now I think about it, how come you didn't invite me?'

Makri is suspiciously cheerful about all this. For a woman who's suffering from several nasty sword cuts and nearly drowned, she's in a surprisingly good mood. I ask her what the fight was about.

'I was just trying to get your money back.'

'What?'

'The money Casax took back from the pot. After all, you said yourself it wasn't fair. Once you make your bet you can't take your money back, no matter what outrage may make you wish to leave the tavern. So I went to get it back for you.'

'Really? And what brought on this display of public-spiritedness?'

According to Makri it was Vas-ar-Methet. After talking for a while about the beautiful epic poem of Queen

Leeuven, they came round to discussing the reason behind her wishing to kill me with an axe.

'Of course, he quite understood why I was so annoyed
at you, insulting me in such a crass manner when really
I was not responsible at all for anything. It's not like anyone ever mentioned to me that menstruation is strictly
taboo in Turai. But after we talked for a while I did see
that you were probably too upset to think clearly. Any
gambler would be, and you of course do have a problem
with your gambling. And you'd been drinking heavily,
which always clouds your judgement. I expect you were
addled with thazis as well. I've noticed it always has a
bad effect on you when you smoke too much. So with the
gambling, the drink and the drugs all making you crazy,
I figured it wasn't really fair of me to hold a grudge,
though your behaviour was bad, even by your standards.
In the spirit of friendship I thought I'd get your money
back for you.'

I inform Makri stiffly that I was far from addled, and
was certainly not crazy. 'It was merely the rational response
of a man who has been pushed past the limit by the ludi-
crous behaviour of a woman who has no idea of how to
behave in polite society. What happened when you saw
Casax? I take it he wasn't too keen to return the money?'

Makri shakes her head. 'Afraid not. He wasn't keen to
see me in the first place and I had to do a fair bit of fighting just to get to him. I grabbed his purse, but there's
only a hundred or so gurans in it. And after that a battle
just seemed to develop between me and his men. I didn't
realise there were so many of them.'

Makri grins happily, hands me the purse, and squeezes
past me to peer out of our porthole.

'The Elvish Isles. Avula, birthplace of Queen Leeuven. And the festival! I can't wait. Remind me why we're going there?'

'You're not going there for anything. I'm going to get my friend Vas's daughter out of jail. She's accused of attacking a tree.'

'Attacking a tree? And they threw her in prison? These Elves certainly love their vegetation.'

'It was a special tree. The Hesuni Tree in fact. No doubt you have learned all about Hesuni Trees at the Guild College.'

'Heart and soul of the tribe,' pronounces Makri.

'Exactly. I don't have all the details yet, but Vas's daughter is in bad trouble. So kindly try not to ruin everything for me. Vas is an old friend and I want to help him. Also I can't afford to look bad in front of Cicerius and Prince Dees-Akan.'

'Is he the dwa-ridden drunken Prince or the sober responsible one?'

'The sober responsible one. Well, sober and responsible as far as Turanian Princes go.'

'You mean he's a lush?'

'He's not quite as bad as his older brother. And don't insult the Royal Family.'

My cheerful mood has vanished. I can see this is going to be a tough journey.

'When we get to Avula I doubt you'll be allowed to go ashore, but if by some miracle you are, for God's sake don't mention your – your – well you know what I'm talking about. You'll panic the Elves.'

CHAPTER
FOUR

On the second day of the voyage Vas-ar-Methet manages to escape from his official duties for long enough to fill me in on the details of the case.

'My daughter's accuser is Lasas-ar-Thetos, Chief Attendant to the Tree. He is the brother of Gulas-ar-Thetos, the Chief Tree Priest. According to Lasas, he caught her in the act of chopping into the tree with an axe, after she had previously tried to set it on fire.'

'What does your daughter have to say about this?'

'She remembers nothing of the incident.'

I raise my eyebrows. I don't expect all my clients to be innocent, but the least they can do is think of a good excuse. 'She remembers nothing at all?'

'No. But she does not deny that she was there. Unfortunately her memory of events appears to be completely empty. She cannot remember a thing from the time she left our house till the moment she found herself in custody.'

'You know that doesn't look good, Vas. Doesn't she even remember why she went to the Tree?'

Vas shakes his head. I ask him if he believes her and he is quite emphatic that he does.

'I am aware that it looks bad for her. She has no defence to present to the Council of Elders who will try her. But I do not believe that my daughter, as fine an Elf as there is on the entire island, would ever commit such a sacrilegious act. It is completely against her character, and besides, she had no reason to do it.'

Despite Vas-ar-Methet's strong desire to see his daughter cleared, I can't learn nearly enough from him. He has no idea of what she might have been doing near the Tree, no idea when she ever visited it in the course of her normal life, and no idea of who else might have wished to damage it.

'Do you think her memory was sorcerously affected? Has anyone checked?'

'Yes. The case has been investigated by Lord Kalith's officials, and that includes Jir-ar-Eth, his Chief Sorcerer. I understand that he found no trace of sorcery being used in the area, although everyone knows that that would be hard to establish anyway. The Hesuni Tree creates a powerful mystical field around it. All sorcery would be affected, and it is impossible to look back in time at any-thing that happened there.'

I nod. I'm used to sorcery not working out too well when it comes to investigating. The idea of a Sorcerer having a look at events, sorting out some clues and producing a neat answer is fine in theory – and it works occasionally in practice – but generally there are too many variables to make it reliable, or even feasible. That's why I'm still in a job. You always need a man who's pre-pared to pound the streets looking for answers. Or, in this case, pound the trees. The Avulans live mainly above the ground, on villages suspended in the tree tops, with walkways connecting them. Last time I visited the Elvish Isles I remember travelling briskly over these walkways, admiring the ground below, but I was a lot younger then, and a lot thinner.

As Vas leaves the scrawny little Elvish girl arrives and tells me that Lord Kalith wants to see me in his cabin. I make my way there, shielding my face against the heavy rain that pounds down on to the deck. Despite the poor weather the wind is in our favour and we're making good progress. The ship rolls gently beneath my feet and the motion brings back many memories. It's some time since I've been on a voyage, but I haven't lost my sea legs.

Lord Kalith's cabin, while comfortable, is not ostentatious. There's little by way of decoration to show that Kalith is the head of his tribe, though I cast a jealous eye at the fine furniture. All I have in my cabin is a bunk, and it makes for a very poor seat, particularly when the ship pitches into a trough.

Lord Kalith himself wears few emblems of his rank, as is common among the Elves. An Elvish Lord would regard anything more than a small circle of silver in his hair to be bad taste. His cloak, while slightly more sumptuously cut than those of the other Elves, is the same shade of green, and untrammelled by any decoration.

'I understand you have been questioning my crew.'

I nod. There's no denying it, though really I have been doing little more than acquainting myself with the background of the case.

'I wish you to stop,' says Lord Kalith.

'Stop? Why?'

'As master of this ship and Lord of my island, I do not have to give you a reason. I merely wish you to stop. My sailors should not be disturbed in their duties.'

I shrug noncommittally. I would have no qualms

whatsoever about outraging Kalith and every other Elf Lord while carrying out an investigation, but I figure there's no point in annoying him yet. If things go badly for me on Avula, I'll annoy him plenty there.

I do take the time to point out to Kalith that I am here at the bidding of Vas-ar-Methet, and was given to understand that he had his Lord's approval. Kalith concedes that this is true, but makes it clear that he never thought it was such a great idea.

'Vas-ar-Methet is of great value to me. I could not refuse his request for help in the matter of his daughter. But I am quite certain that, sad as it may be, his daughter did actually do what she is accused of. On Avula, you have my permission to ask questions, within reason. Here on my ship, I expect you to behave with decorum, and refrain from distracting my crew.'

I nod. I notice that Lord Kalith has a game of niarit set out on the small table by his couch. I glance at the pieces.

'The Harper's Game,' I say, recognising the formation.

Lord Kalith raises an eyebrow. 'You play the game?'

'Often. But I never favour the Harper's Game. I find it's too susceptible to an attack from the Elephants and the Plague Carrier.'

'I have been working on a new variation. It involves some new moves for the Hero and the Sorcerer. Perhaps we shall have a chance to play, later in the voyage?'

As I leave the cabin his farewell is friendlier than it might have been. Keen niarit players always feel some sort of bond with their fellows. Heading back to my cabin, I'm thoughtful. As a warning not to do any investigating, it was reasonably friendly. I've had far worse.

Makri is sitting on my bunk reading a scroll. She's

wearing a green Elvish tunic brought to her by Isuas, the young Elf maid. While none of the other Elves on board has so much as spoken to Makri, Isuas doesn't seem to share their inhibitions. From the way she bounded into the cabin minutes after Makri arrived soaking wet, and offered to find her some dry clothes, I'd say Makri might have made a friend. Makri doesn't seem too impressed.

'At least someone on this ship likes you. I'd have thought you'd be pleased.'

'She annoys me.'

'Why?'

'Because she's so weedy and pathetic. Are all thirteen-year-old Elf girls like that?'

I tell her I don't think so. Isuas does seem a little on the small side, but I don't see that as any reason for Makri's dislike.

'I hate weedy little girls,' says Makri, matter-of-factly. 'Back in the slave pits they just used them for target practice. If I'd been runt-sized like her I'd have been dead long ago.'

'Well, excuse the rest of the world for not all being demented warrior women,' I say, and tell her to shove up on the bunk as I need to sit down. 'Anyway, try not to alienate her. Apart from Vas, she's probably the only Elf on board with any sympathy towards either of us. You know, I've just been warned off by Lord Kalith? Not what I was expecting, I must say. I thought he'd be pleased to have an experienced investigator coming down to sort things out. It's weird the way my cases always get so difficult right from the start. Sometimes I think I'm cursed by the Gods.'

Makri shrugs. She's not big on religion. 'Maybe you

should pray more. Are you still meant to do it three times a day, even on a ship?'

In Turai this is a legal requirement.

'A Turanian citizen should pray at the correct times, no matter where he is.'

'I haven't noticed you doing it,' says Makri.

'Yes, well, my knees aren't what they were. It's hard on a man, having to kneel all the time.'

In truth, I haven't been out of bed in time for morning prayers for something like ten years, and for the other two daily prayer slots I generally just try to hide in my room.

'Anyway it's too late for prayer now, I'm stuck with you.'

'What do you mean, stuck with me?' protests Makri.

'Exactly that. The plan was for me to go to Avula, thereby missing the rigours of the Turanian winter, quickly clear Elith-ir-Methet of Tree desecration, then spend the rest of the time lounging around in the sun drinking beer. Now you've managed to spoil everything. I'm practically confined to my cabin, and when we get to Avula I'll be lucky if the Elves will deign to speak with me – I'm a man with a travelling companion who has Orc blood. And it's no use looking at me like that, you know full well it's true. It beats me why you insisted on coming.'

'I didn't insist on coming. It was an accident. I was just trying to get your money back.'

I still suspect Makri staged the whole thing.

'Shouldn't you be home studying?'

Makri attends the Guild College, a place where those sons of the lower classes of Turai who wish to better themselves take classes in philosophy, theology, rhetoric, mathematics and whatever else it is they teach there. Makri is the first woman ever to study at the College. At first they refused to have her, but she gained entry by extreme force of personality and some threats of legal action by the Association of Gentlewomen. Her ultimate ambition is to attend the Imperial University. There is no chance that they will ever let her in, but she refuses to be put off.

'The College shuts for the winter. I figure this trip will do me a load of good next year. I'll be able to give my professors first-hand accounts of Elvish society.'

'You'll be able to give them first-hand accounts of what it's like to stay on a ship, you mean. There's no chance they're letting you disembark, Makri.'

'But I want to see the festival. Just think, there are going to be three staged versions of the tale of Queen Leeuven.'

'Sounds dull to me. These Elvish plays are all full of heroes battling hopelessly against fate, and they always end in tragedy.'

'What's wrong with that?'

'When I'm at the theatre I like something a little more entertaining.'

Makri makes a face at me. 'You mean you like it when the chorus line sings some obscene drinking song and the heroine's top falls off by accident.'

'That's the sort of thing,' I agree. 'I never enjoyed the classics.'

'They have to let me attend the festival,' says Makri. 'I'm the only one from Turai who'll appreciate it properly.'

'You won't appreciate it if the Elves start rioting because they sense Orc blood in the audience.'

'Do Elves riot?' asks Makri.

I admit I don't know. If Makri sets foot on Avula, we'll probably find out.

By the fourth day of our voyage I'm bored. The ship is making good time over a calm sea with a fast wind behind us, but I'm starting to feel more than a little frustrated. Deputy Consul Cicerius has strongly suggested that I keep myself hidden for the whole of the journey. As a free Turanian citizen I don't have to do what the Deputy Consul says, but I don't want to aggravate him more than is necessary. He could make my life very difficult back in Turai. During the past year I've done some good work for Cicerius, thereby increasing my standing with city officials, but if I end up offending him or the Prince I could have my Investigator's licence revoked and then I'd be in trouble.

I sigh. It's surprising how much of my life is spent being in trouble. I should have studied more when I was young. I could have been a proper Sorcerer.

As for Prince Dees-Akan, he has not yet condescended to visit me. Nor has an invitation to an informal get-together in his cabin come my way.

I've been explaining the case to Makri. Normally I'd do this anyway – Makri is a very smart woman – but I had planned to be mad at her for a lot longer. However, as we have now been thrown together in one small cabin, it seems easier to forget her numerous outrages and revert to being friends.

The facts, as reported by Vas, are puzzling: his

daughter Elith-ir-Methet was found unconscious at the scene of the crime, the Tree was badly damaged and she still had an axe in her hand.

'Is she saying she didn't do it?' asks Makri.

'Unfortunately not. She claims not to remember anything.'

'That's going to make things difficult for you.'

I nod. 'Even if Elith is telling the truth about remembering nothing, it doesn't mean she's innocent. I've known criminals who've blanked out all memories of their crime. Something to do with the trauma, I suppose.'

'So what are you going to do? Distort the facts? Muddy the waters till there isn't enough evidence to convict her?'

'Only as a last resort. I'll at least try to find out the truth first. It's possible she didn't do it. It sounds to me as if there wasn't any sort of proper investigation. The Elves on Avula are not used to investigating. I'm going along with the presumption that's she's been framed.'

The seas have become a little rougher and the ship has started to roll. I notice that Makri is looking a little queasy.

'Feeling the effects?'

'I'm fine.'

A large wave rocks the ship. Makri turns quite an odd colour and rushes out of the cabin. That will teach her to interfere with my mission.

Seasickness doesn't trouble me. My only worry is that I might run out of ale on the voyage. Back in my army days I was used to these hardships, but since I moved into the Avenging Axe I've grown used to beer being available whenever I want it. It occurs that I want beer most of the time.

'Nothing wrong with that,' I say out loud, patting my belly. 'In a corrupt city full of thieves, murderers and drug addicts, heavy beer consumption is the only rational response.'

Makri reappears, groans and flops down on the bunk, where she lies moaning about how terrible it is to be at sea.

'You'll get used to it,' I tell her. 'Feel like a beer?'

Makri spits out an Orcish curse, which would sound strong even in a gladiator pit, and turns her face to the wall. I decide to leave the cabin and wander among the crew. Even taciturn Elves will be better company than a seasick Makri.

I emerge on deck to encounter a light drizzle and a strong wind. A senior member of the crew is shouting instructions to some lithe young Elves who are swarming over the rigging, adjusting the sails to cope with the worsening weather.

I watch them with interest, noting the skill with which they carry out their tasks. I've seen Turanian sailors performing similar work on many occasions, and Turanian sailors are skilful at their craft, but the Elves seem to fly over the masts and rigging as if they are unaffected by gravity's pull.

Someone appears beside me. I'm about to comment on the crew members' expertise when I realise that it is Prince Dees-Akan. This is the first time I've met him on board. I greet him graciously. I may have been sacked from my job at the Palace after getting drunk at Rittius's wedding and generally disgracing myself, but I haven't forgotten how to address the second in line to the throne.

The Prince is around twenty years old, tall and dark, though not reckoned particularly handsome by our nation's matrons, certainly not in comparison with his older brother. The young Prince is fairly popular in our city-state however, and commonly regarded as a much more stable character than his brother, the heir to the throne. That's not saying too much really. Prince Frisen-Akan might have the good looks but he is also a drunken degenerate who'd sell the Palace furniture to buy dwa. Last year he very nearly caused the ruin of the city when he became involved in a plot to import the drug through the agency of Horm the Dead, a half-Orc Sorcerer who damn near destroyed Turai with one of the most mal-evolent spells ever created.

I had a hand in stopping Horm. I also prevented the elder Prince's involvement from becoming known to the public. Cicerius paid me well enough, but I figure he might have been more grateful.

I've never had any dealings with the younger Prince. As he stands next to me I sense a certain awkwardness. On a long sea journey etiquette tends to be relaxed so there is no particular reason why the Prince can't con-verse with even a low-life like myself, but he seems to be unsure of what to say. I help him along a little.

'Ever been to the Elvish Isles before, your highness?'

'No. Have you?'

'Yes. A long time ago, before the last great Orc War. I've always wanted to go back.'

The Prince gazes at me. Is there a glimmer of dislike in his expression? Possibly.

'Deputy Consul Cicerius is worried that you may cause trouble.'

I reassure him. 'Nothing is closer to my heart than the well-being of our great city.'

'You are conducting an investigation. Might that not lead to some unpleasantness?'

'I'll do my very best to prevent it, your highness.'

'I trust that you will. It seems to me a bad idea that you are here at all. Surely our Elvish friends can deal with their own criminals?'

I've quickly gone off the young Prince, but I still try to look respectful.

'And Cicerius informs me that when you are around, bad things tend to happen.'

'Not at all, your highness,' I say, in my most reassuring voice. 'For an Investigator, my life is surprisingly peaceful.'

At this moment an Elf falls from the highest mast and lands dead at my feet. It makes a really loud noise. I swear the Prince looks at me as if it's my fault.

I'm already bending down over the body. Elves are much longer lived than Humans, but even they can't survive broken necks. Members of the crew are running towards us and more are swarming down the rigging to see if they can help. There's some confusion till Vas-ar-Methet arrives on the scene and forces his way through. He kneels over the fallen Elf.

'What has happened?' comes the commanding voice of Lord Kalith, arriving at a fast gait from the bridge.

'He fell from the rigging, sir,' replies one young sailor.

'Dead,' says Vas, standing up. 'His neck's broken. How did it happen?'

I struggle to hear clearly as many Elves speak at once, but from what I can gather the young Elf had lost his hold on the rigging when he went to take a drink from his water bottle. The bottle, made from some sort of animal skin, is still slung from his neck on a long string.

I bend over the body, lift the bottle and sniff the contents.

'That will not be necessary, Investigator,' booms Lord Kalith, sounding quite insulted at the implication that there may have been something other than water in the Elf's bottle. Without making it too obvious, the other Elves get between me and the body and lift it up to take it away.

Throughout all this the Prince has stood impassively at the side of the action, joined now by his bodyguards, and also Cicerius, who hastened to our side at the sound of the commotion.

'That was hardly tactful,' the Prince says to me reproachfully as the Elves depart.

Cicerius asks what he means.

'The Investigator felt obliged to check the unfortunate Elf's water bottle, apparently suspecting that he may have fallen from the rigging while drunk. Lord Kalith was plainly insulted.'

'Is this true?' explodes Cicerius.

I shrug. 'Just a reflex action. After all, he fell off while trying to take a drink. You've seen how sure-footed the Elves are. I just wondered if he might have had a little klee inside him, or maybe some Elvish wine?'

Cicerius glares angrily at me. The Prince glares angrily at me.

'Well, it's my job,' I protest. 'What if he was poisoned?'

Cicerius, never hesitant about giving a man a lecture, proceeds to tell me in strong language that I am to stay well out of the affair.

'Let the Elves bury their own dead, and whatever you do, do not go around asking questions about the accident. You and your companion have caused us enough trouble already.'

I am spared further lecturing by the reappearance of Vas-ar-Methet. He looks worried.

'Very unfortunate,' he confides. 'Please tell Makri to stay well out of sight.'

'Why?'

'A few of the younger Elves are muttering that we're cursed because of her presence.'

'That is ridiculous, Vas, and you know it. It's nothing to do with Makri that one of your crew fell off the rigging.'

'Nonetheless, do as he says,' says Cicerius.

A slender figure in a man's tunic with a great mass of hair billowing in the wind suddenly staggers past us at a fast rate. It's Makri, heading swiftly to the rail at the side of the ship. Once there she hangs her head over and throws up violently. The wind catches some of her vomit and blows it back over her feet. She curses vehemently, and quite obscenely, and bends down to wipe them clean. I notice that her toenails are painted gold, a fashion only worn, to my certain knowledge, by the lowest class of prostitutes in Simnia. Cicerius winces.

'Hey, Makri,' I call. 'The Deputy Consul wants you to stay out of sight.'

Makri's reply to this is fortunately carried away in the wind. She's really going to have to stop using these Orcish insults if she wants to start making friends around here.

As soon as Cicerius and the Prince depart I start asking Vas-ar-Methet about the recently deceased Elf.

'Did anyone see anything suspicious?'

Vas is puzzled. 'I don't think so. Why?'

'Well aren't you curious when one of your crew suddenly plunges to his doom for no apparent reason?'

Vas shrugs. 'These things happen at sea.'

'Maybe. But I seem to recall hearing that Lord Kalith has one of the finest crews in the Elvish Isles. I'd say it warranted a little digging around. Will Lord Kalith instigate an enquiry?'

Vas-ar-Methet seems genuinely puzzled by my curiosity. He doesn't seem to think that there is anything to enquire about. Maybe it's one of these different-culture things. Perhaps Elves accept deaths at sea as natural occurrences. Myself, I'm just naturally suspicious about anyone dying right in front of me.

CHAPTER
FIVE

Next day they hold the funeral of the young Elf who fell from the rigging. It's a long time since I've seen a burial at sea.

'Have a nice time,' mutters Makri from her bunk.

'You're coming too,' I inform her.

'I'm sick.'

'Everyone on an Elvish ship has to attend the funeral of a crew member. It's their custom, no exceptions allowed. So get ready.'

Neither of us is much looking forward to it. I'm trying to put some sort of shine on to my salt-water-encrusted boots. It's a frustrating task and I give voice to some complaints.

'Sail down to Elfland and sort out some minor difficulty over a tree – ought to be as easy as bribing a Senator. Now Kalith is angry with me, the Prince wishes I was back in Turai and the Elves are treating me like I've got the plague. How did everything go wrong so quickly?'

'It's a flaw in your character,' says Makri. 'You generally offend everyone when you're on a case. Sometimes it's because you've drunk too much. Other times it's just because you're an offensive sort of person. But hey, you often get the job done.'

'Thank you, Makri.'

The ship's crew are joined by the Turanian delegation in a sad and solemn gathering at the stern of the ship. Makri and I skulk at the back, trying to keep out of everyone's way. Prince Dees-Akan, standing beside Lord Kalith, ignores us.

'I don't really take to that Prince,' whispers Makri. 'I liked his sister much better.'

We encountered Princess Du-Akai a while back. She hired me under false pretences, told me a load of lies and very nearly got me killed. But she did seem like a pleasant sort of person.

Lord Kalith intones the funeral litany, much of it in the Royal Elvish language which I don't understand although I attended plenty of Elvish burials during the war. It doesn't differ a great deal from a Human funeral – formal attire, brief reminiscences of the departed, some singing – and it isn't any more cheerful. The Elves tend to look at life in a more philosophical manner than we do, but that doesn't make death easy for them.

The ship pitches gently. We're now far south and the weather is improving. The rain has ceased and the sun warms the air. At night all three moons have been visible, large and heavy in the clear sky.

The dead Elf is wrapped in a funeral cloth bearing Lord Kalith's nine-starred insignia. After the oration a singer steps forward and intones a mournful dirge. His voice is clear and strong but the lament is full of sadness and casts a further shadow over us all. When the song is finished the Elves stand in silence. I bow my head, and try not to fidget. Finally the body is lowered over the side and sinks below the waves.

Lord Kalith walks briskly back to his post. The other Elves linger, talking among themselves. I'm already heading back to my cabin, keen to get below deck before Cicerius or the Prince decides it's time to lecture me about something or threaten to take away my Investigator's licence.

'A rather unfortunate family,' says Makri, as we step through my door.

'What do you mean?'

'The dead Elf. Weren't you listening to the oration?'

'Most of it was in the Royal Elvish language. I couldn't understand it.'

Makri slumps on to the bunk, looking ill. She's one of the poorest sailors I've ever encountered.

'I caught most of it,' she says. 'Lord Kalith is a very good speaker. I'll relay his speech to my Elvish language teacher back at the College. He'll like it.'

I get a beer and start hauling my boots off. 'What did you mean about an unfortunate family?' I ask.

'Well, one Elf in jail and another one dead. The Elf who fell from the rigging was called Eos-ar-Methet. Vas-ar-Methet's nephew, and Elith's cousin.'

I finish my beer and start putting my boots back on. I can feel some investigating coming on.

'Her cousin? How about that. An interesting piece of information that no one was rushing to tell me.'

I make to leave. Before I do I ask Makri if she could keep it quiet that she understood all of the funeral oration.

'I think that the fewer people who know you can speak the Royal Elvish language, the better. You might pick up more interesting things.'

I find Vas-ar-Methet in his cabin, a large area that

serves as both his living quarters and his on-board treatment area. As I arrive an Elf is leaving, smiling.

'He was looking pleased. You just heal him?'

'Yes. He was having bad dreams.'

'How do you cure someone of bad dreams? No, you can tell me some other time. Right now I'm looking for some information.'

Vas-ar-Methet immediately seems troubled.

'Thraxas, you know I'm grateful for your help, but . . .'

'But you've heard that with the assorted Lords, Sorcerers and important Turanians on this ship I'm about as popular as an Orc at an Elvish wedding. Don't worry about it, it's often this way. You didn't hire me to make friends. Now, how come you didn't tell me that the Elf who died was your nephew?'

Vas looks puzzled. 'Is it significant?'

'Of course. Doesn't it strike you as strange that the Elf who plummeted to his death for no apparent reason was Elith's cousin?'

'No. What is the connection?'

'I can't say. But trust me, my Investigator's intuition doesn't let me down. I knew there was something strange about that accident. Why would a healthy young Elf suddenly fall from the rigging and break his neck? Doesn't make sense. How many times has he been up there? Hundreds. I saw him myself, moments before, and he wasn't looking like an Elf who was suddenly going to make the elementary mistake of not holding on.'

'What are you suggesting? That he was pushed? There were other members of the crew there. They would have seen something.'

'There are other ways it could have happened. I tried

looking at the body at the time but I was prevented from examining it properly. My first thought was that he might have been drinking, although as far as I could see he only had water in his flask. But it could have been poisoned.'

Vas is very dubious.

'I really don't think that that is likely, old friend. His companions report that he simply lost his grip when he reached for his flask.'

'Do experienced sailors normally wave their hands around when they're up in the rigging? He could have got a drink any time. Speaking of which . . .'

I look pointedly at the inviting decanter on Vas's table and he pours me a glass of wine. As Elvish wine goes, it's okay, nothing more. Lord Kalith ought to take more care when he loads up with supplies.

I admit that the link may appear tenuous, but when I'm grubbing around in the city and odd things start happening I generally find they're connected somehow. I doubt things are any different with the Avulans.

'Did Eos have any sort of connection with the Hesuni Tree? Maybe help with the prayers, hymns or whatever else goes on there? And was he on friendly terms with your daughter?'

Vas considers this. 'It is not impossible. But before this terrible affair of my daughter, I had very little contact with the Tree Priests. I am only slightly acquainted with Gulas-ar-Thetos, the Chief Tree Priest. Whether Eos knew him, I can't say. It seems unlikely. Young sea-going Elves do not normally spend too much time with older members of the religious order. But he was friendly with my daughter. She will be sad to learn of his death.'

He promises that when we reach Avula he will be able to put me in touch with several Elves who will be able to tell me more.

'I hope they're going to be more co-operative than the crew.'

'They will be. They are my friends. I may be the only Elf on Avula who believes my daughter is innocent, but I am not the only one who would be glad if she were.'

An Elf arrives, apparently needing Vas's healing services. He is looking particularly unhappy. Many of the crew look unhappy. Maybe they're all having bad dreams.

The seas are now rough but we're making good progress. It is not just the skill of the Elvish sailors that speeds us onwards; Elvish shipwrights are privy to shipbuilding secrets unknown to their Human allies. Our craft cuts through the water at a rate that would be the envy of any Turanian Captain. Lord Kalith's personal Sorcerer, Jir-ar-Eth, is on the ship and could if necessary use sorcery to change the weather in our favour, but so far there has been no need. He stays below decks, swapping tales with Harmon Half-Elf and Lanius Suncatcher.

The death of the crew member has cast a pall of gloom over the ship. I'll be glad when we reach Avula. The voyage has started to bore me and I'm running short of beer. There is nothing to see apart from the endless grey seas and there is precious little to do. I've carried on with my enquiries as best as I can but because of the reticence of the Elves I've learned very little that Vas has not already told me.

Even young Isuas, for some reason quite in thrall to Makri, tells us bluntly that Vas's daughter is clearly guilty of the crime and is fortunate not to have been punished already.

'Only my father's high regard for Vas-ar-Methet has delayed it.'

'Your father's high regard? What do you mean?'

Isuas looks puzzled. 'Lord Kalith of course. Were you not aware that he is my father?'

'This youth is a spy!' I exclaim, and glare at her. 'So that's why you've been coming here every day, is it? Reporting on my movements to Lord Kalith, no doubt. Makri, send her away immediately.'

'I didn't want her here in the first place,' exclaims Makri, who has notably failed to warm to the young Elf.

'Are you really the daughter of the Elf Lord?'

'Yes. His youngest daughter.'

'Then what are you doing working as a cabin boy? Or should that be cabin girl?'

'Cabin Elf?' suggests Makri.

Isuas doesn't seem to think there is anything strange about it. She's been sailing with her father for the past year. 'He says it will toughen me up.'

'Well that would make sense,' says Makri. 'You certainly are a weedy kid.'

Isuas looks distressed at this. I guess she already knows she got the short straw when it came to handing out health and strength. I still feel suspicious of her presence. Back in Turai, young daughters of rulers don't go around being junior sailors.

'Does no one else believe Elith to be innocent?'

'Why would they? She admits the crime.'

'Not exactly. She doesn't deny it. That's different.'

Isuas does not seem overly concerned with the affair.

Rather, her interest is taken up with one of Makri's swords, which is lying on her bunk, a dark evil-looking weapon that Makri brought with her from the Orc Lands.

'Is that an Orcish blade?' asks Isuas, wide-eyed.

Makri grunts in reply.

'Such a thing has surely never been on this ship before. Can I touch it?'

'Only if you want to lose your hand,' growls Makri, who is never keen to see her weapons pawed at.

Young Isuas again looks distressed.

'Well, could I watch you clean it?' she ventures.

Makri hisses something rude.

'Could I just touch it? Please?'

'Oh, for God's sake, pick the damn thing up,' growls Makri. 'Anything to shut you up. Little brat,' she mutters as she lies on the bunk, groaning and complaining about the rough seas. Isuas holds Makri's sword out in front of her, and tries to look fierce.

'Will you teach me how to fight?' she says, eagerly.

Makri, unable to take any more of this, picks up one of her sandals and bounces it off Isuas's head. Isuas squawks, then flees from the cabin in tears.

'That was a bit harsh.'

'Harsh? She's lucky I didn't hit her with the sword. Now stop talking to me – I'm sick.'

I depart, leaving Makri to her misery. I meet Cicerius on deck. He knows I'm curious about the death of the sailor and this displeases him. The rain has obliged him to wear a cloak over his Senatorial toga but he still manages to look like an important official giving a telling-off to some hapless minion as he informs me that I am to stop making enquiries.

'I have been given strongly to understand that the Elves do not wish the matter to be further investigated.'

'Tell me something I don't know. Am I the only one around here who thinks that deaths should be looked into? I take it you don't actually forbid me to try and clear Vas-ar-Methet's daughter of the crime she's accused of?'

'I believe Lord Kalith regrets giving permission for Vas-ar-Methet to extend the enquiry,' says Cicerius.

Cicerius has the universal reputation of being the most incorruptible person in Turai. Despite his renowned austerity, he is not an unfair man. He tells me that he can understand my need to help my friend and wartime companion.

'Although I regret that you are on this voyage, I realise that it would have been difficult for you to refuse Vas-ar-Methet's request. Ties of friendship should not be taken lightly. But I must insist that you carry out your work without causing offence to our Elvish friends. And keep that woman Makri out of sight. Yesterday she was parading round the ship in a quite shameless manner wearing only a chainmail bikini. I do not believe the Elves were pleased.'

'Well, it was certainly a novel sight for them. Though I think she was fleeing to the rail to be sick, rather than actually parading around. Did you notice the gold toenails? Odd that she's picked up that fashion, because Makri's never been in Simnia, and as far as I know the only other women who do that are Simnian—'

'Just keep her under control,' says Cicerius, icily.

'You know what she's like, Cicerius. Difficult to reason with.'

The Deputy Consul almost smiles. Cicerius is not about to admit that Makri is exactly a good thing, but he would be forced to allow that she had been helpful when I last worked for him. He draws his cloak tighter against the wind and the rain, and contents himself with warning me not to make things difficult.

'There are times when your doggedness has proved useful. This is not one of them. If by any chance you do discover any secrets on Avula, keep them to yourself. As a representative of the state of Turai, I forbid you to say or do anything that may upset the Elves without fully consulting me first. This five-yearly festival is an important affair and the Avulans will be highly displeased if anything bad happens while their island is full of visitors.'

He pauses. 'Have you been drinking?'

I don't deny it. It passes the time.

Cicerius departs with his nose in the air. I notice that he is vain enough to wear a cloak sufficiently short to display the gold edging around the bottom of his toga. Only the upper classes wear togas. I'm dressed in my standard dull tunic with a heavy cloak to keep out the elements. I wander off, wondering who I might profitably spend some time with. It makes sense at least to try to gather some background information. Elith is due to be tried immediately after the festival, which means I'll only have a week or so to investigate the affair once we land.

I decide to see if I can find Lanius Suncatcher and Harmon Half-Elf. So far I have had little contact with them on board and I wonder if they might have picked up anything interesting about the crime. Before I can go in search of the Sorcerers, an Elf I don't recognise plants himself firmly in front of me. I greet him politely. He stares at me in a hostile manner. Though most of the Elves tie their hair back whilst on board ship, his long golden hair swings freely in the wind. His eyes are a little darker than normal and he has a powerful build. We stand looking at each other in silence.

'I am Gorith-ar-Del,' he says, finally.

I stare at him blankly. 'Is that supposed to mean something to me?'

'Callis-ar-Del was my brother. He hired you to help him. Then he got killed.'

Callis-ar-Del. I remember him. Along with his friend Jaris-ar-Miat, he was one of the Elves who hired me to look for the valuable Red Elvish Cloth last summer. They pretended they were trying to recover it for their Elf Lord Kalith-ar-Yil, our ship's Captain, but in reality they were trying to steal it. Both were eventually killed by Hanama from the Assassins Guild. They got in her way, which was foolish.

The way Gorith-ar-Del is staring at me, I have the impression he holds me responsible. I wasn't, but I don't want to go over the details of the case again. Hearing about his brother's criminal activities can only be painful to Gorith.

'I don't believe my brother was trying to steal the Cloth. I believe he was made the scapegoat after being caught up in events in a foreign city. He hired you to help him. Why didn't you protect him?'

The wind is picking up, My hair, tied back in a long ponytail, starts to swing gently like a pendulum.

'He left Turai without telling me. I did go after him, and I caught up with him before his ship left harbour.

Unfortunately he was dead by then. The Assassins Guild. It was no secret.'

'And was any effort made to punish the killers?'

'No one from the Assassins Guild ever gets taken to court.'

'Why not?'

'That would require a longer lecture on Turanian politics and customs than you want to hear. I'm sorry your brother was killed.'

Gorith leans towards me threateningly. 'It seems to me that someone set my brother up with the Cloth then was able to share the profits after he was murdered.' The Elf's eyes are cold. 'I don't trust you, fat man.'

Gorith-ar-Del stalks off, graceful despite the pitching of the ship. I look at his retreating figure. I shrug, and continue on my way to find Lanius and Harmon.

I locate them below decks in Harmon's cabin, which is a whole lot bigger than mine. The Elvish Sorcerer Jir-ar-Eth is with them and they're all seated comfortably, drinking wine. I'm irritated that no one thought to invite me, a fellow practitioner of the mystic arts, for a friendly drink. Harmon Half-Elf greets me affably enough.

'Come in, Thraxas. How are things with you?'

'Better than rowing a slave galley. Not too much better though. The Turanian delegation wishes I wasn't here, the Elves are freezing me out and my cabin is occupied by a woman who only stops complaining when she's throwing up.'

Vas has given Makri soothing herbs and potions, but she seems to be unusually prone to seasickness. There is nothing to do but wait for it to pass.

I've really come here looking for some friendly company,

but the sight of all the friendly company going on quite merrily without me is annoying. Even the Sorcerers are avoiding me. How come I'm the one who's suffering here? Rather than the civilised conversation I had in mind, I find myself pitching into the Elvish Sorcerer with an aggressive line in questioning.

'So, what's up with you Elves anyway?' I demand, fixing Jir-ar-Eth with an accusing look. 'I'm starting to think you all have something to hide. How come no one will answer my questions? Scared I'll dig up something?'

'Not at all,' replies Jir-ar-Eth. 'You can hardly blame Avulans for some reticence in the face of a man they have never met, who brings with him a woman of Orc parentage. But to the best of my knowledge, all the facts about the assault on the Hesuni Tree are known.'

'Oh yes?' I grunt. 'Well, I'm not convinced.'

I'm feeling aggressive. It feels good. I've had enough of crawling around being polite. I take a goblet of wine, uninvited, and bark a few more questions.

Unlike our magicians, who all wear a rainbow cloak as a mark of their guild, Jir-ar-Eth is clad in a standard Elf's green cloak with only a small yellow tree embroidered on the shoulder as a mark of his profession. He looks fairly old for an Elf, with his golden hair turning silver, but vigorous still.

'I understand that Elith can't remember the crime. Very convenient, don't you think?'

'You believe that someone else is responsible? Why?'

'Investigator's intuition,' I reply. 'And I'll trust my intuition against yours any day. Is there any chance of another glass of wine? Thank you. So, why did Vas's daughter damage the Tree?'

The Elvish Sorcerer confesses that he has no idea. Elith has not vouchsafed a motive.

'Rather suspicious, don't you think? Who might have framed her?'

'Really!' protests Jir. 'This is quite uncalled for. You must not apply the standards of your Human city to those of the Elvish Isles.'

'Oh yes,' I state, walking around the cabin waving my hands in the air. 'You Elves are always keen to brag about your high standards. Well let me tell you, I've had to help quite a few high-class Elves out of tough spots in Turai. Generally when they find themselves drunk in some low-class brothel and want it all hushed up from their Elf Lord.'

Jir-ar-Eth looks at me with amazement. Possibly fearing that Jir is about to blast me with a spell for my insolence, Lanius Suncatcher tries his best to smooth things over.

'You must excuse Thraxas,' he laughs. 'Always has to see suspicious circumstances everywhere. Back at the Palace he was famous for it.'

I am unapologetic. It's time I stirred things up a little around here. I've been on this ship for two weeks and I've learned nothing at all. You can't expect an Investigator to take that lying down. (Not this Investigator anyway. Maybe some others with lower standards.)

'I really don't see that you have any cause for suspicion, Thraxas,' says Harmon Half-Elf. 'And I would suggest that you moderate your manner. Cicerius and the Prince will not be pleased to learn that you are insulting our hosts.'

'Cicerius and our Prince can go to hell. I'm fed up with being warned about my behaviour. Who was it saved the city from that mad Orc Sorcerer only last month at the race meeting? Me. I didn't see anyone complaining about my bad manners then.'

'Everyone complained about your bad manners,' retorts Harmon. 'You were just too pleased with yourself to pay any attention.'

The Elvish Sorcerer clams up and refuses to answer any more of my questions. Lanius suggests that perhaps I should go back to my cabin and rest.

'Fine,' I tell him, and pack a bottle of wine into the bag at my side. 'I will. But don't expect me to pussyfoot around when I get to Avula. If anyone tries to hide the facts from me there I'll be down on them like a bad spell.'

I storm out. Back on deck the rain hits me in the face. I ignore it and stride back to my cabin. Inside Makri is sitting on the floor, not looking any better.

'Damned Elves,' I exclaim. 'I'm sick of them already. What can you expect? Sitting round in trees all the time, singing about the stars. Apart from the ones who are threatening me.'

'You were threatened?'

'Yes. Some large Elf called Gorith thinks I was responsible for the death of his brother. You remember, one of the pair whom Hanama killed in Twelve Seas.'

'Hanama. I like her.'

'Yes, for a murderous Assassin she's always excellent company.'

I bring out the wine and take a healthy slug. 'To hell with Gorith.'

The ship rolls suddenly. Makri, unable to take the sight of me guzzling wine in her present precarious state, is once more overcome with nausea. She fails to make it to the side of the ship. She fails even to make it out the cabin, and is sick on the floor. Meanwhile the sudden violent pitching makes me drop the bottle of wine and it smashes. I slip and follow it down. At this moment, while Makri and I are rolling around on the floor of our tiny cabin in a mess of beer, wine and vomit, the door bursts open and Prince Dees-Akan walks in.

He stares, incredulous, at the sight that meets his eyes. It's not the sort of behaviour he's been brought up to expect. As I'm hauling myself to my feet he seems to be having some difficulty in finding the appropriate words.

'Is it true that you just insulted the eminent Elvish Sorcerer Jir-ar-Eth?' he demands.

'Certainly not,' I reply. 'Possibly he got the wrong impression. Not used to being questioned, I expect.'

Makri groans, rolls over and throws up over the Prince's feet.

'Eh . . . sorry, your highness . . . hasn't quite found her sea legs yet.'

'You low-life scum!' yells the Prince.

'There's no need to talk to her like that!' I protest. 'She's never been on a ship before.'

'I was referring to you,' says the Prince.

'Don't worry,' says Makri, grabbing his leg in an attempt to make it back on to her feet. 'I'll have him civilised by the time we get to Avula.'

When Makri first arrived in Turai, fresh from the rigours of the gladiator slave pits, she showed very little sign of a sense of humour. It developed fairly rapidly, but I could have told her that with the Prince looking with horror at his ruined sandals, this was not the time to be light-hearted.

'How dare you address me, you piece of filth!' shouts the Prince.

He departs in a fury. Makri abandons her efforts to rise and lies in a pool of her own sickness. It is really, really unpleasant. I hunt for one of my remaining beers, break open the bottle and start pouring it down my throat. We remain in silence for a while.

'You think we made a good impression?' says Makri finally.

'Pretty good. I may be in for a swift recall to the Palace.'

Makri laughs. I help her to her feet. She shakes her head to clear it. 'I think I'm starting to feel better now. How long till we reach Avula?'

I hand her a towel to clean her face. 'Another two weeks.'

'I'll be pleased to walk on dry land again,' says Makri.

'Me too. And it will be good to get some proper investigating done. Now we've started to make friends in important places, it should be a breeze.'

CHAPTER
SIX

Two weeks later we're close to Avula. We should sight land tomorrow. The weather has improved. Makri's health has improved. We're bored. For want of anything better to do, Makri, with encouragement from me, has given in to Isuas's repeated requests and has given her some lessons in basic sword play. These lessons have all taken place in the cramped privacy of our cabin, partly because Isuas feels her father would not be pleased if he knew, and partly because Makri says she wouldn't like her reputation as a fighter to suffer from anyone learning that she was trying to teach sword-fighting to such a useless excuse for an Elf as Isuas. The cabin being somewhat cramped at the best of times, I haven't actually seen any of these sessions, but Makri assures me that Isuas is the most pathetic creature ever to hold a sword, and seeing the child fumbling around gives Makri the strong desire to pick her up and throw her overboard.

'Not warming to the kid, then?'

'I loathe her. She keeps bursting into tears for no reason. Why did you encourage me to teach her?'

'Because it might do us some good on Avula if we have an ally. She's Kalith's daughter – she might be able to open a few doors for us.'

'Not if I break her fingers,' mutters Makri.

Nothing of note has happened to me. I haven't even been threatened recently. I've seen Gorith-ar-Del several times but he has not spoken to me since his original menacing approach.

I haven't learned anything much though I picked up a little gossip while playing niarit with Osath, the ship's cook. I like Osath. He's an excellent chef. He's also one of the very few Elves who carries a little extra weight round his belly. My tremendous enthusiasm for his food overcame his Elvish reticence and we've spent a few evenings playing niarit together. Most of what I learn sheds no light on Elith's case, but it's interesting background information. Even in a place like Avula, there are political tensions. Lord Kalith has an advisory Council of twelve leading Elvish Elders, and certain of these Elders have been pushing for more influence. It's even rumoured that some wish to abandon the traditional rule of the Elvish Lord and move on to some representative system, which would be unheard of among the Elves.

Furthermore, there are some tensions around the Hesuni Tree. Gulas-ar-Thetos holds the position of Chief Tree Priest but there is another branch of the family that has claimed for several generations that the Priesthood should belong to them. Some sort of complicated dispute about the rules of succession, which never quite goes away.

Even the festival is not without its attendant controversy. The three staged versions of the tale of Queen Leeuven are each put on by one of the Ossuni Elves' islands – Avula, Ven and Corinthal – in the form of a competition, with judges giving a prize to the winning play. It is a great honour to produce the play and on each island leading Elves compete for the position. Apparently the person chosen by Lord Kalith to produce and direct Avula's play this year is not universally popular. There is a feeling on the island that the job has gone to the wrong Elf.

'Myself, I've never cared much for the plays,' confides Osath. 'Too highbrow for me. I like the juggling competition best. More soup?'

Other than this, I sit in my cabin and smoke thazis with Makri.

'I can't wait to get off this ship,' she tells me for the twentieth time, idly prodding at the gold ring that pierces her nose, another sartorial outrage guaranteed to inflame public opinion in Turai. She's just washed her hair and the huge dark mass of it seems to take up a substantial amount of our limited cabin space.

We pass the thazis stick back and forward between us. We have the porthole open to let out the pungent aroma. This gives me the odd feeling that I'm a much younger man, a youth in fact, smoking the mild narcotic in secret. These days in Turai no one bothers to conceal thazis, though it is still technically illegal. Since the much more powerful drug dwa took its hold on the city, the authorities are relieved if thazis is the worst thing you're up to. But I don't want to offend the Elves. As far as I know, they disapprove of all narcotics.

Isuas appears, wide-eyed and timorous as usual.

'Can't you knock?' growls Makri.

I grin at the young Elf. She might be a sickly sort of kid, with straggly hair and watery eyes, but I like her well enough. She has a message for me from Lord Kalith.

'He asks if you would like to spend this last evening playing niarit.'

'Niarit? I must be back in his good books.'

Isuas looks doubtful. 'I think he just ran out of opponents. He's beaten all the other players on the ship.'

I haul myself up. 'Then it sounds like a job for Thraxas. Once I'm through with him, your father will regret ever taking up the game.'

Isuas looks pained. 'My father is renowned as a fine player.'

'Oh yes? Well, when it comes to niarit I am number one chariot. Ask Makri here.'

'Will you teach me some more fighting?' asks Isuas eagerly.

Makri scowls. 'What's the point? When it comes to sword play you're about as much use as a eunuch in a brothel.'

Isuas gapes, shocked by this crude expression. She hangs her head. 'I'll try to do better,' she mumbles.

'Well, I'll leave you to it, Makri. Have fun.'

'Are you going to go and leave me with this brat for company?'

'I am indeed. A true niarit player never refuses a challenge. If there's any wine going spare I'll bring you back a bottle.'

I depart, keen for some action. I wonder if Lord Kalith might wish to place a small wager on the outcome? I have a package with me, just in case.

I enter Kalith's comfortable cabin for only the second time on the voyage. One might have thought that as a guest of the Elves I would have been invited there more frequently, but no. While Princes, Deputy Consuls and assorted Sorcerers have freely enjoyed the Elf Lord's hospitality, Thraxas the Investigator has sadly languished in a tiny cabin at the unfashionable end of the ship, fruit-lessly awaiting an occasional invitation to socialise with the upper classes.

Stifling my resentment, I greet Kalith politely enough. 'You wished to see me?'

'I wondered if you might care for a game?'

Lord Kalith gestures with his hand towards the niarit board set out in front of him. The two opposing armies are lined up against each other, the front rank com-prising, from left to right, Foot Soldiers, or Hoplites, then Archers, then Trolls. The rear rank is made up of Ele-phants, Heavy Mounted Knights and Light Mounted Lancers. Each player also has in their army a Siege Tower, a Healer, a Harper, a Wizard, a Hero and a Plague Carrier. A the very back of the board is the Castle, the object of the game being to defend your own Castle and storm your opponent's. Lord Kalith's board is the same as that used all over the Human Lands, except that one of the armies is green instead of white, and the Castles at each end of the board are instead represented by large fortified trees.

'I generally take green,' says Lord Kalith.

'Fine. They call me Thraxas the Black. And I generally take wine.'

No servant is in attendance. Faced with the possibility of actually standing up and pouring me some wine him-self – which would be asking rather a lot of an Elf Lord – Kalith looks suddenly puzzled and asks me if I know where his daughter is. I tell him she's hanging around with Makri, which doesn't please him.

'All I hear from my daughter these days is Makri this or Makri that. I do not approve.'

'Yeah, as a role model Makri is the woman from hell. Don't worry, she hates your daughter anyway.'

Somehow that didn't come out quite as I intended. Kalith is not pacified. To save him any embarrassment I get my own wine, filling a goblet from the decanter nearby. And once again I have to say that, as Elvish wine goes, it is not of the finest. Makes me again suspect that Kalith is not liberal with his hospitality, and probably doesn't have a spare barrel of beer waiting in the store-room for anyone who might wish to partake of it.

'Care for a small wager?'

Kalith raises his eyebrows a fraction. 'I have no wish to take money from you, Investigator.'

'You won't.'

'I will assuredly defeat you.'

'That's what your cook said before I sent his army down to Elvish hell.'

Kalith smiles. 'I have heard that you outplayed Osath. I, however, am a rather better player. But I repeat, I have no wish to take money from you.'

I unwrap my package.

'A stick?'

'An illuminated staff. One of the finest. Given to me by the renowned Turanian Sorcerer Kemlath Orc Slayer.'

I speak a word of power and the staff lights up with a brilliant golden hue. It really is a fine illuminated staff, the best I've ever had. Even to an Elf Lord, it can't be an unattractive bet.

Lord Kalith picks it up and holds it, watching as the golden light streams out of it, lighting all corners of the cabin.

'A fine staff. Though I seem to remember hearing that

Kemlath Orc Slayer was obliged to leave Turai in disgrace.'

'He had the misfortune to have me investigate some crimes he'd committed.'

'Very well, I accept your bet. What shall I wager in return? A golden goblet?'

Elves always think that humans are slaves to gold. Fair enough. I've done plenty of questionable things for gold. But that's not what I'm looking for right now.

'Would you rather I staked some mystical item? My chief Sorcerer Jir-ar-Eth has many fine articles.'

'No, I'm not needing any fine articles. I was thinking more about Makri.'

Kalith frowns.

'I want her on Avula with me. She helps me investigate. If I win, I want you to let her land, no questions asked. And guarantee that the Avulans will be hospitable to her.'

'There is no possibility of my people being hospitable to her.'

'Well at least not openly hostile. Do you accept my bet?'

The Elf Lord shakes his head. 'I cannot allow her on my island.'

I stand up.

'A pity. I was looking forward to playing. It's not often you get the chance to show an Elf Lord that no matter how many excellent variations he works out for the Harper's Game, he's got about as much chance against Thraxas as a rat against a dragon. And I mean a small rat and a big dragon.'

A pained look comes into the Elf Lord's face. I doubt that he has ever before been compared to a rat.

'Sit down,' he says coldly. 'And prepare to lose your staff.'

We start to play. Lord Kalith apparently does not fully trust his new variation because he starts off with the Hoplite advance, a solid if unexciting strategy. I respond in a conventional manner by harrying them with my Light Cavalry, meanwhile forming up my own Hoplites to resist and bringing up my Trolls for some heavy support. It has all the makings of a stiff battle on the centre of the field, which will suit me fine, when Lord Kalith surprises me by sending his Hero striding out in front of his army, straight into my Light Cavalry.

This seems foolish. The Hero carries a lot of weight on the board and can deal with most things, but not an entire division of Cavalry backed up with Hoplites and Trolls. I surround him and get ready for the kill but I'm keeping a watchful eye out for whatever else Kalith might have planned.

When I'm about to slay Kalith's Hero he suddenly advances his Archers up towards my right flank, backed by his Elephants. Coming alongside them are his Harper and his Plague Carrier. I'm momentarily puzzled. Apparently Lord Kalith now wishes to rescue his Hero, but I can't see how even this strong force can reach him in time. His Harper sings to my troops, which has the power of paralysing them, and his Plague Carrier starts to do some damage, but I form up my Trolls in a strong defensive line and send over some of my Heavy Cavalry for support, with my Healer and my Wizard in attendance. Lord Kalith's relief force fails to penetrate and I kill his Hero, which, I think, puts me at a strong advantage.

All of a sudden I notice that for some reason his

Harper seems to be continuing to advance and far too many of my troops on my left flank are succumbing to his singing. In an unexpected move, Lord Kalith sends his Light Cavalry streaming through the gap. I remain impassive at the board, but inside I'm uttering a few curses. Kalith has indeed worked out a new variation on the Harper's Game, sacrificing his Hero. He apparently had no intention of rescuing him, but merely used the gambit as a distraction.

There are a tense few minutes as I struggle to re-inforce my left flank. Even here I'm still a little doubtful, fearing that I may be missing something. I don't want to overcommit and find Kalith suddenly breaking through somewhere else. It takes some fine swift calculations on my part to reorganise my defences and in the process I lose the services of my Harper when he is trampled by a rampaging Elephant.

Finally, however, I hold the line, and start pushing Kalith back up the board. With his Hero gone, his Wizard nearly out of spells and his Trolls hemmed in by my Heavy Cavalry, he has no option but to retreat. As play crosses back into his side of the board I start to inflict heavy losses on his army and manage to isolate and kill his Wizard. I've got him beat. No one comes back from this position, not against me anyway.

Makri chooses this moment to burst into the cabin, followed firstly by a frightened-looking Isuas and secondly by two irate Elvish attendants. She strides over to us and plants herself right beside Lord Kalith's chair.

'What's this your daughter tells me about you issuing orders that I can't leave the ship?' she demands.

I quickly glance at Makri's hips and am relieved to see

she has not actually brought a sword with her. Not that this is any real guarantee that she is unarmed. Makri is always liable to produce a dagger or a throwing star from some unexpected place. I never met anyone so keen on walking round with a knife in each boot.

'I did indeed issue such an order,' says Lord Kalith, regally. If he's at all concerned about the sight of a furious Makri towering over him he's not showing it, and when his attendants hurry forward he holds up his hand to show that everything is under control.

I rise to my feet. 'Don't worry about it, Makri, I've arranged things.'

I wave at the niarit board, then give Kalith a look.

'I presume you do not wish to carry on with the game.'

Again, I have to say that Lord Kalith takes it well. Good breeding. He can't be at all happy that's he's just lost to me at niarit, and he has made it perfectly plain that he is utterly opposed to Makri landing on Avula, but from all the emotion he shows you might imagine he was having another excellent day at the Tree Palace.

'I concede. Well played, Investigator. I see that my variation needs further work.'

He turns his head toward Makri. 'You may land on Avula. Do nothing that may disturb my Elves. And stay away from my daughter.'

'What's going on?' asks Makri. I tell her I'll explain later and usher her out before she causes any further offence.

Back on the deck we run into Cicerius.

'Have you— ?' he says.

'Yes. Thoroughly offended Lord Kalith. Major diplomatic incident. Better go and sort it out. See you on Avula.'

CHAPTER
SEVEN

B y the afternoon of the next day we're riding inland to
the heart of the island. Avula is extremely lush, densely
forested with tall trees that cover the shallow hills that
rise towards the centre. I'm a little taken aback by the size
of the trees. I'd forgotten how large they were. Even
the great oaks in the King's gardens in Turai are mere
saplings in comparison. And without getting too mystical
about it, the trees on an Elvish island give the impression
that they're more alive than your average tree.

Landing on the island involved less ceremony than I
was expecting. A delegation of important Elves, including
Kalith's wife, Lady Yestar, was at the quay to greet their
guests, but there was not the tedious formality that such
an event would have occasioned in Turai. Brief intro-
ductions were made and we set off inland. Even Makri's
appearance failed to cause a commotion. Kalith presumably had sent word of her arrival, and his subjects,
while not looking thrilled at the sight of her, at least
didn't make a fuss. Makri greeted Lady Yestar in her
flawless Elvish, as genteelly as any lady of the court,
if the Elves have a court that is, which I'm not certain
about. I know Kalith has some sort of palace in the trees.

I ride beside Makri at the back of the column, far
behind Lord Kalith and Prince Dees-Akan. Makri looks

around her with interest but I'm too busy thinking about my work to fully appreciate the splendour of the island. I have the tiniest feeling, far away at the very edge of my Investigator's intuition, that something is wrong all around me. Something intangible that I can't put a name to. Whatever it is, it prevents me from gaping at the giant butterflies.

Avula is one of the largest of the Elvish Isles. During the last Orc War it provided many troops and ships for the defence of the west, but as we travel inland it's not exactly obvious where all these Elves live. There are no extensive settlements at ground level. Here and there wooden houses stand secluded in clearings in the forest, but in the main the Elves prefer to construct their houses high up in the trees. These are cunningly crafted so that they appear to be more like natural growths than artificial objects. Even some of the larger collections of these houses, connected by walkways high above our heads, blend in with the environment in a manner that makes it easy to believe that the land is devoid of inhabitants. Only the regular, well-maintained path we travel on betrays the fact that many Elves live in these parts.

Somewhere or other there must be some sort of industry, workshops where the Elves make their own swords, harnesses and other such things, but we see nothing of this. Just trees, treehouses and the occasional Elf looking down with interest at the procession.

We're riding on horses provided by the Elves. Vas tells me that on the far side of the island the land is more open, and their animals are pastured there. We pass several small rivers, each running with bright water that glints in the sunlight.

Lord Kalith's Tree Palace is situated at the centre of the island, the highest point on Avula. The Hesuni Tree is next to the Palace. The important guests are to be quartered nearby. I wonder how Cicerius will manage living in a tree. I notice that the sombre mood of our Elvish hosts has lightened as they find themselves once more in their familiar surroundings, but I still have the feeling that all is not well.

Cicerius is riding beside me, upright in the saddle like a man who once fought in the army. Cicerius never managed to cover himself in glory at war, but he did at least do his duty against the Orcs, unlike most of our present-day Turanian politicians, many of whom bought their way out of military service. I lean over and whisper to him.

'Is it just me or do you feel something wrong here?'

'Wrong? What do you mean?'

'I don't know exactly. I just get the feeling that something is wrong. Shouldn't these Elves in the trees be waving to us or something?'

'They are waving.'

'Well maybe they're waving a bit. I still figure they should be happier to see their Lord back. Singing maybe. Don't Elves sing a lot? There's some kind of gloom over this place.'

'I don't feel it,' says Cicerius.

I always trust my intuition and it's kept me alive for a long time.

We pass through a clearing and view an unusual spectacle. Thirty or so Elves in white cloaks are moving around in unison under the direction of another Elf. He seems to be shouting at them in an exasperated manner.

'The chorus for one of the plays,' our Elvish companions inform us.

The irate screaming gets louder.

'The directors of the plays are often given to excesses of emotion.'

Passing through another clearing we distinctly hear choral singing, again from a group rehearsing for the festival, and in the distance we catch sight of some jugglers practising. The whole atmosphere becomes more festive. I wonder again if I might solve the case quickly and thereby have some time in which to enjoy myself. Along with Osath the cook, I'm quite looking forward to the juggling competition. Whatever happens, I don't have that long in which to investigate. Elith is due to be tried immediately after the festival, which begins in seven days' time and lasts for three.

Vas-ar-Methet is riding some way in front of us. Several hours into the journey he sends a message back to me that we are close to his brother's abode. The messenger is to take Makri and me there while the procession rides on. The deputation is to receive the full hospitality of Lord Kalith. We aren't.

'Would it be any use telling you not to make a nuisance of yourself?' asks Cicerius as we prepare to go our separate ways.

'You'll hardly notice we're here,' I promise.

'Whatever you do,' says Cicerius sternly, 'don't meddle with anything that is calanith.'

'Cheer up, Cicerius,' says Makri, appearing beside us. 'I'm an expert in Elvish taboos. In fact, I am an Elvish taboo. I'll keep Thraxas out of trouble.'

Makri sits well on her horse. When she arrived in

Turai she was already a good rider. Makri is good at most things. It's annoying. Since leaving the ship her spirits have improved.

'I'm as happy as an Elf in a tree,' she says, laughing, and then looks thoughtful. 'Although I have noticed that the Elves up in the trees don't actually look all that happy. Good choral singing though.'

Our guide leads us down a narrow path. For an Elf he seems remarkably dour. My efforts at conversation come to nothing. Apart from learning that his name is Coris-ar-Mithan and he's a cousin of my friend Vas, I learn nothing at all from him.

We don't have to endure each other's company for long. Coris brings us swiftly to another small clearing where three other Elves, two of them elderly, are waiting for us. Coris greets them briefly, bows formally to us and rides off.

'Greeting, friends of Vas-ar-Methet. Welcome to our home.'

They introduce themselves to us as Vas's brother, mother, and sister.

'You must be tired after the long journey. We have pre-pared food and your rooms are waiting. Please follow us.'

They head for a tree. Lying flush with the trunk is a ladder that goes upwards for a long way. I look at it doubtfully and turn to Makri.

'How do you like heights?'

'I'm not wild about them.'

'Me neither.'

We grit our teeth and start to climb. We climb a long way. I try not to look down. As a man who can have diffi-culty mounting the outside steps to my office, I don't find it the most convenient place for a home. I'm relieved when we reach the top and step on to a platform. The Elvish house stretches over the highest branches of the tree, and over to the next tree. We're on the very outskirts of the large central township of the Elves, and from here to the centre of the island houses are strung over most of the forest, increasing in density as they approach the centre. From here is should be possible to walk all the way to the centre of the island without once touching the ground.

Once we step inside we find a comfortable and welcoming dwelling place. The rooms, though simply constructed, are brightly lit, decorated in warm colours with tapestries and rugs. There are pitchers of water and we are invited to wash and make ourselves comfortable before our meal.

'Nice house,' says Makri after they've left us.

I agree. 'Pity it isn't on the ground. I'd have a hard time making it up that ladder every day.'

It is now late in the afternoon. After eating I'm planning on heading out quickly to investigate.

'I'm going to see Elith. Time to question the suspect and get things moving. I figure if I can clear her name quickly I might be able to get a bit of rest before heading back to Turai. I need a rest, I've been working way too hard recently.'

Vas has arranged that his brother will take me to the place where Elith is held and I'm keen to set off as soon as I can. Carith, slightly younger and less distinguished than the healer, is pleased to find I'm eager to get started.

'No one in our family believes that Elith is guilty of this terrible crime.'

Leaving Makri to look around, I accompany Carith on the long journey through the walkways over the trees towards the centre of Avula, where Elith is incarcerated. He tells me that she is held in a rarely used prison building at the rear of Lord Kalith's Tree Palace.

'Have you considered a jail break?'

Carith seems shocked by the suggestion. 'No. We are presuming that her name will be cleared.'

'Don't presume. After all, she might be guilty. I'm planning on knocking a few heads together to find out the truth. But it never hurts to have a back-up plan.'

The wooden walkways lead us past more houses. Elves stare as I pass. I'd imagine it's a long time since they've seen anyone with my impressive figure. They're a thin race, the Elves. Even in old age they rarely seem to settle into comfortable obesity. I ask Carith if there are any taverns on Avula. He tells me that there is nothing that would actually qualify as a tavern, but they do brew their own beer and gather in glades to drink it, which doesn't sound too bad. I tell him that I have now run out of beer, and instruct him that I must have some as soon as possible.

We pass over a large clearing, the largest open space I've seen since we reached the island.

'The tournament field,' explains my guide. 'It is often in use – Lord Kalith likes to keep his Elves well prepared. It is here that the plays will be staged. There will also be a tournament, for the younger Elves. Will you be staying for the whole festival?'

'I'm not sure. Depends how the investigating goes.'

'A curious way to make a living,' ventures Carith.

'Not in Turai it isn't. Where I live you can't turn round

without bumping into something that needs investigating.'

'Are you paid well for the service?'

'No,' I reply, truthfully. 'But I make up for it at the chariot races.'

Carith laughs. I like him, he's affable like his brother. He's heard about my triumph over Lord Kalith at the niarit board and has the good grace to tell me that the Avulans cannot remember when their ruler was last defeated at the game, which pleases me immensely.

The evening is cool and pleasant. Walking through the tree tops isn't so bad when I get used to it and the journey takes less time than I anticipated. Carith comes to a halt, pointing out to me a large wooden construction visible a short way ahead.

'The Tree Palace,' he informs me.

To one side there is a tree so large and impressive that it has to be the Hesuni Tree. It seems healthy enough, with plenty of golden foliage. Beside it are two pools of still water, one large and one small. We walk over a narrow suspended bridge towards the Palace, but when we're almost there a commotion breaks out and several Elves appear at the doorway, talking together in an agitated manner. When they see us they run up and start speaking to Carith accusingly. He looks confused, and turns to me to explain, but I need no explanation. Elithir-Methet has vanished from her prison.

'Escaped?'

The Elvish guards nod. They recognise Carith and they find it very suspicious that her uncle just happens to be strolling by at this very moment, but before they can pursue it further a great wailing breaks out from

the direction of the Hesuni Tree. Carith and the other
Elves are taken aback and peer over the walkway in
an attempt to find out what is happening. Sensing that
his niece may be in trouble Carith starts to run in the
direction of the Palace. I follow him as best I can, though
I have difficulty keeping up. All around Elves are
shouting, torches are being lit and the general uproar
grows ever more furious. Close to the Tree Palace Carith
spots an Elf he recognises on a walkway some way below
us and leans over to shout at him, trying to find out what
is happening.

'It's Gulas-ar-Thetos,' shouts the Elf. 'He's dead. Murdered beside the tree. Elith-ir-Methet has killed him.'

Carith almost falls off the walkway, such is the shock
that this intelligence gives him. For a while he is
incapable of speech and gasps for breath as the outcry
intensifies. The Elves' Tree Priest has been murdered and
I don't need to be told that this is the most sensational
event ever to happen on Avula.

'Elith!' gasps Carith. 'How could she?'

'We don't know that she did,' I tell him harshly. 'Now,
take me to the scene of the crime, and quickly. If I'm
going to sort things out I'll need to know a lot of things
and I'll need to know them fast.'

I give him a push, none too gently. It's enough to get
him back into action. We hurry round the outskirts
of the Palace and make our way down a ladder to the
Hesuni Tree, where already a great many Elves are con-
gregating, and everything is noise and confusion.

I pat my sword, secure at my hip, and take out a small
flask of klee I've saved for emergencies. As it burns its way
down my throat, it strikes me that for the first time in

over a month I'm feeling properly like myself. Thraxas
the Investigator. I'll show these Elves a thing or two when
it comes to investigating.

CHAPTER
EIGHT

By the time we reach the ground about fifty Elves are standing in a circle between the large pool and the towering Hesuni Tree, and they're making enough noise to wake Old King Kiben. Camith hangs back but I barge my way through. Standing forlornly in the centre of the circle is a tall young female Elf I take to be Elith-ir-Methet. Lying next to her is another Elf, this one dead, with blood seeping from an ugly wound in his chest.

Elith is holding a blood-stained knife.

'Elith-ir-Methet has killed the Tree Priest,' say the Elves over and over again, horror and incredulity in their voices.

Things are looking worse for my client.

The surrounding Elves seem at a loss. No one is making any moves to drag the culprit away, examine the body, or do anything really. I stride forward.

'Thraxas,' I announce. 'Investigator, guest of Lord Kalith.'

I examine the body. The light is fading and I'm not as familiar with deceased Elves as I am with murdered Humans, but I'd say he's only been dead for a matter of minutes.

'Did you do this?' I ask Elith.

She shakes her head. Then she faints. I curse. I was hoping for a little more information. Three tall

Elves wearing the nine-starred insignia of Lord Kalith's household arrive on the scene and start to take control. When the crowd appraise them of the facts one of them departs immediately, presumably to inform Kalith of events, while the other two pick up Elith. Her long golden hair trails to the grass as they start to carry her away.

'Where are you taking her?' I demand.

They decline to answer. I follow them. The crowd troops along in our wake and I lose sight of Camith. I notice that one Elf in particular seems to be doing a lot of wailing, something about his poor brother. Before we reach the great wooden ladders that lead up to Kalith's Tree Palace more of his household appear. While their manner holds none of the undisguised hostility that the Civil Guards in Turai would display in similar circumstances, they make it clear that this matter is now in the hands of their Lord and the crowd is not to advance any further.

'Thraxas of Turai,' I say imperiously as they bar my way. 'Assistant to Deputy Consul Cicerius.'

I try to look important. It gets me through. My weight can lend me a certain grandeur. Elith is carried up the ladder and I climb up right behind her.

We ascend a long way, past platforms decorated with carvings of eagles intertwined with ivy and woven with streamers of golden leaves. The trees that support the Palace seem to reach up forever and my limbs are aching by the time we reach the top. As we clamber on to the final platform Kalith is there to greet us.

His attendants place Elith in front of him. She stirs. Lord Kalith glares down at her.

'You have killed Gulas-ar-Thetos, Priest of the Hesuni Tree!'

Elith blinks, and makes no reply. She appears dazed, maybe just from shock, but maybe from something else. Her pupils seem to me to be dilated, though with Elves it's hard to tell, the whole race generally having such big eyes anyway.

'Well, so it is alleged,' I say, moving to her side. 'But nothing has been proved against her.'

The Elf Lord is positively displeased to see me. 'Leave my Palace.'

'I never desert a client. And shouldn't someone be getting her a healer? She looks as if she could do with some attention.'

'What sort of attention did she give my brother?' roars an Elf behind us, and he makes an effort to rush at Elith. His companions restrain him.

I don't like this at all. My client is surrounded by a horde of hostile Elves and the ruler of the island seems in no mood to listen to pleas on her behalf. Simply because Elves have a reputation as just and tolerant, it doesn't mean that Kalith won't decide that the best thing to do with the murderess is to throw her off the highest platform and have done with it. I'm relieved when Vas-ar-Methet arrives. He doesn't do much except stand there looking anguished, but I figure that his daughter is at least less liable to summary justice with him in the picture.

Kalith orders Elith to be taken to a secure place and guarded well. He allows Vas to go with her, to minister to her sickness, then tells his guards to bring him witnesses to the event so that he can have the full story from people who saw what happened. Then he orders me to get out of his sight.

I depart without an argument. I could do with talking

to some witnesses myself. I'm about to fortify myself with klee for the journey back down the ladders when I get a mental image of the Elf falling from the rigging, so I put the flask away and make the descent sober.

Back at the Hesuni Tree the crowd is still gathered. A few of them are wearing the white robes that denote their status as actors.

'More evil has befallen us,' moans an Elf to her friends, and they moan back in agreement.

I can understand why they're upset. If the most important religious official in the land has to get murdered, you really don't want it to be right at the moment you have a host of foreign guests to impress. No wonder Lord Kalith is furious. That, however, is a problem for the Elves. My problem is gathering information and clearing Elith's name. Unless she turns out to be irredeemably guilty, in which case I've a jail break to plan. For desecrating the Hesuni Tree, Elith was facing banishment. For murder of the Tree Priest, she's facing execution. I will not allow Elith to be convicted of murder. For one thing, I owe her father. For another, Lord Kalith has really started to annoy me.

I introduce myself to a group of Elves and ask them if anyone actually saw Elith sticking the knife into Gulas-ar-Thetos. They don't know. It all happened before they arrived on the scene. The next group gives me a similar reply. Some Elf – no one knows quite who – arrived to find Gulas dead and Elith lying beside him with a knife in her hand.

I'm hindered in my investigations by the activities of the Elves sent by Kalith to gather witnesses, and more than once I'm just about to question someone when he or she is hustled off to the Tree Palace, but at least the attendants don't send me away, or threaten me with arrest. As darkness falls I've learned about as much as I can and I decide it's time to talk to Vas-ar-Methet. I head back towards the Tree Palace but in the gloom I bump into an Elf coming the other way. He raises his head and beneath the hood I see a face I recognise. It's Gorith-ar-Del, and he doesn't look any happier to see me now than he did during the voyage.

'Interfering again?' he demands.

I decline to answer, but as I hurry away I'm struck by the murderous look he had in his eyes. There is an Elf who hasn't been spending much time singing in the trees. There's something about him that doesn't quite add up and I make a mental note to check him out later.

Back at the ladders that lead up to the Tree Palace I have the good fortune to arrive just after Prince Dees-Akan and his entourage. The guards part to let them through and I hurry after as if I'm part of the official party. Making the climb for the second time tonight I develop the strong conviction that it is a mistake to live up in the trees. My limbs wouldn't take too much of this. Prince Dees-Akan catches sight of me.

'Were you invited to the Tree Palace?' he demands.

'Yes, your highness,' I lie, and saunter past. The door-men look doubtful. An Elf with drooping shoulders and downcast gaze comes towards us and I march past crying out Vas's name.

'I'm here. Take me to the patient.'

I grasp the startled Vas-ar-Methet's arm and steer us through to the first courtyard.

'Where is she?'

'Thraxas, it is all so terrible, I cannot—'

I interrupt him impatiently. 'Never mind that just now. Just take me to her. If I don't get to speak to her now I might never get the chance.'

Vas nods. Back in the War he wasn't an Elf to hang around dithering when action was needed. He leads me through the courtyard and up another ladder to a higher platform. From there a walkway stretches over most of the length of the Palace. Lord Kalith's attendants are dotted around, but no one tries to get in the healer's way.

'She's being held in a building at the back of the Palace. I can get us close, but I doubt they'll let you in.'

'I'll think of something.'

We are now high above the Palace, further from the ground than I would wish to be. I look down at the blanket of trees below us, and imagine how easily I would plummet down through them if I lost my footing. We reach the end of the walkway and descend into another courtyard, this one darker and less ornate than those at the front of the building. Vas points to a door in front of which three Elves are stationed, each of them armed. These are the first Elves I've seen on Avula to carry swords openly.

'They are guarding Elith,' whispers Vas. 'I didn't want to leave her, but Lord Kalith sent word that I was to be dismissed before he came to question her himself.'

'Where is he now?'

'Hearing the accounts of those who witnessed the affair. I imagine that he will be here before long. The death of our Tree Priest is a catastrophic event, Thraxas. I will not wish to continue living if my daughter is found to be guilty of his murder.'

'Well, don't do anything rash,' I tell him. 'I'm going in.'

The guards challenge me. I speak the one solitary spell I'm carrying with me, the sleep spell. It works well, as it always does. The three guards sink gently to the ground. Vas-ar-Methet gasps in amazement at my action.

'You worked a spell on Lord Kalith's guards?'

'What were you expecting? A few cunning lies? I need to see Elith and I need to see her now.'

'But when Kalith—'

I don't stay around to listen to the rest but hurry into the cell, where Elith is sitting on a wooden chair, gazing out of the barred window.

I greet her and introduce myself as a friend and war-time companion of her father.

'Why are you here?'

'Your father hired me to investigate the damage to the Hesuni Tree. He says you're innocent, so I believe him. Now there are a few more things I have to deal with. Fine, I'll deal with them. Tell me everything and make it quick. What happened to the Tree and what's the story of you not remembering anything? How did you escape from prison, and why were you found with the knife right beside the dead Priest?'

Elith is taken aback. Since the ministrations of her father she's looking healthier but, not surprisingly, she's extremely distracted. I look her straight in the eyes and tell her to snap out of it.

'There's no time for rambling, so get to the point. Lord Kalith is on his way here; three of his guards are outside sleeping off a spell, thanks to me, and he's not going to be very pleased about it. So in the brief time we've got I need to know everything. Don't sigh, don't cry and don't stray from the point. Just tell it like it happened.'

At this, Elith-ir-Methet manages a weak smile.

'I remember Father speaking of you now,' she says. 'You appear in many of his war stories. It was good of you to come. But really, you can do nothing to help me.'

'I can. Tell me about the Tree. Did you damage it?'

She shakes her head slowly. 'I don't think so. But I might have. I really can't remember. They said I did it.'

'Who said?'

'Gulas, the Tree Priest. And his brother Lasas.'

Why can't you remember?'

She looks blank and tells me she just can't. Already I'm starting to dislike her as a client.

'What were you doing near the Tree?'

'Just walking. We live nearby.'

I'd like to question her plenty more about this, but time is short and there's the murder to consider.

'How did you get out of your cell tonight?'

'I wasn't in a cell. Kalith had merely confined me to a room in the Palace and I gave my word I would not try to leave.'

'So why did you change your mind?'

She shrugs. I grow impatient.

'Is this hopeless-Elf-maiden routine the best you can do? You realise how much trouble you're in?'

Elith just sits there: tall, slender, golden-haired and apparently suffering from a severe attack of amnesia. I ask her what happened after she left the Palace.

'I descended to the forest and went to the Hesuni Tree.'

'What for?'

'I wanted to see Gulas-ar-Thetos. It was he who was

my main accuser in the matter of damaging the Tree.'

She stops. Tears start to trickle down her pale face.

'What happened then?'

There's no reply. I change tack. 'Your cousin Eos-ar-Methet died on the voyage from Turai to Avula. Were you friendly with him?'

Elith is startled. 'No,' she says. 'Well, yes, I knew him. Why?'

'Because I'm wondering about his death. You know any reason he might have been acting strangely?'

Elith goes quiet, and I'm fairly certain she's hiding something. I ask her again what happened when she left the Palace earlier this evening.

'She killed Gulas, that's what happened,' roars a voice as the door flies open and Lord Kalith marches in, flanked by four Elves with swords.

'How dare you interrupt an Investigator in private conference with his client?' I roar back. 'Have you no idea of the due process of law on Avula?'

Kalith strides up to me and puts his face near mine, which involves some bending over on his part. His men meanwhile surround me and point their swords in my direction.

'Are you responsible for putting my guards to sleep?' he demands.

'Guards? I didn't see any guards. Just wide open space and a comfy cell at the end. Now would you mind giving me a little time alone with my client? I really must insist—'

The attendants make to grab me. Not wishing to be grabbed, I step back quickly and prepare to defend myself. Elith prevents an ugly scene by laying her hand on my arm.

'Stop,' she says, quite softly. 'I appreciate your trying to help me, Thraxas, but you can do nothing for me. Lord Kalith is right. I did kill Gulas-ar-Thetos.'

'Disregard that statement,' I say quickly. 'The woman is under stress and doesn't know what's she's saying.'

'She knows very well what she is saying,' retorts Kalith. 'She murdered our Priest. Three Elves witnessed the event. At this moment they are giving sworn statements to my scribes.'

It's a bad turn of events but, as people have been known to say in Twelve Seas, Thraxas never abandons a client.

'Witnesses have been known to make mistakes,' I point out.

Kalith smiles, which surprises me. He's regained his composure.

'Thraxas, I could almost like you, were you not such a buffoon. One certainly has to admire your persistence. You enter my Palace without an invitation, you sneak over to this cell and you put three of my guards to sleep with a spell. You question Elith-ir-Methet against my express wishes. Then, despite the fact that she admits the crime, and that there are independent witnesses to testify that she is guilty, you persist in standing here blustering about client–Investigator privileges. You have never thought me sympathetic to your case, but believe me, if my trusted healer Vas-ar-Methet had not spoken so highly of the character you showed during the Orc Wars, I would never have even allowed you on board my ship. And he was right, in some ways at least. He told me that you were disinclined to give up on anything you started. An admirable trait in time of war, but not so now. Elith is guilty. Nothing you can do will change that fact. And you must now leave it to me to dispense justice, as is my right and duty.'

I protest, but he holds up his hand, forbidding further speech, and gestures to his guards. 'Enough, Thraxas. These Elves will escort you from the Palace. No doubt we will meet again at the festival.'

And that, for the moment, is that. The four armed Elves escort me out of the cell, along the courtyard, back up to the high walkways, and out of the Palace.

Once back on the ground, I turn towards the Hesuni Tree, having no intention of going home just yet. The large clearing is now empty of life. Light from the moons reflects from the still water of the twin pools and the Hesuni Tree stands majestically at the far end of the water. I decide to take a look at the Tree, and march over.

To me it looks like any other large tree. I can't pick up any traces of its spiritual power, but that's only to be expected, me being Human rather than Elf, and not very spiritual. I can't sense any sign of sorcery in the air either. I can't learn anything, in fact. Studying the grass in the area where Gulas lay dying reveals nothing except that a lot of Elves have since walked all over it.

'Are you looking for something that will save Elith?'

It can be annoying the way these Elves approach without making a sound. I whirl round and lift my staff, illuminating an Elf by the Tree.

'Lasas-ar-Thetos?'

He bows slightly. I wonder at him being here on his own. As his brother has just been murdered, I might have expected him to be comforting the family, or mourning, or something.

'I must assume my new position and minister to the tree,' he says, as if in answer to my thoughts.

'Why did Elith kill your brother?'

'She is insane. We knew it from the moment she damaged the Tree.'

'Is that the only reason?'

'I believe so. Now, please, leave me. I must communicate with the Tree.'

'Yeah, I guess the Tree must be pretty upset, with all this going on. Do you know Gorith-ar-Del?'

Lasas scowls at me, frustrated by my persistence.

'No,' he replies. 'I do not.'

It seems to me that Lasas is lying. I'm about to question him further when he starts chanting softly, his eyes closed, his head swaying gently from side to side. Torchlight and voices from the other side of the clearing announce the arrival of some Elves from the Palace. I depart. It feels like a long walk back to Camith's house. I climb wearily up to my temporary dwelling and find Makri sitting in my room, studying a scroll.

'How's the case going?' she asks.

'Getting difficult,' I confess. 'Elith-ir-Methet has just been accused of murdering the Tree Priest.'

I haul my boots off. 'And I still can't find any beer. I think the Elves are hiding it from me out of spite.'

CHAPTER
NINE

Vas-ar-Methet's brother has treated Makri and me hospitably from the moment we arrived and we're grateful for this. We can eat our meals with Camith's family or on our own if we prefer, and they make no attempts to hinder us in our coming and leaving. If they think it is strange or disreputable to have someone with Orc blood under their roof, they don't show it. Makri tells me that her faith in Elfkind is partially revived.

'After that voyage, I thought I was going to hate them all. But Vas-ar-Methet's relatives are nice. When you were out they asked if there was anything they could bring me and then Camith invited me up to the top of the tree to look at the stars.'

Elves are partial to the night, rising late in the day and staying up to enjoy the pleasures of the midnight sky. Well, most of them. Perhaps farming Elves have to rise early to plant crops. I ask Makri about this, but she doesn't know.

'At the Guild College we only learn Elvish myths, stories, histories of their wars and things like that. The subject of Elves having to get up early to plant crops or milk cows never came up. Strange really, because only last term Professor Azulius was stressing how important the average citizen was in the history of the city-state. "History is not all Kings , Queens and battles," as he likes to say. Do you think there are low-class Elves who clean the sewers at the Tree Palace?'

'I expect so. They can't all be composing epic poems and gazing at the stars. You know, I've been close to losing my faith in Elfkind as well. I appreciate that I'm causing them difficulties, but right from the first day of the voyage they've been about as friendly as a two-fingered troll. Much less welcoming than my hosts on my last visit to the islands.'

'That was a long time ago,' Makri points out. 'Maybe they became more suspicious of strangers after the last War. Do you know the whole island is suffering from bad dreams?'

'Really? Everyone?'

'Apparently,' says Makri. 'Camith certainly is. I don't think the Elves like to talk about it though. Discussing illness with strangers is calanith.'

'Is it only the Avulans or are their guests from the other islands suffering as well?'

Makri doesn't know. She's hoping the other Elves are in good health because she's looking forward to the theatrical performances. I remain unimpressed at the prospect.

'Three versions of the tale of Queen Leeuven. Couldn't they come up with something else?'

'Of course not. The plays at the festival are always about Queen Leeuven. That's the point.'

'It sounds dull to me.'

'Well, they do choose different episodes from the saga. But it's all quite formal, you know. The stories are already well known to the audience; it's the way they are told that makes all the difference. At the last festival the Venian Elves presented such a tragic account of Queen Leeuven accidentally killing her brother that the entire audience was moved to bitter tears. They won the prize. The Avulans are keen to take it this time.'

I see that Makri has wasted no time in learning more about the culture of the island. I ask her if she knows anything about the juggling competition. She informs me that it's part of the light entertainment put on before the plays, to get the crowd in a festive mood.

'Is there a favourite to win? I might be able to get a bet down.'

'Do you have to bet on everything?'

'Yes.'

'I don't think they have bookmakers on Avula,' says Makri.

'Don't you believe it. Just because the festival features high-class tragedy doesn't mean there isn't someone running a low-class gambling operation somewhere. If you can get a hot tip for the juggling competition, I've no doubt I can place some money on it.'

With her mind occupied by the theatre, Makri has little enthusiasm for juggling, but she does express an interest in the tournament. She's sorry that it is only for the under-fifteens and would have preferred to see the true Elvish warriors battling it out, but considers that any fighting is better than none.

'I've never seen a tournament,' she says.

She is disappointed when I inform her of the probable nature of the event.

'It's only practice really. Nothing too vicious. They use wooden swords and there are restrictions on what you can do. No stamping on your opponent's groin for instance, and no attacks to the eyes.'

'No groin-stamping? No attacks to the eyes? What's the point of that?'

'They're all under fifteen, Makri. The Elves don't want to maim their kids, just give them a little practice in sword play. And don't tell me that when you were fifteen you were already killing dragons. You mentioned that already. But being a gladiator is not the same thing as entering a civilised tournament.'

Makri is still dissatisfied. 'Sounds like a waste of time to me.'

I'm eating my dinner from a tray. Obviously realising that I am a man of healthy appetites, my hosts have sent me a great amount of food. It's not quite the gargantuan meal I'd take in back at the Avenging Axe after a hard day's investigating, but it comes close. As I drink the last of the bottle of wine they sent along with it I feel a little more in tune with the world.

'Did Camith have any idea why everyone was having bad dreams?'

'Not exactly. He thought it might have something to do with the damage to the Hesuni Tree. The Avulans are all connected to it in some way.'

'Isn't it healthy again? It looked okay to me.'

Makri nods. The tree healers have brought it back to full health. Something is still causing the Elves to have nightmares, though, which is interesting.

'So what now? If Elith did kill the priest, what can you do? Are you serious about breaking her out of jail?'

'Maybe. The way these Elves run things it would be as easy as bribing a Senator. Her last cell didn't even have any bars on the window. Elith just gave her word she wouldn't escape.'

I pause. It is very, very unusual for an Elf to break her word. It's something they just don't do. It's calanith. Vas would rather die than disgrace himself in such a way. It strikes me that there must have been some over-whelmingly powerful reason for Elith-ir-Methet to leave the Palace.

'But I'm not convinced she's guilty. I don't like the way she can't remember anything about damage to the tree. It means she's either lying or under pressure from some-one. Or else her memory has been affected by sorcery or drugs. I'm not happy about her murder confession either. She was acting very strangely the whole time I was with her. The first time I saw her she fainted right away and you know, Elvish women don't faint a lot. They're tougher than that. I've seen them fighting Orcs. When I was asking her questions I swear her mind was somewhere else. There was a very strange look in her eyes.'

'What kind of look?'

I can't exactly describe it. 'Something like a person on dwa.'

Makri is dubious. 'You said dwa hadn't reached the Elvish Isles.'

'It hasn't. Anyway, it doesn't affect them the same way it affects Humans. I've seen the occasional decadent Elf in Turai who's taken it, but they never get the same hit off the drug as a Human. Nothing like enough to be so out of it they'd forget about committing some major crime. I'll go and see Kalith's Sorcerer, Jir-ar-Eth, and see if he might have picked up any lingering traces of magic.

Lord Kalith has probably had him examine Elith by now, though if he's found anything I doubt he'll be eager to tell me. Things would be a lot easier if these damned Elves would cooperate. Still, I knew it was going to be tough.'

I consider the situation. Things look bad for Elith-ir-Methet, but things have looked tough for my clients before. It's not as if anyone has provided a motive for the killing, and I can't see why a respectable Elf would just up and kill the Tree Priest for no reason. As for the witnesses, I'm keeping an open mind. There are plenty of reasons why witnesses might get things wrong. Like wanting to please an Elf Lord for instance. I'll start nosing around the Hesuni Tree and see who else might have had something against Gulas-ar-Thetos. And I'll ask a few questions about Gorith. I'm suspicious of him, if only because he seemed so hostile towards me.

Makri stretches. 'Camith gave me this scroll; it's all about the local plants. He used to learn from it when he was at school. Elves go to school in trees, which is no real surprise. Tomorrow I'm going to look around at the local plant life and then see what the Elves have in the way of swords, knives and axes. You think they might give me some free stuff, seeing as I'm their guest? Thank God that spineless brat Isuas isn't here to bother me any more.'

'Eh . . . hello,' says the spineless brat, entering the room timidly. She's wearing a green floppy hat that comes to a point at the end, rather like a pixie might wear in a children's story. It makes her look even younger than usual. As Isuas walks towards Makri she catches her foot in a rug and plummets to the floor. It's quite a pathetic sight, but Makri looks on stonily as I help the youngster up. She rubs her head and tries not to cry.

'I thought I'd see if you were all right,' she says, fumbling with her hat.

'I was a minute ago,' says Makri sharply.

I'm still of the opinion that being friends with Kalith's daughter would be no bad thing, so I cover up for Makri's rudeness by asking Isuas if she's pleased to be home.

'Feel good to be back on dry land?'

Isuas shrugs. 'Okay. But everyone's busy at the Palace.'

I have the impression that everyone being too busy for Isuas might not be that uncommon.

'Will you save Elith even though she killed Gulas?'

'I will. And I'm not convinced she did kill him.'

'I hope not,' says the young Elf. 'I like Elith.'

'Will you teach me more fighting?' she says to Makri, unexpectedly.

'No,' replies Makri. 'I'm busy.'

'Please,' says Isuas. 'It's important.'

Makri sticks her nose in her scroll.

'Why is it important?' I enquire.

'So I can fight in the junior tournament.'

Makri emerges from her scroll to have a good laugh. 'The junior tournament? With wooden swords?'

'Yes. For all the Elves under fifteen. My oldest brother won it six years ago. My next oldest brother won it the year after that. And my next oldest brother won it the year—'

'We get the picture,' says Makri. 'And now you want to enter but you can't because you're too puny and haven't a chance of making it past the first round even if your father lets you enter, which no doubt he wouldn't. You being so puny. And clumsy.'

Isuas stares at the floor. Makri seems to have summed it up neatly enough.

'They never let me do anything,' Isuas mumbles.

'Who can blame them?' says Makri.

'Please,' wails Isuas. 'I want to enter the tournament.'

Makri again finds something to interest her in her scroll. I frown. I wish she didn't display her dislike of the child quite so openly.

'What do your parents say about you entering the lists?'

'My father refuses to listen.'

'Well, perhaps we could have a word with your mother,' I suggest. 'If Lady Yestar had no objections, I'm sure Makri could continue your lessons.'

Isuas's face lights up. She is of course too young to realise the cunning way in which I have just guaranteed our entrance to the Tree Palace as an aid to investigating. Unfortunately Makri isn't. She grunts at me.

'Forget it, Thraxas. I'm not getting stuck with the kid just so as you can wander about asking questions.'

'Makri will be delighted to help,' I say. 'Would tomorrow in the afternoon be a good time to talk to Lady Yestar?'

Isuas nods, and manages to raise a smile. 'I'll have the servants prepare a meal.'

'Excellent, Isuas. Do you think they could rustle me up some beer?'

'Beer? I don't think we have that at the Tree Palace. But maybe we could send out for some. I know that Mother will be pleased to meet you.'

I doubt that very much.

'I've practised what you showed me every day,' says Isuas to Makri before she departs.

Makri places her scroll on a table and looks at me rather wryly.

'Yes, very clever, Thraxas. Now you can enter the Palace as a guest of the Royal Family and make a nuisance of yourself to your heart's content. Provided you don't just concentrate on emptying the island of beer, that is. But I'm not playing along. I refuse to teach that kid any more. She's a hopeless student. Anyway, I don't like her. It was all I could do not to knock her head off on the ship. I only went along with it because I was bored. There's plenty of other things I want to do on Avula rather than play nursemaid to the Royal Family's unwanted runt.'

'I still don't see why you dislike her so much, Makri. She's not that bad.'

'I can't stand the way she's always bursting into tears. When I was her age tears were punishable by immediate execution. And she keeps falling over. It's infuriating. And she's so weedy. Also, it gives me the creeps the way she keeps getting more friendly the more I insult her. It's not natural. What she needs is a good beating.'

'Are you sure she doesn't remind you of yourself at her age?'

'What do you mean?' demands Makri. 'I was never like that.'

'So you say. But the way you take against her gives me the strong impression that at one time in your life you were an extremely frightened and weak child. And you don't like being reminded of it.'

'Nonsense,' says Makri, crossly. 'Stop trying to be analytical, Thraxas, you're really bad at it.'

I shrug. 'Anyway, if you were teaching her how to fight, wouldn't that give you some reason for handing out a beating? It would certainly toughen her up.'

'I've a reputation to protect,' objects Makri. 'You think I want to send her out to fight as my pupil and have all these Elves laugh at her? Think how bad it would make me look. I'm not going to be able to teach her enough in six days to prevent her from being a laughing stock.'

'Don't forget, she's been practising every day. She might have improved. Anyway, when it comes right down to it, Lord Kalith and Lady Yestar aren't going to let her enter the tournament. So just pretend you're willing. It'll get me a day or two at the Palace. After the way I outraged Lord Kalith by putting his guards to sleep, I can't see any other way I'll get back in.'

The most I can persuade Makri to do is to turn up with me there tomorrow.

'If I end up having to teach her, there's going to be trouble,' Makri warns me.

'You won't,' I assure her. 'Kalith wouldn't let Isuas within a mile of any fighting. Okay, you're laughing about using wooden swords, but these things can still be tough. There were junior tournaments in Turai when I was young. Not big affairs, like they have for Senators' sons of course, just small affairs for the offspring of the local workers. Prepared us for life in the army. One day I went up against the son of the blacksmith and he broke my arm with a wooden axe. My father was furious. Said I'd let the family down. He made me go back out and fight with my arm in a sling.'

'What happened?'

'I kicked the blacksmith's son in the groin and then

stepped on his face. Which was going a bit far even by the relaxed standards of the tournament. I was disqualified. But my father was pleased with me.'

'Quite right,' says Makri. 'I don't see why they disqualified you. You have to do whatever is necessary.'

Makri tells me some stories of her early fighting experiences, most of which involve inflicting terrible damage on Orcish opponents, all much older and heavier than her. She cheers up. Talking about fighting always puts Makri in a good mood. It must be the Orcish blood. Keeps her savage, even when studying botany.

CHAPTER
TEN

I'm planning to make an early start next day. As the Elves rise late I should be able to examine the scene of the crime without interruption. Unfortunately, after securing another bottle of wine from Camith, I find myself swapping war stories with him late into the night and by the time I wake the sun is overhead and the morning is gone.

'I did not wish to disturb you,' says Camith as I struggle through for a late breakfast. 'I know that Turanians are conscientious about their morning prayers.'

'Yes, it often holds me back,' I admit, and settle down to a loaf or two, washed down with the juice of some Avulan fruit I can't put a name to.

I ask Camith if he knows Gorith-ar-Del.

'I know of him. I don't believe we have ever spoken. He's a maker of longbows and lives on the west of the island, where the trees are suitable for his craft.'

'Can you think of any reason why he might be skulking round the Hesuni Tree, looking unfriendly?'

Camith can't. He's never heard anything disreputable about Gorith although he is aware of the trouble his relatives found themselves in when they visited Turai.

'I've been wondering about this Hesuni Tree, Camith. Just supposing it wasn't Elith who damaged it, and also supposing it wasn't just some random act of vandalism, which seems unlikely, what motive might any other Elf have for doing it? I mean, who could gain from it?'

'No one.'

'Are you sure? Makri tells me that not only are all the Avulans connected to it in some way, but the Tree Priests can actually communicate with it.'

'In a way,' agrees Camith. 'Though the communication is not what you would have with another Elf. More a sense of the life around the Tree, I believe.'

'What if something dubious was going on on Avula? Might the Tree be able to tell the Tree Priests about it?'

This makes Camith smile. 'I do not think so. It's not that sort of communication.' He looks serious. 'Yet there is a relationship. Perhaps the Tree Priest might learn some things that were beyond the ken of other Elves.'

'Which might be motive for someone to try and kill it. Bumping off a witness, so to speak.'

Makri is sceptical. 'You can't get a witness statement from a Hesuni Tree, Thraxas. You're grasping at straws here.'

'Okay, I'm grasping at straws. But last summer I found myself in conversation with dolphins in Turai, so I'm keeping an open mind about a talking tree. What about this other branch of the family I heard about? The rival claimants to the position of Tree Priest?'

This makes Camith uncomfortable. 'There is a rival claimant, Hith-ar-Key. The dispute over the succession goes back some centuries. I believe that their claim is weak but it is not something that would be much discussed, apart from in the Council of Elders.'

'Why not?'

'Any dispute over the Priesthood is calanith to everyone except the Elders and the priestly families. It is up to them to sort it out and no other Elf would interfere or even refer to the matter.'

I'm already getting the impression that far too many things on Avula are calanith, which might turn out to be awkward, given the Deputy Consul's strict admonition not to rub up against any Elvish taboos the wrong way. I let the subject drop.

Makri is eager to set off.

'I haven't seen the Tree Palace yet. Look, I painted my toenails again.'

'Lady Yestar will be thrilled. Are you planning on wearing that tunic?'

'What's wrong with it?'

'The same as with everything else you wear. It doesn't cover enough of you. Haven't you noticed that the Elf women cover their legs? Couldn't you borrow some demure Elf clothes?'

'I think not,' says Makri, sagely. 'As the philosopher Samanatius says, "Never try to pretend to be someone else."'

'I don't trust Samanatius.'

'Why not? You've never heard him speak.'

'He teaches for free, doesn't he? If he was any good he'd charge admission.'

Makri shakes her head. 'Thraxas, you take ignorance to new depths. Anyway, Yestar would probably be disappointed if I turned up looking like an Elf. Isuas will have told her what a Barbarian I am.'

As if to emphasise the point, Makri has her twin swords strapped to her back. I instruct her not to unsheathe

the Orcish blade under any circumstances. The dark metal is instantly recognisable and waving an Orcish weapon around is liable to get us run off the island.

Camith sees us off. 'You notice how he was yawning all through breakfast?' I ask Makri.

'Still bored by your war stories, no doubt.'

'Camith was not bored by my war stories. Rather, he was honoured to have such a distinguished soldier under his roof. If we hadn't stood firm in Turai, there would have been no stopping the Orcs. They'd have been down here with the war ships, dragons at the ready. The Elvish Isles might well have fallen. Really, when you think about it, these Elves owe me for protecting them.'

'I thought the Elves came to your rescue?'

'They helped. I expect we'd have managed anyway. But the point I was trying to make before you started interrupting was that Camith was yawning having presumably had a bad night's sleep. More nightmares, I imagine. So when we get in the vicinity of the Hesuni Tree, keep a look-out for anything that might be affecting it enough to make it start sending out bad feelings to the Elves.'

'Like what?'

'I've no idea. Just look. You're well versed in Elvish lore, you might spot something I'd miss.'

We set off across the walkways towards the Palace. Even at this elevation the vegetation is dense, with vines tangled over the tops of the trees. There are few places where the ground is visible and such small clearings as we cross are covered with flowering bushes. There are plenty of butterflies and small birds that make a lot of noise, and occasionally a monkey swings over to examine us before disappearing back into the forest. Makri studies them with interest but I've never been fond of monkeys.

Above our heads the sky is blue. Although this is the winter season on Avula it's still warm and pleasant, in contrast to the icy misery of Turai, far away to the north.

'Poor Gurd, he'll be as cold as a frozen pixie right now. Of course as a northern Barbarian he doesn't feel it as much as a civilised man like myself.'

We pass over the tournament field. Some young Elves are practising for the big event. Camith had laughed when we mentioned that Isuas had asked Makri for fighting lessons. Isuas is not unpopular among the Avulans, but her lack of physical prowess is something of a standing joke among them.

'But Kalith has four strong sons and three hearty daughters,' Camith pointed out. 'No one minds that his eighth child is a weakling. I believe that Lady Yestar encourages him to take her on his voyages in an effort to harden her, but from what I saw of her yesterday it has had little effect.'

Along the way we pass small settlements. When an Elvish child runs indoors in a panic at the sight of Makri, she professes that's she's starting to feel depressed again.

'Now I think about it, it might not be so great at the Tree Palace. Full of high-class Elves making comments about my toenails, I expect.'

'Well, you would insist on painting them.'

'I need some fortifying,' she announces. 'You bring any thazis out with you?'

'Thazis? This is the Elvish Isles. A paradise on earth and a drug-free environment.'

'I know. So did you bring any?'

'What do you need it for? Can't you just enjoy the clean air?'

'It's wonderful. So? You bring any thazis?'

'Of course. You expect me to wander about a strange island without any thazis? Hell, who knows when I might next get a beer.'

I pass Makri a thazis stick and she lights it with a satisfied sigh. I do the same. I don't know if this mild narcotic is illegal on Avula but I doubt Lord Kalith would be pleased to learn we'd been using it on his island. We finish it off on a lonely stretch of walkway. The sound of choral singing floats past us pleasantly. Entrants to the festival are rehearsing anywhere they can find space.

'Now I'm relaxed,' says Makri.

Eight masked Elves carrying long vicious spears appear round the corner and advance towards us menacingly.

'Damn it,' says Makri. 'Why did you make me smoke that thing?'

I can't believe that we are about to be attacked right here in the middle of Avula.

'They must be practising for the tournament.'

'They don't look like they're under fifteen.'

The walkway is wide enough for four. The eight Elves are drawn up in two ranks, in battle formation. Eight spears point towards us, leaving no way through. They break into a run. You can't fight eight Elves with spears in a confined space like this, certainly not without a hefty shield to cover yourself.

'Got any spells?' says Makri, unsheathing her twin blades.

'Didn't think to load any in.'

'Can't you just remember one?'

Unfortunately it doesn't work like that. Once you use a spell it's gone from your mind. To use it again you have to reread it from your grimoire. We've no time for further discussion. They're almost upon us. Even against such odds Makri would normally refuse to retreat. Probably she'd try and outflank them. On the narrow walkway, there's no way to do that. When the spears are only a few feet away Makri and I sheathe our swords simultaneously and leap into the trees. I offer up a prayer for a sturdy branch to hold on to, a prayer that unfortunately seems to go unanswered as I plunge down through the branches. I grab frantically at everything I can reach but nothing will support my weight and I fall a long way without making contact with anything firm enough to halt my descent. Eventually I thud heavily into a sturdy branch, only ten feet or so from the ground. I'm severely winded and badly scratched, but otherwise undamaged.

There are crashing noises above me, and some swearing. Makri found a firm handhold further up and is now swinging herself down to my level. We drop to the ground and draw our weapons, waiting for our assailants to come after us. There's no sign of them.

'Let's go,' I say, and we move off, but moving off in the dense undergrowth is difficult. Makri snarls as she cuts her way through the vegetation. Fleeing from an opponent always puts her in a bad mood.

'Don't worry. I figure you'll get a chance to meet them again.'

'Who were they?'

Neither of us has any idea. Eight masked Elves, all silent, with no identifying marks.

After a long period of hacking our way through the thick plant life, hunting unsuccessfully for a path, Makri rounds on me with a savage look in her eyes.

'Give me more thazis,' she demands.

'Not really what we need right now, is it, Makri?'

'Just give me the damned thazis,' she snarls.

'Hey, okay, don't get crazy about it. I know you hate running from opponents, it's not my fault they had us outweaponed in a narrow place.'

Makri's anger suddenly leaves her and she sits down heavily.

'Now I'm depressed. In fact I'm as miserable as a Niojan whore. Damn these mood swings.'

I ask her what is going on.

'It's a month since we left Turai,' she replies.

'So?'

'So it's my period again. Any complaints?'

I sigh. 'No. None. But try not to bleed over the Tree Palace. Kalith will be furious if that happens.'

'To hell with Kalith,' says Makri, lighting up her thazis stick. 'Of course I don't have anything with me, seeing as I didn't get a chance to pack before I leaped into the ocean. Maybe Lady Yestar can lend me a towel or something.'

By this time I'm in need of a little relaxation myself. I smoke another thazis stick and consider the situation. There has to be a path around here somewhere. There's nothing for it but to keep chopping our way through till we find one. I'm not certain if the Avulan forest contains any dangerous predators. It certainly contains a lot of insects, several of which seem to have decided that nothing tastes better than Thraxas the Investigator.

'If this blunts my blades someone is going to pay dearly,' states Makri. 'I hate this. My legs are getting scratched. Why didn't you tell me to wear something more suitable? You want to go in front for a while, I'm sure I'm doing all the work here. Put some effort into it, Thraxas, we're going to be here all day at this rate.'

It's exhausting work and I am soon dripping with sweat. Eventually we break through into a small clearing. I slump heavily to the ground.

'To hell with this.'

'Give me another thazis stick,' says Makri.

I was planning to ration my thazis carefully, but the situation seems to call for it so we light up some more, smoke it, then set off again. We're heading in the general direction of the Palace. At least I hope we are. I'm trying to navigate by the sun but the sun is rarely visible through the trees. Makri's mood continues to alternate between anger and depression. I'm fairly furious myself.

'Damned spearmen. If I'd known this was going to happen I'd never have jumped.'

'We should have stayed and fought them. I'll kill them when I get my hands on them. Hell, I just got stung.'

After what feels like several hours of hacking, chopping, cursing and complaining, we finally find a clearing in which a ladder ascends to a walkway above.

'Thank God for that.'

We climb. When we finally make the top I sit down exhausted. Makri has drawn her swords, eager for another sight of the spear carriers, but the walkway is empty. She sheathes her weapons angrily.

'I'm in a really bad mood,' she says.

I pass her a thazis stick. We smoke them and walk on.

'Where are we?'

'No idea. Look, there's an Elf sitting in that tree.'

We shout to the Elf, asking which way the Palace is. He points, and we head in that direction.

'I'm in no mood to talk to Lady Yestar,' Makri says. 'Better give me another thazis stick, mellow me a little.'

I figure this is a good idea. No point in being flustered when we arrive. We light two more thazis sticks and smoke them as we walk. Wherever we are, it seems to be a sparsely populated part of the island, and we pass no further Elves.

'I hate this stupid forest,' says Makri.

I pass her another thazis stick. We walk on.

'Look. Elf houses. Don't you think they look sort of funny?'

Makri giggles. 'Houses in trees.'

It does seem quite funny, now she mentions it.

'We better have some more thazis before we hit the Palace. Don't want to arrive there in a bad mood, what with me menstruating and everything.'

'Absolutely,' I agree, and light us up a stick each. I remember my flask.

'Some klee?'

'Thank you,' says Makri.

The walkway brings us into the centre of the island, ending in a long ladder down to the central clearing. The Tree Palace is visible on the other side. Elves stare at us as we pass. We greet them warmly.

Once we reach the clearing Makri halts, looking thoughtful.

'You say thazis isn't used among the Elves? You think they might not like it? We'd better smoke some behind this tree, before we get to the Palace.'

This sounds like a good idea.

'You are good at having good ideas,' I tell Makri.

'I know. I think about things a lot,' replies Makri, inhaling the thazis smoke. 'Important things.'

'I think about important things too.'

'It's good to think about important things.'

After all the thazis my mouth tastes funny. I take some klee to clear away the taste and pass the flask to Makri. She coughs as it burns her throat. We sit under the tree and gaze at the beautiful blue sky for a while. Butterflies flutter around our heads.

'I never realised how beautiful butterflies are,' says Makri.

'Neither did I. Aren't they pretty?'

We watch them for a long time. A few clouds drift across the sky.

'Where were we going?' asks Makri, eventually.

I think about this.

'The Palace.'

'Right. What for?'

'You know. Just to see it. Talk to the Elves.'

Makri blinks. 'Right.'

We sit under the sun.

'Should we go?' says Makri, after a while.

'Go where?'

'The Palace.'

'If you like.'

Our discussion is interrupted by a furious debate. A large group of white-robed Elves appears out of the forest, all talking heatedly at once.

'We cannot omit the scene where King Vendris butchers his children,' says one of the actors, angrily. 'It traditionally appears after the Tree-burning scene . . .'

'Then it is time for a change,' counters a grey-haired Elf, whom, from the way he seems to be taking the brunt of the anger, I take to be the director.

'And who are you to change the telling of the ancient tale of Queen Leeuven?' demands an actress, possibly Queen Leeuven herself, from the gold tiara in her hair.

'I am the man appointed by Lord Kalith to put on the play,' retorts the grey-haired Elf.

'A terrible mistake!' cry several of the actors, with feeling.

'Just do as I tell you if you want that prize . . .'

The group carries on across the clearing, finally disappearing back into the forest, still arguing.

We stare at them as they go.

'You know, Makri, I kind of thought that traditional Elvish actors would be more dignified. That Elf with the tiara reminded me of a chorus girl I once knew. I had to help her flee from Turai after she burned down the theatre.'

We lapse back into silence.

'I haven't had any thazis since we landed on Avula,' says Makri. 'Did you bring any?'

'I think so,' I reply, hunting around in my bag.

We saunter towards the Palace, thazis in hand. More Elves walk by. They stare at us, but say nothing. When we're walking between the two pools by the Hesuni Tree Makri stops to admire the view.

'I'm thirsty,' she says, and kneels down to drink.

'Me too. You know, I think that thazis might have affected me a little.'

Makri says she feels fine. I figure I'll be fine too after I've had some more water. I almost imagine that someone is shouting at us, but it's only a fleeting impression. Makri bends down to splash water over her face and I do the same. It's cool and refreshing. I drink some more, and feel the intoxication passing from my body. I realise that someone is indeed shouting at me. It's an Elf I recognise, looking angry.

'Don't you know it's forbidden to drink from the sacred pools that feed the Hesuni Tree?' he cries.

'Sorry,' I say.

'No one mentioned it,' adds Makri.

Our Elvish inquisitor looks at us with disgust. It's Lasas, brother of the murdered Tree Priest.

'Pray you are pure of body and spirit, both of you. Else be very wary of the effects of the sacred water.'

Sensing that nothing I can say is going to pacify Lasas, I apologise again and make off briskly for the ladders that lead up to the Tree Palace.

'Another social blunder. How were we meant to know they were sacred pools? They should put a sign on them or something.'

I'm expecting difficulty with the guards at the ladders, but they wave us up almost affably.

'Lady Yestar is expecting you.'

We start to climb.

'What do you think that Elf meant by "be very wary of the effects of the sacred water"?' says Makri.

'Who knows? Just trying to scare us, I expect. I mean, it can hardly be poisonous as it's feeding the Hesuni Tree.'

'Hesuni,' says Makri. 'That's a funny name.'

She giggles. I realise that the thazis has not entirely worn off and make a supreme effort to concentrate as we reach the platform on which stand the great wooden doors to the Palace. Again we gain entry without difficulty.

'You have to hand it to Isuas,' I say. 'Having her put in a good word for us certainly makes things easier.'

'Absolutely,' agrees Makri. 'She's a fine kid. I always did like her.'

We pass through several well-lit rooms and corridors. The Tree Palace, while larger than the other Elvish dwellings on the island, is far smaller than the sort of palaces built for Human Kings and gives the impression of comfort rather than luxury. A pleasant aroma permeates the whole building, either from incense or natural fragrances in the wood. We're shown into a reception room, which again is far smaller than an equivalent room at the Imperial Palace in Turai, but warm and welcoming, with a tapestry on the wall depicting some deer drinking from a pool.

'Lady Yestar will be here presently,' says the attendant.

'Can you get me a beer?' I ask, hopefully.

The attendant looks doubtful. 'I don't think we have any beer in the palace.'

At that moment Lady Yestar enters the room. A small silver tiara is the only mark of rank she wears. Isuas is hanging on to the side of her dress. When she sees Makri the child shouts with glee and tugs at her mother's dress in her eagerness to introduce her.

'This is Makri,' she cries. 'She killed a dragon when she was a gladiator slave and she once fought eight Trolls at once and then she slaughtered everyone and escaped and went to Turai and now when Thraxas is out investigating she kills people as well. And she let me point her sword. She's got an Orcish sword! She got it when she slaughtered everyone. She's been teaching me how to fight. She was the champion gladiator!'

At this introduction Lady Yestar surprises me by bursting out laughing. It's the first time I've seen an Elf laugh since the start of this affair. I'd almost forgotten they were capable of it.

CHAPTER ELEVEN

L ady Yestar is not at all as I had anticipated. As she is the wife of Lord Kalith and a very aristocratic Elf in her own right, I had expected her to be cool and aloof, distant in that particular way only an Elf with a long lineage can be. Some of the great Elvish families can trace their ancestry back as far as the Great Flood, an event that, though only mythical to the Human nations, is historical to the Elves.

Yestar certainly looks the part; she's tall, pale-skinned and tending towards the ethereal. At first sight she gives the impression of being an Elf to whom the affairs of a Turanian Investigator will be well below her notice. In this I am mistaken. She turns out to be a friendly, cheerful, intelligent Elf who greets us warmly while laughing at the enthusiastic antics of her daughter. I notice that she wears eye make-up, which is rare among the Avulans.

Isuas herself seems transformed in the presence of her mother. She still trips over rugs but her shyness largely disappears and she no longer seems like the hope-lessly inadequate child of a very busy and important family.

Lady Yestar rises further in my estimation when, in reply to my polite question about the availability of beer on Avula, she informs me that, while it is generally not drunk in the Palace and other similarly elegant establishments, it is brewed and enjoyed by many of the common Elves.

'I could ask my attendants where you might meet with other Elves who partake of it.'

By this time I've shaken off the effects of the thazis binge but I'm not so sure that Makri has. I'm surprised to see her patting Isuas affably on the head and admiring her floppy green hat.

'Would you like it?' enquire Isuas.

Makri would, and accepts it with glee.

'Bezin hat,' she says, cramming it over her head, where it looks ridiculous.

Bezin is a pidgin Orcish word that Makri uses of things she approves of. It's utterly unsuitable for use in a place like this but fortunately Lady Yestar has never encountered pidgin Orcish and it passes unnoticed.

'You must have had an interesting life,' says Yestar. 'Isuas is full of stories about you.'

'Very interesting,' agrees Makri. 'Champion gladiator of the Orcs and now barmaid at the Avenging Axe. Also I'm studying at the Guild College. And I help raise money for the Association of Gentlewomen. They're trying to raise the status of women in Turai. Do the males on Avula treat the females like lower forms of life? Turanian men are dreadful; you wouldn't believe some of the things I have to put up with as a barmaid.'

This is all quite inappropriate as an opening speech to Avula's Queen, but Yestar only laughs. More than that, she conveys the impression that yes, she has met a few dreadful males in her time. I sip some wine, and let them talk. Lady Yestar obviously likes Makri and that is all to the good. I'm hoping Makri's benevolent mood lasts long enough for her to pretend to be willing to teach Isuas how to fight. Though Yestar will undoubtedly pour cold water on the idea, it will show us in a good light if Makri can at least feign some enthusiasm. It seems like the subject might never come up as Makri and Yestar talk about particularly useless males they have encountered, then move on to the tale of Queen Leeuven, till Isuas, bored with this, interrupts them.

'Tell Mother about you jumping in the ocean. You know Makri wasn't on board when we sailed? She ran on the quay, fighting all these men. And she killed most of them and then jumped in the sea and Thraxas went out for her in a boat.'

'Really? How extraordinary. Did you miss the embarkation?'

'I wasn't invited on the voyage,' explains Makri.

Yestar asks why she was not invited. I don't like what this might be leading to.

'Well, Orcish blood, you understand,' I break in. 'Didn't want to cause any embarrassment—'

'Thraxas was mad at me because I cost him a load of money gambling at cards,' says Makri, interrupting me. 'He's a terrible gambler.'

'What did you do?'

'Opened her mouth when she shouldn't,' I say, glaring threateningly at Makri.

'Makri can train me for the tournament,' cries Isuas, unable to contain herself any longer. Yestar smiles. She has a beautiful smile. Perfect white teeth.

'Ah yes. The tournament. Isuas is keen to enter. All her

older brothers fared well in the junior tournament, as did one of her sisters. Unfortunately . . .'

Not wishing to say anything demeaning to her daughter, she leaves the sentence unfinished.

'You think she might do badly, not being used to sword play?' suggests Makri. 'Well, if that's the only problem, leave it to me. I'll bring her up to the required standard.'

I'm amazed. Makri must really be under the influence. Strange, she's normally no more liable to the effects of thazis than I am. I wonder if the water from the sacred pool might have affected her in some way.

Isuas whoops with glee and starts dancing round her mother. Lady Yestar seems dubious.

'I do not really think I can allow it. Isuas is small for her age, and inexperienced. Surely she could not put up a good showing against boys older and more experienced than her?'

'She'll do well,' says Makri. 'Only way to get experience, just plunge right in. I tell you, I can train that child to put up a fine show. Why, even on the ship she was making excellent progress.'

Isuas beams. Lady Yestar considers it.

'Well, if you are sure . . . I would not like to risk my daughter being hurt, but I have been encouraging her to sail with my husband, to make her tougher.'

She turns to Isuas. 'Are you sure you wish to do this?'

Isuas bounds around, very sure that she wants to do it.

'Excellent,' says Makri, adjusting her hat, which has slipped over her eyes. 'We'll get started as soon as possible.'

'Might Lord Kalith possibly object?' I venture.

'We won't mention it to him just yet,' says Yestar. 'Keep it as a surprise.'

'I have a practice sword,' says Isuas, still unable to control her excitement. 'Come and see it.'

Makri allows herself to be dragged away to see the practice sword. I know she's really going to regret this when she wakes up tomorrow.

'Do many women in Turai have pierced noses?' enquires Yestar politely.

'Only two. One's a travelling musician who dyes her hair green and the other is Makri. I expect the green hair will follow along in time.'

'Such things can surely not help her in her quest to be thought a suitable candidate for the Imperial University?'

'So I keep telling her. But she's full of contradictions. All that mixed blood, I expect.'

'Are you hoping to question me about the sad affair of Elith-ir-Methet?'

I'm surprised at the abruptness of this.

'Yes,' I reply. 'I am. Do you go along with the popular opinion that she is guilty of everything?'

The Elvish Lady sits in silence for a while.

'Perhaps. I have heard all the reports. And there are witnesses who claim to have seen her stab the Tree Priest. But I have known Elith for most of her life. I find it very difficult to believe that she would kill anyone. Have you any reason for imagining her to be innocent, apart from your desire to upset my husband?'

I assure Lady Yestar that I have no desire to upset her husband.

'Only a few days ago we shared a friendly game of niarit, and . . . eh . . .'

'You defeated him.'

I apologise. Lady Yestar doesn't mind. I tell her I have a powerful desire to help Vas-ar-Methet.

'I know he'll go into exile if his daughter is found guilty and I don't want to see my old companion-in-arms reduced to hawking his healing services around some third-rate city in the west.'

'Have you learned anything that may assist her?'

I admit that I have made little progress.

'I can see far, in many directions,' says Yestar. 'I gazed at the troubles of Elith-ir-Methet, but I was unable to penetrate the mists that surround them. Yet your presence here brings new energy to the affair, Investigator. Perhaps I should look again.'

She lapses into silence. She stares into the distance. The sun streams in through the windows, and the sound of birdsong. It strikes me that of all the rooms in palaces I've ever been in, I like this one best. I like Lady Yestar too. I wonder what she is looking at. Who knows what a powerful Elvish Lady might be capable of?

Finally her attention returns. 'I see that you might have been a powerful Sorcerer,' she says, 'had you been prepared to study when you were young.'

There doesn't seem to be any answer to this so I remain silent.

'You know we have been plagued by bad dreams? I see that they are connected with Elith in some way. And the Hesuni Tree, though our healers assure us that it is again healthy.'

Yestar stares into space. A smile comes to her face. 'The juggling competition? Even here on Avula, you wish to gamble?'

I feel uncomfortable. If Lady Yestar possesses powers of farseeing, I'd prefer her to concentrate on the matter of Elith rather than my bad habits. Any moment now she'll be advising me to drink less.

She lapses into her semi-trance once more. From another room I can hear the sound of a child's voice, excited. Isuas is screaming about something or other.

'And Makri may regret her offer of help when her mind clears. Did you drink of one of the pools?'

I nod.

'You're not supposed to.'

'I'm sorry. Is it calanith?'

'No. We just don't like it.'

The Elvish Lady frowns, and concentrates some more. 'Something was sold next to the Hesuni Tree.'

'Pardon?'

'Something was sold.'

This is interesting, but Yestar can summon up nothing more. She can't tell me who sold what, or to whom, but she has the distinct impression that a transaction was made. I ask her if in all her farsighted gazing she received any impression as to Elith's guilt or innocence.

'No. I could not see who killed our Tree Priest. But, as you know, the Hesuni Tree casts a dense cloud over all mystic effects in the area.'

Yestar, now fully back in the real world, fixes me with a stare. 'If you are able to clear Elith-ir-Methet I will be pleased. However, if it transpires that she is guilty, neither I nor my husband will stand for any attempt to forge evidence in her favour, or to spirit her off the island.'

I don't bother to defend myself against this one.

'She will be executed if found guilty,' I point out, and I can see that the prospect of this does not please Lady Yestar.

'I'd like to talk to someone who could tell me about the rival factions for the position of Tree Priest,' I say.

'That would be calanith.'

'But possibly very helpful.'

Yestar studies me for a while longer. Whether she's influenced by my honest face, or by her abhorrence at the thought of Elith being executed, she finally tells me that Visan, the Keeper of Lore, may be willing to explain it to me, if Yestar gives him permission.

Our conversation is interrupted by Isuas, who erupts into the room with Makri in tow.

'Makri just showed me a new attack,' she yells.

It's time for us to leave. Makri promises to return tomorrow to start the training. Lady Yestar will direct her to a private clearing where they will be undisturbed. An attendant leads us through the Palace.

'Still happy to be teaching the kid how to fight?'

'Guess so,' says Makri.

Whatever is influencing Makri's behaviour is lasting a long time. I study her eyes, and I see that they have the same glazed sort of look I saw in Elith-ir-Methet's.

'Bezin hat,' she says, still pleased.

Makri's continued intoxication leads to a brief comedy when we are led through a corridor with doors going off on each side. One of the doors opens and Jir-ar-Eth rushes out, plunging headlong into Makri, who stands there looking surprised as the Sorcerer tumbles to the floor.

'Careful,' she says solicitously, helping him up.

Jir-ar-Eth is displeased and rises with the air of an Elf
who feels his dignity has been encroached upon.

'Can't you look where you're going?' he demands before
hurrying off. I'm disappointed. From Lord Kalith's Chief
Sorcerer, I would have expected a better rejoinder.

Our attendant leads us on. Before I follow him I bend
down to quickly scoop up a slip of paper that I purposely
covered with my foot when it fluttered from the Sorcerer's
pocket. It's probably only the Royal Laundry List, but I
always like the opportunity to study the private papers of
important people. And Elves.

At the end of the final corridor, before the huge outside doors, the attendant leans over to whisper in my ear.

'I believe that if you go to the clearing at the stream
and three oaks, you will often find a convivial gathering
of those who enjoy beer,' he murmurs.

I thank him profusely, then ask a question.

'We saw some actors in the clearing below. They all
seemed to be arguing with a grey-haired Elf. The director
of the play, maybe?'

'That would be Sofius-ar-Eth, appointed by Lord Kalith
to produce and direct Avula's entry at the festival.'

'Sofius-ar-Eth? Any relation to Jir-ar-Eth, the Sorcerer?'

'His brother.'

That is interesting.

'Didn't feel the desire to be a Sorcerer too?'

'He did, sir. Sofius-ar-Eth is one of Avula's most powerful Sorcerers. It was a surprise to many when he was
appointed to take charge of our play.'

The doors are opened and we stroll out, only to meet
with Cicerius, Prince Dees-Akan, Lanius Suncatcher and
Harmon Half-Elf, a full Turanian delegation here on busi-

ness. I greet them politely and step aside to let them pass. Both Sorcerers enter the Palace but Prince Dees-Akan halts in front of me with an expression of dislike on his face.

'Have you been bothering our hosts again?'

I regret his unfriendly tone. It's going to make life in Turai difficult having a Royal Prince down on me like a bad spell.

'Guests of Lady Yestar,' I explain.

'You are not to disturb Lady Yestar with your pointless questions,' commands the Prince.

Makri wanders up to us, obviously still under the influence of thazis.

'The second in line to the Turanian throne,' she says, benignly, 'doesn't have any power to issue orders to Turanian citizens while in another country. No legal basis for it. I studied the law at the Guild College. Passed the exam only last month. Do you like my new hat? I think it's bezin.'

The Prince is outraged. 'How dare you instruct me on the law!' he says, loudly.

'Well, you need instructing. Cicerius will tell you. He's a lawyer.'

All eyes fall on Cicerius. He looks uncomfortable as he grapples with the difficult notion of trying to grant that Makri is correct without infuriating the Prince. Prince Dees-Akan shoots him a furious glance, turns on his heel, and marches into the Palace.

'Thank you for that,' says Cicerius, icily.

I apologise. 'Sorry, Deputy Consul. Didn't mean to put you on the spot. But we were invited here by Lady Yestar. We could hardly refuse to come, could we?'

The Deputy Consul draws me away from the gates and lowers his voice. 'Have you discovered anything?'

'Nothing startling. But I'm still suspicious of everything.'

'This really is awkward for Lord Kalith you know. It's most unfortunate that all this has happened at festival time. He has many important guests to welcome and even before the murder of the Tree Priest he was in an embarrassing situation. I understand that certain members of his Council of Elders are saying in private that the disgrace of having their Hesuni Tree damaged reflects so badly on the Avulans that Lord Kalith should abdicate. Since Gulas-ar-Thetos was killed that disgrace has grown considerably worse, though Kalith is putting a brave face on it. I repeat, Thraxas, I understand your desire to help your friend and wartime companion, but one can hardly blame the Elf Lord for wishing to bring things to a swift conclusion.'

'I suppose I can't, Cicerius. And I don't blame you for supporting him either. I know that Lord Kalith is an important ally of Turai. But doesn't it strike you that I may be doing him a favour? His prestige won't be helped if the wrong Elf suffers for the crimes.'

'That,' says Cicerius,' would depend on whether anyone found out.'

'Meaning a swift conviction of Elith would be best all round, whether she did it or not.'

'Exactly.'

I study Cicerius's face for a few moments. Over in the trees behind us colourful parrots are squawking cheerfully at each other.

'Cicerius, if we were in Turai, you wouldn't want an

innocent person to be punished for a crime they didn't commit, no matter how convenient it was for the state. Even though you're a strong supporter of the Royal Family you've defended people in the law courts that the King would much rather have seen quickly hanged. Hell, you're far more honest than me.'

Cicerius doesn't contradict me. He gazes over at the parrots for a minute or so.

'You would be far better leaving matters as they are,' he says, finally. 'Were it not for the fact that Lord Kalith knows it would only look worse for him to have a Human guest of his own favoured healer languishing in prison during the festival, you would have been locked up for putting a spell on his guards. You would be unwise to push him any further.'

He pauses. The parrots keep squawking. 'But you might be interested to know that Palace gossip says that Elith-ir-Methet was having an affair with Gulas-ar-Thetos. That, of course, would be a taboo affair that neither of their families would have allowed to continue. Tree Priests cannot marry outside of their clan.'

'Does Palace gossip say that's why she killed him?'

Cicerius shrugs.

'I never repeat gossip,' he says, then walks swiftly away through the gates of the Palace. Makri is quiet as we walk back to Camith's tree dwelling. Even the inquisitive monkeys don't attract her attention. We're almost there when she suddenly comes to a halt.

'What the hell was in that thazis stick?' she demands, shaking her head.

'Just thazis.'

'I feel like I've been journeying through the magic space.'

'I noticed you weren't your usual self.'

Makri shakes her head again and a breeze catches her hair, displaying her pointed ears.

'Did I really agree to teach that horrible child how to fight?'

'I'm afraid so.'

She sits down and dangles her legs over the edge of the walkway. 'Now I'm really depressed.'

'You should be. You've only got six days to get her ready.'

'Give me some thazis,' says Makri.

CHAPTER
TWELVE

We eat our evening meal with Camith and his family in relative quiet. Camith discusses the festival with his wife but Makri is mute and I'm too busy concentrating on the food to talk. Once again, I am well satisfied with the fare. The venison is of the highest quality and the fish is freshly caught that morning by a cousin of the family who has his own fishing boat.

In Turai Elves mean only one of two things to most people: either mighty warriors helping us against the Orcs, or makers of fine poetry and songs. We never think of them as owning fishing boats, somehow. Or having arguments when they're trying to put on a play.

Makri is unusually quiet. Later she tells me that she has been feeling strange ever since drinking the water at the Hesuni pools.

'I'm almost back to normal now. I wonder why it didn't affect you?'

'Maybe it only affects Elves? Or those with Elvish blood?'

Whatever the reason, I'm betting it has some connection with Elith's memory loss, and I'll be investigating the pools at the first opportunity. I wonder what Lady Yestar meant about something being sold in the vicinity?

'I'm heading off to the clearing at the stream and three oaks.'

'What for?'

'Beer. Apparently it's a gathering point for night-time drinking.'

'Do you always have to move heaven, earth and the three moons just to find beer?'

'Yes. Do you want to come?'

Makri shakes her head. She's muttering about the injustice of being mysteriously drugged and then tricked into teaching Isuas how to fight.

I'm puzzled about this. I could see that Lady Yestar liked Makri but after all the fuss about a person with Orcish blood even landing on the island, one might have thought that the Queen would be hesitant about immediately commissioning this person to train her child in the art of war. How are the population going to react? What about the already dissatisfied Council of Elders? Surely Lord Kalith will be furious when he hears the news.

'I'm not worried about Lord Kalith,' says Makri. 'I'm concerned about my reputation as a fighter. How am I meant to train that child? She's about as much use as a one-legged gladiator. She couldn't defend herself against an angry butterfly.'

'Well, be sure and go easy on her,' I say. 'Yestar won't thank you if you send her home with a black eye and a bloody nose. And remember, no attacks to the groin, eyes, throat or knees. It's against the rules.'

'No attacks to the groin, eyes, throat or knees?' cries Makri, despairingly. 'This gets worse all the time. What's the point? It's hardly like fighting at all.'

'I told you, they don't want their children maimed. If Isuas trots out to her first engagement and proceeds to poke a dagger into her opponent's eye she'll be disqualified, and no one is going to be very pleased about it.'

'But I was depending on the dagger attack to the eyes,' complains Makri. 'Otherwise what chance does she have?'

'You'll just have to teach her some proper sword play. You know, the sort of thing gentlemen do.'

'It's all ridiculous. These tournaments are stupid.'

I agree with her, more or less.

'I'd never enter one,' states Makri. 'If I'm going to fight, I'll do it properly or not at all. What about these fighting competitions in the far west I've heard about? Are they all pussyfooting around?'

'No, not all of them. Some of the tournaments in the far west are very vicious affairs. They fight with real weapons and no one minds who gets hurt. The warriors' competition in Samsarina used to be notorious for the number of deaths each year. Still is, I expect. It attracts the finest swordsmen from all over the world, because of the handsome nature of the prize.

Makri is interested in this. 'You've been in Samsarina, haven't you? Did you see the competition?'

'I was in it.'

'Really? How did you do?'

'I won it.'

Makri looks at me suspiciously.

'You won the warriors' competition in Samsarina, against the world's best swordsmen?'

'I did.'

'I don't believe you.'

I shrug. 'I don't care if you believe me or not.'

'How come no one in Twelve Seas ever mentions it? Surely they'd have heard of such a notable feat?'

'It was a long time ago. Anyway, I was entered under a different name as I was on some unscheduled leave from the army at the time. What are you looking so dubious about?'

'I thought you spent your youth being thrown out of the Sorcerers' school.'

'I did. And after that I learned how to fight. You think it's just an accident I've lasted so long as an Investigator in Turai?'

As I'm putting on my cloak I remember the slip of paper I filched from Lord Kalith's Sorcerer. I can't read it, so I show it to Makri.

'Royal Elvish?'

She nods. 'Where did you get hold of this?'

'It fell out of Jir-ar-Eth's pocket when you knocked him to the ground. Can you translate it?'

Makri studies the paper for a moment or two and pronounces it to be a list. I guessed it would be something dull.

'What sort of list? Laundry?'

'No. This is a summary of Jir-ar-Eth's report to Lord Kalith. It's a list of all possible suspects for the killing of Gulas-ar-Thetos. He's been using sorcery to scan the area and he's identified everyone who was close enough at the time to have stuck a knife into Gulas. You're on it, and Camith.'

'We were on the walkway above. Who else?'

'Elith-ir-Methet,' reads Makri. 'Lasas-ar-Thetos, Gulas's brother. Merith-ar-Thet, listed as a cousin of Lasas and Gulas. Pires-ar-Senth, a Palace guard. Caripatha-ir-Min, a weaver. And Gorith-ar-Del.'

I take back the paper.

'Makri, did I ever say how much I valued your intellect, particularly your fine command of languages?'

'No. But you did once say that pointy-eared Orc bastards had no business learning Royal Elvish.'

I chuckle indulgently.

'A joke you took in good part, as I recall. When the Association of Gentlewomen sends round its next collection plate for educating the struggling masses of Turanian women, you can count me in for a few gurans. With this paper, my investigation just became a whole lot easier.'

'How come you get such a lucky break?' enquires Makri.

'I practise a lot.'

I leave Makri and seek out Camith for directions to the clearing at the stream and three oaks, which he provides.

'A haunt of armourers and poets, I believe.'

'Armourers and poets are fine with me, providing they have beer.'

I take my illuminated staff to light my way, and set off briskly over the walkways.

'Follow the Dragon's Tail and you can't go wrong,' Camith instructs me. The Dragon's Tail comprises five stars that form a line. It's visible from Turai, though I think it points in a different direction up there. I don't know why that would be.

I traverse the walkway with care, not wishing to plunge off the edge in the darkness. It's something of a relief when I come to the distinctive tree that carries a ladder down to the ground. From here I'm to keep to the path till I come to a fork, where I'm to take the left path till I reach the clearing.

Even though this is an Elvish island on which there
are no evil creatures of the night and no criminal gangs
– at least in theory – I still feel slightly apprehensive
walking through the forest on my own in the darkness. I
wouldn't admit it to anyone, but the forest bothers me
in a way the city never does. It feels like it's alive, and it
knows I don't belong here. I boost my illuminated staff
up to maximum power and hurry along, cheering myself up with the thought that I'm finally going to get
myself a beer, and that it is long overdue.

I'm concentrating on following the path so when a
voice comes from right behind me I practically jump into
the nearest tree.

'It's an enormous Human with an illuminated staff!
How interesting!'

I spin round, not pleased to be taken unawares. Standing there, grinning at me, is a slender young female Elf
of eighteen or so. Her hood is thrown back and her hair
is cut unusually short for an Elf.

'How do you do?' she greets me. 'Are you looking for
beer, enormous Human?'

I scowl at her. 'The name's Thraxas.'

'I know,' she says, smiling pleasantly. 'Everyone on Avula
knows that there is an Investigator called Thraxas going
around asking questions. Are you going to the three oaks
to ask questions, enormous Human?'

'No. I'm going for a beer. And will you stop calling me
enormous? Is that a polite way to address a guest?'

'Sorry. I was being poetic. But I suppose "enormous"
isn't a very poetic word, when applied to a Human. Would
"impressively girthed" be better?'

'No, it would still be lousy,' I reply.

'Kingly proportioned?'

'Could we just forget my weight for a moment? What do you want?'

'The same as you. Beer.'

She falls in at my side and we walk on.

'I take it you are a poet rather than an armourer?'

'Definitely. I'm Sendroo-ir-Vallis. You can call me Droo.'

'Pleased to meet you, Droo.'

Having got over my surprise, I don't mind a little company. Droo, obviously an Elf who has no problems in talking to strangers, tells me that she comes to the three oaks most nights to meet other poets.

'And drink beer.'

'I thought Elvish poets would drink wine.'

'Only the older ones,' Droo informs me. 'And I daresay it was fine for composing epics. But poetry moves on, you know. Look, there's the clearing. There's a hill where you can look at the stars through the fine mist from the waterfall. It's very inspiring. Poets have always loved the spot.'

'What about the armourers?'

'They use the fast-flowing water for their forges. I've never found that very poetic, but we get on well with them. Is it true that you travel with a woman with Orc blood and a ring through her nose?'

I see that Makri's reputation has spread as swiftly as my own. 'I never go anywhere without her. Apart from tonight. She's home resting.'

Droo seems disappointed, though she owns that's she's pleased to meet a detective.

'I need new experiences, and there are so few opportunities for a young Elf to get off the island. I wanted to sail on the ship to Turai but my father wouldn't let me. Are you going to ask everyone questions?'

'Maybe a few. But mainly I'm looking for beer.'

We arrive at the clearing and I've rarely seen a more welcoming sight. Benches are laid out under the three mighty oaks and from inside the hollow stump of a huge dead tree an Elf is handing out tankards. Two large tables are occupied by brawny Elves in leather aprons whom I take to be armourers, and a further table nearer to the stream is surrounded by younger, thinner Elves, presumably poets. They wave to Sendroo as she appears, and some of the weapon-makers also shout greetings. The atmosphere is convivial, sufficiently so that my arrival, while provoking some comment, doesn't cast any sort of shadow over the place.

I march up to the Elf in the hollow tree, take out some small pieces of Elvish currency, and request a beer. He hands it over in a black leather tankard. I drink it down in one, hand back the tankard, and request another. He fills the tankard from a barrel at the back and hands it over. I down it in one and give him back the tankard.

'More beer.'

I take the third tankard, empty it straight down and hand it back. By this time the Elf is looking slightly surprised.

'Would you like to try—'

'More beer.'

As I'm draining the fourth tankard there is some good-natured laughter from the armourers behind me.

'He is a mighty drinker,' says one of them.

I finish off a fifth tankard, and take a six and seventh over to their table.

'Better bring me a couple more,' I say to the barkeeper, and hand him a few more coins. 'Make that three. Four. Well, just keep them coming till I tell you to stop.'

'Any room for a thirsty man at that table?' I ask.

I figure that while the poets might be interesting in their own way, the armourers will make for better company while I'm in such desperate need of beer. They look like the sort of Elves who enjoy a few tankards themselves after a hard day at the forge. They're brawny, as Elves go. Not as brawny as me, but at least they don't make me feel quite as oversized as most of the Elves do.

The weapon-makers move up, letting me in at the bench. I drink down one of my tankards, make a start on another, and look round to check that the barkeeper is on his way with more.

'A hard day?' enquires the nearest Elf jovially.

'A hard month. I ran out of ale on Kalith's ship and I've been searching ever since.'

When the barkeeper arrives I order a round of drinks for the entire table, which goes down well.

'He's trying to bribe us with drinks,' cry the Elves, laughing. 'Are you here to ask the armourers questions, Investigator?'

'No, just to drink beer. And isn't it time someone was calling that barkeeper over? Anyone know any good drinking songs?'

You can't ask an Elvish weapon-maker if he knows any good drinking songs without getting a hearty response. I know that. I remember these Elves, or Elves very much like them, from the war. I feel on much firmer territory than I have been with Lord Kalith-ar-Yil and his retinue. A drinking song starts up, and after it's gone round a few times one of the Elves further down the table actually shouts that now he remembers me.

'I was up in Turai during the War! You used to fight with that Barbarian – what was his name?'

'Gurd.'

'Gurd! Bless the old Barbarian!'

The Elf slams his tankard cheerfully on the table.

'Thraxas! When I heard we had a Human Investigator heading our way, I never realised it was you.'

He turns to his companions.

'I know this man. Fought well and never let us run out of drink!'

It's true. I raided the cellars after the Orcish dragons burned down the taverns.

'Is that you, Voluth? You didn't have a beard back then.'

'And you didn't have such a belly!'

Voluth roars with laughter. I remember him well – a shield-maker by trade, and a doughty warrior. He calls for more beer, and starts telling war stories, stories in which I'm pleased to see I feature well. I smile at everyone genially. This is more the sort of thing I had in mind when an expedition to the Elvish Isles was mooted. Beer, drinking songs and convivial company.

Which is not to say I'm not alert for anything that may be helpful. Talk naturally swings round to the matter of Elith-ir-Methet's killing of Gulas. If they were having an affair, word of it hasn't reached the armourers, though several of them do say that Gulas was very young to be Tree Priest. His brother is younger, and, I gather, less popular.

The poets are meanwhile sprawled over the ground at the foot of the small hill, looking at the moons and reciting lines to each other. Droo is talking animatedly with another Elvish youth. In fact they seem to be arguing. I can't hear their conversation, but it seems to be growing more heated. Suddenly the sound of singing fills the glade.

'Choirs are practising late,' say the armourers, and listen with the air of Elves who have a fine judgement of such things.

'Sounds like the choir from Ven. Not bad, though I fancy Corinthal may have the edge this year.'

'Is competition fierce in all the events?' I enquire, reasoning that if it is I may well find out if there's any gambling in these parts.

'Very fierce,' says Voluth. 'With the festival only taking place every five years, these choirs spend years practising and no one wants to put up a bad performance on the day. It's even worse with the dramatic companies. It's an immense honour winning the first prize. Ten years ago the Avulans won with a spectacular rendition of the famous episode where Queen Leeuven goes to war against her stepbrother. Lord Kalith made the director an Honoured Knight of Avula, an award previously only given to Elves who distinguished themselves on the battlefield. He's never had to buy himself a goblet of wine or haunch of venison to this day.'

'We didn't do so well last time though,' another Elf puts in. 'Staid performance. No emotion. The whole island was disappointed.'

'What happened to the director?'

'He sailed off in a bad mood, saying the judges wouldn't know a good play if Queen Leeuven herself handed it down from heaven. We haven't seen him since.'

This leads to a lot of talk about the relative merits of the three entrants in this year's competition. As far as I can gather there is no clear favourite, but public opinion slightly favours the Corinthalians.

'But Ven will put up a good show too. Some singers from Avula went over there earlier this year and they came back with some very impressive reports of a rehearsal they'd seen.'

'What about Avula this year?' I ask.

All around the table there are pursed lips, and a general air of disgruntlement.

'Not giving yourselves much chance?'

'Not much. We've got some fine performers, but who ever heard of a Sorcerer for a director? I don't know what Lord Kalith was thinking of, appointing Sofius-ar-Eth to the post.'

The Elvish armourers are unanimous on this point.

'Not a bad Sorcerer, we admit, but a director? He's had no experience. No chance of winning the prize with him at the helm. There's been dissatisfaction in Avula ever since it was announced. There's talk of some fierce arguments in the Council of Elders over the affair. No one wants to see our play turning into a shambles, and from what we hear that's what's going to happen.'

It's odd. No one can explain why Lord Kalith made such an unexpected appointment.

'It's said that Lady Yestar was far from pleased. But they're always arguing, everyone knows that.'

I turn the conversation round to the question of juggling, and this produces some furious debate. The merits of various jugglers from Avula, Ven and Corinthal are discussed at length, with no clear favourite emerging.

The best Avulan juggler is apparently a young woman called Shuthan-ir-Hemas, but opinion is divided as to whether she can defeat some of the more experienced practitioners from the other islands.

I lower my voice, and mutter a few words in Voluth's ear. He grins. 'Well, you might be able to place a bet though Lord Kalith doesn't approve of anyone gambling on events at the festival.'

'Is it calanith?'

'No, he just doesn't like it. But it's been known to happen. I can't really recommend anyone for the juggling, but if you want a safe bet on the junior tournament, go for Firees-ar-Key. Son of Yulis-ar-Key, finest warrior on the island, and a chip off the old block. Firees won the tournament for under-twelves when he was only nine, and he's practically fully grown now, though he's only fourteen years of age.'

I file that away as a useful piece of information. I'm about to cast around for some more betting tips when Droo interrupts by squeezing in beside me at the table. She's looking rather unhappy but her expression brightens as the armourers greet her genially.

'It's young Droo! Up to no good, no doubt.'

'Do your parents know you're out writing poems and drinking ale, youngster?'

Droo returns their greetings, equally genially. They all seem to know her and like her. I try to think of anywhere in Turai where weapon-makers and poets mingle happily together. I can't. The race track, maybe, except poets never have any money to place a bet.

'You've met Thraxas already? Are you writing a poem about him?'

'Certainly,' grins Droo.

'Better make it an epic,' calls Voluth. 'There's a lot of him to write about.'

They all laugh. I call for more beer.

'I came over so I could be questioned too,' says Droo. 'I didn't want to miss out.'

'He hasn't been questioning us,' the armourers tell her.

'Why not?'

Everyone looks at me. I tell them frankly that as this is the first time I've been able to relax with a beer for weeks, I can't be bothered doing any investigating. This seems to disappoint them. In fact, as the ale keeps flowing, almost everyone seems to be keen to express an opinion about the case, and I find myself drawn into some investigating anyway, pretty much against my will. A chainmail-maker at the end of the table knows Vas-ar-Methet well and refuses to believe that his daughter is responsible for any crime. A blacksmith's apprentice beside him is of the opinion that some odd things have been happening around the Hesuni Tree for some time, and everyone knows that this is why the Elves have been having bad dreams. Maybe, he suggests, it was bad dreams that drove Elith to commit the crimes?

There is some sympathy for Elith, mainly because of the high opinion in which her father is held, but the general view is that she must be guilty as charged. Indeed, a blacksmith, who is, incidentally, the largest Elf I have ever seen, tells us that he knows Elith is guilty of the murder because his sister was close to the Hesuni Tree at the time and she was certain she'd seen the fatal blow being struck.

'You should talk to her, Thraxas. She'll tell you what she saw.'

I learn something of note about Gorith-ar-Del. As a maker of longbows he's known to the armourers but he isn't making fine longbows any more. He's given up the business. No one knows why, or what he does with himself these days when he's not sailing with Lord Kalith-ar-Yil.

Some white-robed actors appear in the clearing, leading to more general good-natured greetings. I recognise them as members of the Avulan cast I saw earlier close to the Tree Palace. They've been rehearsing in the vicinity.

'How is the tale of Queen Leeuven coming on?' call the weapon-makers.

'Badly. We need ale,' reply the actors, making comic faces and hurrying to the hollow tree for refreshment. They mingle with the poets and, from the fragments of their conversation I can catch, they're feeling no happier with their director.

I turn to Droo, and notice that she has a rather sad expression on her face.

'Bad time with the boyfriend?' I say sympathetically.

She nods.

'He left after we argued.'

'What were you arguing about?'

'Are you investigating me?' says Droo, brightening at the prospect.

'No. Well, not unless you or your boyfriend defaced the Hesuni Tree and murdered the priest.'

'He didn't,' says Droo, and looks gloomy again. 'But his behaviour is so erratic these days, it wouldn't surprise me if he did something equally stupid. And he was really mean about my new poem.'

I sympathise, which just goes to show how mellow this evening's gathering has made me. Under normal circumstances, I don't have much time to spare for the problems of teenage poets.

Elves start drifting away as the night wears on. Droo departs with her friends and I decide that it's time to go. I have drunk a great amount of beer, and it's a fair walk back to Camith's house. I ask at the bar if they have any beer in flasks or bottles I can take away with me.

'We can let you have a wineskin full, if you like.'

'That'll do fine.'

I pay for my drink, say goodbye to my fellow drinkers, and start off on the journey home. I don't want to admit that I can't see as well as the Elves at night so I wait till I'm some way along the path before lighting up my illuminated staff. On the way home I'm merry. The forest no longer feels threatening.

'Well, of course, that was the problem,' I say out loud. 'How's a man meant to relate to an Elvish forest without a few beers inside him? Now I'm in the right state of mind, it's quite a cheery place.'

I greet a few of the trees as I pass. I'm quite close to home. I remember that I have to climb up a long ladder to get there. Damn. I'm not looking forward to that. The path becomes narrow. I'm humming a bright ditty as I turn the next corner. There, in front of me, are four masked Elves with spears. They let out a battle cry, and sprint towards me, weapons lowered for action.

I'm startled. I'd forgotten all about the hostile spear-carrying Elves. Once more I'm at a severe disadvantage on the narrow path. I mutter the word and my illuminated staff goes out and I hurl myself sideways into the trees. Here in the forest, they won't be able to attack me in formation. I scramble some way into the depths, then halt and listen. There is no sound.

I'm not in the mood for skulking. I'm not in the mood for struggling through the trees either. I had enough of that on the first occasion they forced me off the walkway. I get angry. A man should be able to walk around Avula without being chased by spearmen everywhere he goes. I decide to risk creeping back towards the path. I go as quietly as I can, which is very quietly. When I'm close to the path, I stop, hardly even breathing for fear of making a sound. The moonlight illuminates the path in front of me. There, easily visible, are the four Elves, standing silently, waiting.

I'm unsure what to do. Attacking them would be rash. I'm scared of no one in a fight but back on the path they would have the opportunity to form their phalanx against me. Besides, even if I hurled myself on them and managed to cut them down, Lord Kalith isn't going to be too pleased with me. I wasn't invited here to kill Elves.

All of a sudden the Elves vanish. Just like that. They disappear into thin air. I'm stunned. I've seen plenty of sorcery in my time, but it was the last thing I was expecting. I'm seriously perturbed. If four invisible Elves start hunting for me in this forest I'm doomed. I strain my senses, trying to catch any scent of them. I can't pick up anything but get the faint impression of voices receding into the distance.

After a while I venture back on to the path. Nothing there. I light up my staff and bend down to examine the grass. It looks to me as if the Elves just went on their way after becoming invisible. I don't understand any of this, but I'm not going to hang around and wait for them to come back. I set off homewards rapidly, not stopping till I reach the welcoming sight of the ladder that leads up to Camith's treehouse, which I ascend a good deal more briskly than I had anticipated.

CHAPTER
THIRTEEN

Next day I'm feeling sprightly, despite the hefty intake of beer.

'Must be the healthy air,' suggests Makri. 'I'm feeling good myself. What are you doing today?'

'Questioning a blacksmith's sister who saw the fatal stabbing. And talking to Visan the Keeper of Lore, whoever he may be. Yestar suggested he might be able to tell me more about the rivals for the Tree Priesthood.'

'Wouldn't that be calanith?'

'What isn't on this damn island? You'd think it might be calanith to execute a woman without a proper investigation, but apparently not.'

'Does Elith really face execution?' asks Makri.

'So they say. It would be the first on Avula in over a hundred years, and it's going to happen right after the festival unless I come up with something quick.'

'Well, have fun. I'm teaching that idiot child how to fight.' Makri is wearing her swords and has thrown a few other weapons in a bag. 'I only had two knives when I jumped in the ocean, but I've borrowed a couple more from Camith. And a practice sword.'

Makri looks at the wooden blade with frank distaste. I tell her not to worry, she can still kill Isuas with it if she hits her hard enough.

Makri is meeting her pupil some way over to the west of the island, at a clearing used only by the Royal Family, where they will not be disturbed. Although we've seen young Elves practising their fighting all over the island, Makri is to teach Isuas in private. This suits Makri.

'If no one sees anything, my reputation might survive the debacle.'

She is still unhappy at the way things have turned out but supposes she should just make the best of it.

'Okay, teaching the brat will be a disaster, but I'll get some exercise and weapons practice myself. And maybe a chance to use the Royal Elvish language.'

After some study of my grimoire, I load the sleep spell into my mind, and another one that may prove useful. We leave together, heading west. Rather than tramp over the walkways we borrow two horses from Camith and make our way round by means of one of the main paths in the forest. As we travel we pass performers of various sorts at regular intervals, all rehearsing for the festival, now only five days away. I pause to look at a young Elf who is putting on a fine juggling performance under a tall silver tree. She's keeping four small wooden balls in the air at once and her partner, or possibly her trainer, tosses another one at her, and then another, so that she now has six balls flying in an arc from one hand to the other.

'She looks like a woman who might be worth a wager,' I mutter, and trot over to ask her name. She's called Usath, she's from Ven, and her green tunic is decorated with silver crescent moons. Although she is at first surprised at our approach, and visibly sniffs the air as she catches scent of Makri's Orc blood, she is not distracted for long and soon gets back to practising. Obviously a dedicated performer. Her assistant, another young female Elf, throws a seventh ball to her, but it goes wrong and the balls cascade on to the grass.

The young juggler lets out a coarse oath, and stoops to pick them up. Already she's forgotten our presence.

'Well, she made a hash of the seventh ball, but even so, she was pretty impressive with six,' I say.

'Might be worth a bet,' agrees Makri. 'I'll see if Isuas has any information about the other jugglers.'

Realising what she has just said, Makri frowns.

'How come I'm keen to bet on a juggling competition? I used to disapprove of gambling.' She twists in her saddle. 'It's your fault, you corrupted me.'

'Nothing corrupt about it, Makri. Gambling is good for you.'

'How?'

'I don't know. But I'm sure it is. You know, thanks to me, you are a much finer person than the raw young gladiator who arrived in Turai only a year and a half ago. Beer, klee, thazis and gambling. I taught you them all. Now I think about it, you weren't very good at lying till I showed you how.'

Soon after this we go our separate ways, Makri to Lady Yestar's private clearing and myself on to the collection of treehouses where the blacksmith's sister dwells. She is a weaver by trade and should now be working at her loom. A few enquiries lead me to her place of work, a small wooden hut at ground level that contains four looms and two elves. One of these is Caripatha, the Elf I'm looking for. She's sitting at her loom, though rather than working she's staring into space. I introduce myself, mention my conversation with the blacksmith, and ask her if she'd mind answering a few questions.

She nods, vaguely. I'm surprised at her lack of reaction. From her indifference you might think that a Human detective appearing at her workplace to investigate a murder was an everyday occurrence.

'You were in the clearing when the murder took place?'

She nods.

'Would you mind telling me what you saw?'

'Elith-ir-Methet sticking a knife into Gulas-ar-Thetos.'

'Are you sure it was her?'

'I'm sure.'

'It was dark when it happened. Could you have been mistaken about her identity?'

Caripatha is quite certain that she was not mistaken. I ask her what she was doing in the clearing. She tells me that she just likes to be close to the Hesuni Tree every now and then, the same as all Avulans.

'Do you know of any reason why Elith-ir-Methet might have done it? Can you tell me anything about her relationship with Gulas?'

'I have to go now,' says Caripatha suddenly.

She rises from her stool and walks out. I'm astonished. Her friend, or workmate, has so far sat in silence.

'Where did she go?' I ask her.

The other Elf shakes her head. 'I don't know. Her behaviour has been erratic recently. She hasn't woven anything in a month.'

'Does she often just disappear like that?'

Apparently she does. I'm puzzled. One minute she was answering my questions, the next she suddenly departed. There was no sign that my questions had perturbed her.

It just seemed like she'd remembered something more important she had to do.

Outside my horse is waiting for me. I mount up and ride off, deep in thought. These Elves. Is it just me, or are they all acting strangely?

I ride back towards the centre of the island. Two groups of mounted Elves pass me, each with cloaks and tunics a slightly different shade of green than those of the Avulans. The island is filling up as guests and spectators arrive from the nearby islands for the festival. As I pass the turning that leads to the Queen's private clearing, I'm overcome with curiosity about Makri and Isuas. I lead my horse up the path. As far as I know, Makri has never taught anyone before. I wonder if she has an aptitude for it. I hope so. As long as Isuas is happy, I'm guaranteed entry to the Palace.

There are no guards or fences to prevent other Elves from entering the clearing. They just don't. Avulans are, on the whole, far better behaved than the people of Turai. The murder of Gulas-ar-Thetos is the first killing to happen on the island for twelve years. In Turai someone is murdered every four hours.

When I sight the clearing I dismount, tether my horse, and advance softly, wishing to arrive unannounced. I poke my head quietly round the last tree at the edge of the path.

Makri and Isuas are facing each other. Each has a wooden sword in one hand and a wooden dagger in the other. Isuas is wearing a green tunic and leggings, which look new. Probably her mother provided her with new clothes for the venture, which would be regarded as lucky by the Elves. Makri has discarded her Elvish tunic and sandals and is looking exotic, though not very savage, in bare feet, chainmail bikini and floppy green hat. Her hair is as voluminous as usual but she's plaited the strands at the front into braids to prevent it from flying into her face while in combat.

Makri is giving instructions. I remain silent, and strain to hear her words. Her voice sounds aggrieved, as if things have not been going well.

'Attack me. Sword then dagger, and try to get it right this time.'

Isuas lunges gamely at her. It's not a bad effort for a beginner, but Makri parries her blow with some contempt and Isuas's sword flies from her hand. The young Elf has made an effort to follow through with the dagger as instructed, but Makri simply twists her body to avoid it then hits Isuas on the head with the pommel of her own dagger. Isuas falls down heavily.

'That was terrible,' says Makri, raising her voice. 'Now, get up, and do it right.'

'You hurt me,' wails Isuas.

Makri reaches down, yanks the kid to her feet and tells her to stop complaining and pick up her sword.

'Attack me again and try not to throw your sword away this time.'

Even at this distance I can see the glint of tears in Isuas's eyes, but she does as she's told and again executes a reasonable thrust in Makri's direction. Makri is a master of the twin-bladed technique, which is not so common in the west or the south as it was in her gladiator days in the east. She parries both of Isuas's blades simultaneously, steps forward, smashes her right hand into Isuas's face, kicks her legs from under her and whacks her with the flat of her sword as she's on the way down. The young Elf crumples as if hit by a bolt from a cross-bow and starts to scream, a scream that is cut off as Makri places her foot on Isuas's throat and glares down at her in a very hostile manner.

'What the hell was that?' she demands. 'I didn't tell you to wave your sword at your mother, you useless little brat. I said attack me with it. You're pathetic. I used to have a little puppy dog that could hold a weapon better than you.'

Makri has abandoned all efforts to practise her Royal Elvish language, instead choosing to curse and abuse Isuas in an ungodly mixture of Common Elvish and Orcish, and even the Orcish epithets she chooses belong not to the Common Orc tongue but to the much cruder pidgin Orcish that was the lingua franca of the gladiator pits. All in all it makes for a terrifying verbal assault. I am mean-while standing open-mouthed at this exhibition. I did fore-see that Makri would be no easy task master, but I wasn't expecting her to half kill her pupil on the first day.

Possibly sensing that the youngster is about to expire, Makri removes her foot from Isuas's throat. Isuas sobs. This seems to infuriate Makri even more.

'Stop crying, you ignorant little whore. You wanted to learn how to fight. Well, get up and fight, you cusux.'

Cusux is pidgin Orcish. It's about the rudest thing you can possibly say to anyone. If Isuas ever repeats it to Lord Kalith he'll send up his fleet to sack Turai. Isuas, having made two game attempts at attacking, now seems a little unwilling to try a third. She rises, but slowly, so Makri kicks her savagely in the ribs, making her howl, as she falls over again.

'Don't hang around on the ground, stupid. You think your opponent is going to wait all day for you to get ready? Pick up your weapons and attack me and this time you better do it properly or I swear I'll put this sword in through your mouth and out through the back of your throat.'

Feeling that this is going rather too far, I hasten forward.

'Makri,' I call, endeavouring to make my voice jovial rather than appalled. 'Just called in to see how things are going.'

Makri whirls round. She's not pleased to see me.

'Can't talk, Thraxas, I'm busy.'

'So I see.'

Isuas is lying on the ground, holding her ribs and sobbing.

'Possibly time for a little break?' I suggest. 'Maybe smoke some thazis?'

'No time for that,' says Makri dismissively. 'I have to teach this imbecile to fight. Goodbye.'

Makri turns back to her pupil and screams at her to get up. Isuas breaks down completely, and starts bawling. I lay my hand on Makri's shoulder.

'Don't you think you're being a little—'

Makri spins to face me again, a truly savage expression on her face.

'Get out of here, Thraxas,' she yells angrily. 'Go investigate. And don't bother me again.'

I'm taken aback. I've seen Makri in a foul mood plenty of times before but I wasn't expecting such passions to be raised in the matter of the junior tournament. I decide to withdraw. After all, it is really Makri's business and not mine. I just hope Lady Yestar doesn't ban me from the Palace when she learns of Makri's barbaric behaviour.

I walk back to the path, turning my head for a last look before leaving. Makri has hauled Isuas to her feet and forced her to attack again. As I watch, Makri smacks her practice sword on to Isuas's fingers, making her shriek with pain and once more drop her blade.

'Keep hold of your sword, you miserable cusux!' yells Makri, accentuating each word with a vicious blow. I shudder.

Riding back along the path, I try to remember what my early weapons training was like. Quite rough I think, but nothing in comparison with the lessons Isuas is receiving from Makri the madwoman. I prey that Isuas makes it through the day in one piece. If she does, I'm certain she won't be back for a second.

I ride round the island till I reach one of the paths that lead towards the middle of Avula. It runs along the banks of the river that rises in the central hills. From here I can ride most of the way to the Palace, though I'll have to walk the last part as it is forbidden to take horses into the central clearing. I haven't seen this part of the island before. It's less heavily wooded, with some areas of grassland and a few cultivated fields. Although the majority of the houses I pass are still high up in the trees, there are a few more buildings at ground level. These are of simple construction, but all bear the signs of fine craftsmanship. Everything on Avula does. They don't seem to build anything shoddily.

'The Ossuni Elves perform all work with love and perfection,' I remember Vas-ar-Methet saying a long time ago.

I wonder about his daughter having an affair with Gulas-ar-Thetos. If she was, does it make her more or less likely to have damaged the Tree? Get back at your lover by damaging his precious Hesuni Tree? Maybe. I've known stranger ways of taking revenge. But then, why kill him later? It seems like far too extreme a thing for Elith to have done.

Much as I hate to admit it, I can't run away from the fact that I have now spoken to a witness who actually saw the murder. Though the weaver Caripatha showed some signs of erratic behaviour, she didn't sound to me like an Elf who was lying or unsure of what she saw. Things are looking worse for Elith. I might yet be forced to fall back on finding some extenuating circumstances to save her from execution.

Cursing all witnesses who make life difficult for my clients, I ride on. Why are so many of the Elves acting strangely? It's not just Elith. Gorith-ar-Del, for instance. I can understand his dislike for me, but why did he suddenly quit his work as a longbow-maker? Most un-Elf-like. I think back to the sailor who plunged to his death from the rigging. Very strange. As was the behaviour of Caripatha, who hasn't woven anything for a month, and suddenly decided she had to be somewhere else, rushing off without a word of explanation to her companion. What's the matter with them all?

An Elf on horseback approaches me on the path. Rather than riding past he draws his horse up in front of mine and halts, staring at me intently. He's an old Elf, the oldest I've seen on the island. He sits upright in his saddle but his hair is white and his brow is a mass of fine wrinkles.

'I am Visan, the Keeper of Lore,' he says. 'I believe you wish to talk to me?'

'I do.'

'Then talk.'

'I'd like to know about the disputed succession of the Tree Priesthood.'

'Talking about that to a stranger would be calanith. Also, it is a very old and obscure story regarding junior branches of cousins' families that you would neither understand nor enjoy.'

'I haven't enjoyed much since I arrived here. I don't need to know the whole history, just what might be happening now. For instance, did anyone have it in for Gulas?'

'Yes,' says Visan, surprising me with his directness. 'Hith-ar-Key, who claims that the Priesthood should be his. His complaints to the Council of Elders are never-ending.'

'How strong is his claim?'

'That is calanith.'

Visan declines to answer my next few questions on the same grounds. I can see I'm not going to learn any secret details here.

'Well, might Hith have damaged the Hesuni Tree to discredit Gulas?'

Visan sits astride his horse, elderly and sedate, and considers my question.

'Yes,' he says finally. 'He might.'

'Was it looked into at the time?'

Visan shakes his head. 'Certainly not. Such an outrageous idea would not have occurred to anyone on the island.'

'But now I've suggested it . . . ?'

'It's possible.'

Visan nods to me, then rides off. Whether I've upset him by trampling on something calanith or just tired him out with my questions, I can't say. At least I've dragged another suspect on to the scene.

I ride on till I reach a place where nine or ten horses roam free in a large paddock. Here I have to leave my mount and continue on foot. I don't travel far before I run into a large crowd of Elves who are staring expectantly at a tree. Thinking that this is probably some private tree matter that only Elves will fully appreciate, I make to walk on by till suddenly a voice calls out, 'Avula's greatest juggler – in preparation for the festival – Shuthan-ir-Hemas!'

The watching Elves applaud as Shuthan-ir-Hemas steps nimbly out along a branch and bows to them all. She's a slender young Elf with bare feet and extremely long hair, and from the excited words of the crowd I can tell that they're expecting great things of her. Still keen for some information on which way to bet, I hang around to study her act.

Shuthan starts confidently, juggling three balls and performing some standard tricks while making faces at the crowd. I've seen this sort of thing often enough in Turai, but she quickly ups the tempo, adding fourth and fifth balls, still juggling easily while hopping back and forward along the branch. The crowd cheers and shouts encouragement. Obviously Shuthan-ir-Hemas is a popular favourite.

Unfortunately things go badly wrong when she tries to add a sixth ball to the routine. She fails to catch it, the sequence goes wrong, and the balls tumble from her hands. In an effort to retrieve the situation Shuthan trips clumsily over her feet and plunges to the ground, landing heavily on the heads of the onlookers. There are groans of disappointment from the audience.

'She's not at her best,' they say with disappointment.

'Just hasn't got the same skill she used to have.'

Others mutter that this is going to be a bad festival for Avula. Their play is being directed by an incompetent Sorcerer, their choir is nowhere near the standard of that of the Venians, and now even their top juggler is about to let them down.

'If Firees-ar-Key doesn't win the junior tournament we'll be the laughing stock of the Ossuni Islands,' mutters one disconsolate Elf to his companion.

I walk on. I feel sorry for the Avulans, but that's one juggler I won't be placing a bet on.

It's late in the afternoon. The weather is mild and a light breeze blows small ripples over the pools of water at the Hesuni Tree. The clearing is busier than usual, with Elves from other islands paying their respects to the Tree. They ignore me as I stroll over the grass. I'm not the only Human in view. Over by the smaller of the pools some Elves are pointing out features of the local scenery to a delegation of visitors from Mattesh.

I've been suspicious of the large pool ever since Makri found herself so powerfully affected by drinking the water. I'm here to work a spell. I know the Elves won't like it. I considered coming here in the early hours of the morning when it might be quieter, but I suspect that Kalith will have set his attendants to watch over it and I'd be easily spotted. Here in the crowd I'm hoping I might just work some sorcery unnoticed.

I sit down next to the pool. I casually dip my finger into the water then sprinkle a few drops on to a small scrap of parchment. I look round. No one is paying any attention to me. Just another large detective taking a rest from his exertions.

I drift slowly into a state of concentration. I utter the arcane words of the Spell of Not Belonging. I've used this spell in the past and found it simple and effective, though it's possible that the mystic field projected by the Hesuni Tree will render it useless. I watch the pool, and wait. After a minute or so I notice something bobbing to the surface, quite close to me. I get up, stretch and saunter round the edge, a man without a care in the world. Floating on the surface is a small package. I reach down to adjust my boot, quickly scoop up the package, then walk on.

I'm well pleased with myself. I might not be much of a Sorcerer, but it takes a cool head to successfully work a spell like that in public without a soul noticing anything.

'Easy as bribing a Senator,' I mutter, strolling over the grass.

I duck behind a tree and take out the package. I unwrap the waterproof oilskin. Inside is some white powder. I dip my finger in, taking a tiny pinch to my lips to taste it.

It's dwa. The most powerfully addictive drug on the market. The scourge of the Human Lands, and now available at the most exclusive locations in Elfland. I'm just congratulating myself on finally making some progress when a hand falls heavily on my shoulder.

'I arrest you in the name of Lord Kalith-ar-Yil.'

I'm surrounded by nine Elves in Kalith's regalia, swords at the ready.

'Try to say a spell and we'll run you through before you utter a word.'

Their leader snatches the packet from me.

'Do you have an explanation for this?' he demands.

I do, but I'm not going to waste it on him. They're going to take me to Kalith-ar-Yil anyway, so I might as well save my breath till I get there. I'm led through the clearing and up the long ladders to the Tree Palace, where they put me in a small cell with one chair and a nice view of the tree tops through the barred window.

'There are guards outside the window with bows. If you try to escape they have instructions to shoot. We do not take kindly to peddlers of drugs on Avula.'

I'm left alone. I sit on the chair. Somehow none of this has come as a surprise. I've been thrown in jail so many times in Turai and elsewhere in the west that it was probably only a matter of time before I ended up in an Elvish prison.

CHAPTER
FOURTEEN

The prison cell is clean and airy. There's a pitcher of water on the table and shortly after I arrive a guard brings me a loaf of bread. The sun streams in through the window and from somewhere in the forest below I can hear a choir practising. In terms of comfort it doesn't compare too badly with my rooms in the Avenging Axe.

The first person to visit me is Ambassador Turius. I have not yet encountered our Ambassador to Avula, so I greet him warmly and thank him for arriving so swiftly.

'It's reassuring to know that our Ambassadors are resolute in their task of protecting Turanian citizens unjustly incarcerated in foreign lands. Once you get me out of here, I shall speak very highly of you to Deputy Consul Cicerius.'

'I haven't come to get you out,' says the Ambassador.

'You haven't?'

'No. As far as I'm concerned you can stay here for the rest of your life. Everyone advised to you keep out of Elvish affairs. You refused to listen to this advice. Now you're in a cell, which is exactly what was to be expected.'

'Aren't you bothered about whether I actually committed a crime?'

The ambassador shrugs. 'If you did, Lord Kalith-ar-Yil will punish you. If you didn't, he'll let you go in due course. He's a fair-minded Elf.'

'Then why the hell did you bother coming to see me?'

'A Turanian Ambassador always does his duty. I see you have food and water. Excellent. Your needs are being well catered for. Now goodbye.'

Turius departs. I swear he enjoyed that conversation. I sit down and listen to the choir, and wonder who Turius bribed to get his cushy job as Ambassador to Avula.

My next visitor is an Elf of advanced years who informs me that his name is Rekis-ar-Lin and he is a member of the Council of Elders. He's accompanied by a scribe who takes down our conversation.

'I have been given responsibility for investigating this matter. Why were you found with a package of dwa?'

'I took it out of the pool.'

'How did it get there?'

I tell him I've no idea.

'And how did you come to find it?'

'I looked.'

'Why?'

'Investigator's intuition.'

Councillor Rekis is dubious, but I don't want to tell him that I used a spell to locate the dwa because I know that will only lead to more trouble. However the Councillor has difficulty believing that, with all the Elves in the area, it just happened to be me who found a packet of dwa in the pool.

'It seems to us more likely that you brought the dwa with you from Turai.'

'Why would I do that? Everyone knows Elves don't go for dwa. Doesn't work on them.'

'You would no doubt be aware that there would be many

Humans on the island at the time of the festival. Perhaps
you wished to sell it to them. Perhaps you yourself are so
addicted that you were unable to travel without it. Either
way, you are not telling me everything you know. You
will provide me with a precise description of your actions
since landing on Avula.'

I clam up. Any time I'm in a cell, I just get wary about
giving precise descriptions of my actions. We're interrupted by the arrival of Jir-ar-Eth, Kalith's Chief Sorcerer.
He stares at me for a few seconds.

'He used a spell,' he says. 'But I can't tell which one.'

Councillor Rekis stares at me coldly.

'You used a spell in the vicinity of the Hesuni Tree? On
Avula, that is calanith. It is also a crime. What was it?'

'A love spell. I'm looking for romance.'

Jir-ar-Eth speaks a few words and there is a slight cool-
ing of the air in the cell.

'I've dampened the area,' he says to Rekis. 'The prisoner
will not be able to use sorcery to escape. He has very little
power anyway.'

The Sorcerer stares at the necklace I'm wearing.

'A spell protection charm? With Red Elvish Cloth? Where
did you get that?'

'Just picked it up along the way.'

They leave me alone. I eat bread. I'm feeling hard done
by. For the rest of the day my only other visitor is the guard
who brings me some food. I demand to see Lord Kalith.
The guard, rather politely, informs me that Lord Kalith is
busy.

Night falls. I've been in so many cells it doesn't particularly bother me, but I'm annoyed at the waste of my
time. Shouldn't someone have been here to help? Deputy

Consul Cicerius for instance. Or Makri. She ought to at least have visited me. Maybe she's still tormenting the unfortunate Elf child. I go to sleep madder than a mad dragon and I wake slightly madder.

It's approaching lunchtime and it's getting to the stage where I'm seriously considering slugging the next person who comes into my cell and risking a jail break when Lord Kalith finally gets round to paying me a visit.

'Dwa is a filthy drug,' he says, getting right down to business. 'It is a curse on the Human Lands. It has never been seen on Avula before.'

'Only because you didn't bother to look. And don't lecture me about using a spell in the vicinity of the Hesuni Tree. If I hadn't done that you'd never have known about the dwa.'

'You still claim that you did not bring the substance with you?'

'Of course I didn't. Do you seriously believe I did?'

'Why would I not?' says the Elf Lord. 'You have hardly shown yourself to be a man of sober habits. You brought a barrel of beer on to my ship and when you finished that you resorted to theft to meet your craving. You may have thought you were unobserved when you removed three large wineskins from Osath's kitchen, but I assure you that you were not. Since arriving on Avula you have mounted an almost continual search for beer, culminating in what I am reliably informed were scenes of unheard-of excess at the haunt of the armourers. And this only the day after you and your female companion ingested so much thazis as to be unable to remember your own identities. The story of you talking to the butterflies has been widely reported all over Avula.'

'I was not talking to the butterflies,' I reply, with some dignity. 'And is there any point to all this?'

'The point is that you are a corrupting influence. Thazis is not illegal on Avula, but we discourage its use. Now one of my most respected councillors informs me that not only did he find three thazis sticks in his daughter's room, but she has informed him that she wishes to travel to Turai to write poetry. His wife is now terrified that their daughter will return home with a pierced nose and an Orcish love-child.'

We seem to be straying from the point here. I tell Lord Kalith-ar-Yil that he can criticise me as much as he likes, but he can't deny that I've dug up evidence of some strange goings-on on his island.

'And what exactly are these goings-on?'

'I need to investigate more.'

'Nothing you find will change the fact that Elith-ir-Methet was seen stabbing Gulas-ar-Thetos. You yourself have talked to a witness.'

'I still need to investigate more.'

Lord Kalith is not minded to let me out. There are three days left till the start of the festival and I'm running out of time.

'You cannot execute Vas-ar-Methet's daughter without the fullest investigation,' I insist.

'Her punishment has not been decided.'

'But her guilt has. You must allow me to continue with my investigation.'

Kalith is offended by my tone and tells me sharply that his patience with me is wearing thin.

'Fine,' I say. 'Though I must admit to being very surprised at an Elf Lord being such a poor sport. In Turai, the aristocracy does not stoop to such low tactics when faced with defeat.'

Kalith's head jerks in surprise.

'What do you mean by that?'

'Well, it's pretty clear that this is all down to me beating you heavily at the niarit board. Ever since then it's been nothing but trouble all the way for me. You've hindered my investigation at every turn simply because you can't stand losing to a Human.'

I move towards the window, raising my voice so the guards outside can hear.

'I guess it was just too embarrassing for the niarit champion of the Ossuni Elves to have his conqueror walking around the island, telling everyone about the bad variation of the Harper's Game he'd played. The armourers warned me you'd probably throw me in jail rather than risk facing me over the board again . . .'

From outside my cell comes something that sounds very like muffled laughter. Lord Kalith, an Elf who proved his bravery and honour time and again against the Orcs, can't take any more of this. And so it is that minutes later I find myself sitting at the table facing an angry Kalith-ar-Yil over a niarit board, hastily brought by a guard in response to his Lord's furious instructions.

'Don't bother locking the cell,' I call after the jailer. 'I'll be walking out of here soon enough. So, Lord Kalith, are we—'

'Enough talking,' says Kalith. 'Play.'

I start moving my Hoplites forward. Kalith counters warily. But I notice he's getting his Elephants ready, and his Heavy Cavalry.

The sun shines cheerfully into the cell. Parrots squawk

merrily in the trees. Outside it's another bright day in
Avula. Inside, things are not so good, at least for Lord
Kalith. Not too long after the start of the game his forces
lie in ruins, mere dust under the wheels of the un-
stoppable Thraxas war chariot. Kalith, after his tentative
opening, was unable to resist a wild assault on my forces
using his heaviest troops, an assault that I withstood
for just long enough to bring his army exactly where I
wanted it before falling back with my centre, outflanking
him on both sides and carrying out what could only
be described as a massacre. His Hero, Plague Carrier,
Harper, Wizard and Healer lie dead beneath a sad tangle
of dead Elephants and decimated Trolls.

Kalith looks grimly at the miserable remains and concedes defeat. I am now free to go, as per our pre-game
agreement.

'Any chance of some food?' I ask, as I sling my cloak
over my shoulders.

'You may visit the kitchens,' replies Lord Kalith,
summoning up the last reserves of his good breeding.
'The guards will show you the way.'

'Thank you. I take it that I will be allowed to speak
with my client again?'

Lord Kalith allows that I can, which is a relief. I wasn't
looking forward to trying to break back into prison.

In the short walk between the cell and the main Palace
building, I pass two stern-looking Elves marching another
prisoner into the lockup. I recognise the captive, though
I don't know his name. It's the young Elf whom the poet
Droo was arguing with in the clearing at the three oaks and
river. His eyes are blank and he isn't walking very steadily.
The guards help him along, shepherding him into a cell.

I'm shown to the kitchens. There I find Osath the cook, whom I haven't seen since I disembarked. He's delighted to see me. He knows how much I appreciate his cooking.

'Thraxas! They let you out? The word in the kitchens was that Lord Kalith was going to throw away the key. What happened? Did your Ambassador stand bail?'

'The Turanian Ambassador is about as much use as a one-legged gladiator. No, I was forced back on my own resources. I beat Kalith at niarit again.'

Osath laughs heartily at this, as do his assistants. Again the Elves are amused at Kalith losing. Which just goes to show that even a well-loved and respected Elf Lord shouldn't go around bragging about his prowess at the niarit board. It annoys everyone.

Osath begins to pile up food in front of me and I start shovelling it in.

'I have to ask you a few questions, Osath.'

The chef looks doubtful. 'We can't tell you anything about Elith, Thraxas. It would be awkward for us to discuss it . . .'

'I wasn't talking about Elith. Are you and your fellow low-lives in the kitchens planning to bet on the juggling competition?'

This brings Osath and his helpers clustering round keenly.

'We are. I was going to bet on young Shuthan-ir-Hemas,' replies Osath. 'I've seen her put up some sensational performances. But I hear she's gone off the boil.'

'She has. Yesterday I saw her trip over her own feet. Didn't look like a woman who was about to win. I did see a young woman called Usath, from Ven, juggling seven balls and looking good for a few more. You know anything about her past form?'

'Junior champion at the competition two years ago in Corinthal,' says a young cook. 'She's still inexperienced, but she might do well. I think she might be worth a gamble, but there's another juggler from Corinthal called Arith-ar-Tho who's built up a fine reputation recently. Be best to check him out if you get the chance.'

I thank them for their help.

'What's this we hear about Makri teaching Isuas how to fight?'

'I thought that was meant to be a secret.'

'There are no secrets in a Palace kitchen,' says Osath. 'Lady Yestar might not have told Lord Kalith about it, but we're the ones that have to make up food for them every day. Is there any chance of Makri teaching the kid well enough to enter the tournament? Would it be worth a bet? Isuas is so weak we'd get a good price on her winning even one fight against the most hopeless opponent. In fact, you'd get a good price on the kid even staying on her feet for thirty seconds.'

I consider this, while mopping up some fragments of venison pie with a hunk of bread.

'I think Isuas will give up before the tournament. Makri's treating her pretty rough. But if things change, I'll let you know. Make sure you don't let on to anyone that Makri's teaching her though, or the price will drop.'

Having cemented my good relations with the lower Elvish order by some solid gambling talk, I emerge from the Palace well fed and in good shape for investigating, which is just as well as I've lost time I couldn't afford and have a great deal to do.

I find Lasas-ar-Thetos in a small hut in a tree near to the Hesuni. Around his head he has a yellow band denoting his new rank as Chief Tree Priest. He's heard about recent events and displays a deep sadness.

'To think that such a substance could be polluting the sacred water of the Hesuni Tree. It brings shame to the whole island. I cringe at the thought of what my dear brother would have made of it. '

At least Avula's new Tree Priest doesn't blame me.

'When Lord Kalith informed me of the matter I told him that you were not a man who would bring dwa to our island. Indeed, we should be grateful to you for uncovering it. Do you know where it came from?'

I admit that I don't, but I'm still working on it. It's something of a relief to find an aristocratic Elf who doesn't seem to hold me responsible for everything that's been going on around here. Now that Lasas has got over the immediate shock of his brother's death, he's proving to be a calm and responsible Elf. I ask him again if there's anything he might have forgotten to tell me.

'No strange goings-on? No hint of who might have been in the vicinity with dwa?'

'Nothing, I am afraid. I have been keeping my ear to the ground, but really since my brother was killed I have been too busy with preparations for the funeral and with taking up the reins of the Priesthood.'

At least we seem to have got to the root of the bad dreams the Avulans have been suffering from. Lasas is firmly of the opinion that a powerful alien drug, contained in the water that feeds the Hesuni Tree, would be more than enough to give the Elves nightmares.

'All Avulans communicate with the Tree. As it was

ingesting poison, so it produced nightmares. We must be grateful to you for finding it. I am now attempting to cleanse the area by means of ritual.'

Tramping back across the clearing, I'm frustrated. Everyone knows that something strange has been going on but no one quite knows what. And no one can suggest a motive for Elith killing Gulas. Even Elith, who admits to doing it, can't think of a motive. Before I leave I ask Lasas if he has encountered Gorith-ar-Del yet.

'Should I have?'

'Probably not. It's just I keep noticing him hanging round the area. Would you let me know if he contacts you in any way?'

Lasas says that he will, and I depart. I find Harmon Half-Elf and Lanius Suncatcher in the enclave of houses next to the Turanian Ambassador's residence. I know that Harmon Half-Elf has seen the prisoner and I want his opinion on whether she has been attacked or bemused by sorcery.

'I did not get that impression,' he tells me. 'Although with the Hesuni Tree in the vicinity, it is impossible to be certain. However, I think that if she had had her memory wiped or been victim of some spell that over-powered her will, forcing her to kill the priest, there would be some trace of it remaining. I know that Jir-ar-Eth has searched very thoroughly for any sign of this and has been unable to locate anything.'

'And congratulations on getting out of jail,' adds Lanius Suncatcher.

The two Sorcerers are not entirely unsympathetic to my cause.

'If only because you are refusing to give up. Despite

the fact that everyone knows Elith is guilty, I think the Avulans are starting to respect you for the way you keep on trying to help Vas-ar-Methet. They value friendship. But really, Thraxas, what can you hope to achieve now? Elith-ir-Methet is guilty. People saw her kill Gulas. She admits it.'

They offer me some wine. I drain the goblet and rise to my feet.

'If I find some reasonable motive, she might not be executed.'

Stuck for inspiration, I seek out Makri. My horse is in the paddock where I left it, so I saddle up and ride round the island. Every clearing is now filled with choirs, actors, jugglers, all practising for the festival. As the path narrows between the encroaching trees I keep a keen eye out for masked Elves with spears who might be about to attack me, but none appear. So far I have not managed to gather the slightest clue as to who they are or who they might be working for. As far as I know, the Elves have nothing that is equivalent to the Assassins in Turai, but someone is certainly out to get me. Someone with powerful sorcerous backing. Once more I'm grateful for my excellent spell protection charm. It will protect me from most magical attacks, though not from invisible Elves suddenly appearing and gutting me with their spears.

I dismount near the private clearing and again advance cautiously. I'm wondering if Isuas has given up. Before long I hear Makri's voice raised in anger.

'Fight, you cusux! If you trip over your feet one more time I swear I'll kill you. You want to see my Orcish blade? I'll let you see it, you useless brat, I'll pin you to that tree with it.'

This is followed by the sound of a wooden sword cracking over a young Elf's head, and some wailing.

I peer into the clearing. Isuas has shown some spirit in returning for more lessons, but Makri doesn't seem to appreciate it. The young Elf is struggling to her feet under a rain of blows, while Makri continues to scream abuse at her.

'Didn't I show you how to parry? Well, parry this!'

Makri hits Isuas with a stroke that must come close to breaking her shoulder. Isuas yells in pain. This annoys Makri even more.

'I didn't say cry like a girl, I said parry. Now do it.'

Makri slashes at the young Elf. Isuas makes a reasonable attempt at deflecting the blow, but Makri simply uses her other blade to whack Isuas on the side of the head, sending her once more thumping to the ground.

I'm fairly aghast at this. The sight of Makri using her full fighting skills against the weak little Elf would distress the hardest of hearts. Isuas lies on the ground sobbing, where she is in receipt of a further torrent of abuse.

'You useless exin miserable zutha pathetic cusux,' screams Makri, using a string of vile Orcish epithets, some of them unintelligible to me and some quite possibly never heard in the western world before.

Makri drops her swords and yanks Isuas to her feet.

'Are all Elves as pitiful as you? God help you if the Orcs ever sail down to Avula. Pah! You're so pathetic I don't even need a weapon.'

Isuas suddenly looks angry. The insults are getting to her. She leaps to attack Makri, showing a surprising turn of speed. Makri stands her ground, merely twisting her body to avoid the blades before stepping lightly to one side.

Isuas tries to turn and face her, but Makri, displaying new heights of savagery, actually kicks her in the head. Isuas crumples, which doesn't prevent Makri from getting in another two kicks before she hits the ground. This time the young Elf lies still. I hurry forward, alarmed.

'Goddammit, Makri, you've killed her.'

Makri looks round, unconcerned.

'No I haven't. She's just dazed. What are you doing here?'

'I came to talk to you. If you can spare a moment in between tormenting that unfortunate youth.'

'Unfortunate?' says Makri, puzzled. 'She's being taught to fight by the undefeated champion gladiator of all the Orc Lands. I'd call that a privilege.'

Isuas groans. Makri, who possess surprising strength despite her slender frame, hoists her into the air and tosses her in the direction of a water bottle under a tree.

'Take a drink,' she says. 'And stop crying.'

'Is it really necessary to be this brutal?'

Makri shrugs. 'I'm trying to teach her a lot in a hurry. Anyway, we're using wooden swords. How brutal can you be with a wooden sword?'

'Pretty brutal, from what I saw. When Lady Yestar gave her permission for this I doubt very much if she quite foresaw that you would be kicking her daughter in the head. Shouldn't you be doing something about the bleeding?'

'The island is full of healers. They'll sort her out later. What are you here for?'

'To talk. I'm still baffled by this case and I'm running out of time. I figured I might get some inspiration if we talked it out.'

'I can't spare the time right now. I'll be back at Camith's after dark – can it wait till then?'

I suppose it can.

'Try not to kill Isuas.'

'Death in training isn't so bad,' states Makri, firmly. 'Better than disgracing yourself in the arena. Which,' she adds, turning menacingly back to the young Elf, 'no pupil of mine is going to do. So get up and fight.'

I leave them to it.

I call back to Makri from the edge of the clearing.

'What does zutha mean?'

Makri gives me a translation. I wince. It's even worse than cusux.

CHAPTER
FIFTEEN

I return to Camith's peaceful home, where I wash, eat and stare out of the window. I'm in need of some inspiration. None is forthcoming. Somewhere outside, an Elvish choir is singing, a long slow tribute to one of Lord Kalith's ancestors. It's meant to be soothing, but I'm too pressurised to appreciate it.

It's late into the night when Makri returns. She brings a tray of food into my room and tells me with a disgruntled air that she again encountered masked Elves with spears.

'On that quiet bit of walkway where you never see anyone. I turned the corner and there they were, marching towards me, spears at the ready.'

Makri, unwilling to flee again, had drawn her swords and made ready to repel her attackers.

'But then they disappeared. Just vanished into the air.'

I nod. A similar experience to mine.

'So what's going on with them?' demands Makri. 'Do they want to attack us or not? I wish they'd just get on with it. I can't be doing with all this appearing and disappearing. It's no way to fight.'

'Speaking of fighting, how is Isuas?'

'Bruised and bloody,' replies Makri. 'I told her to visit Vas-ar-Methet for some healing before she saw her father. Lady Yestar is still keeping it all a secret.'

I again express my doubts about the ferocity of Makri's training and Makri is again unrepentant. With so little time to prepare she is of the opinion that there is no alternative.

'And that's not the only reason. I'm strengthening her spirit. If she ever gets in a fight for real, she'll be glad I showed her the Gaxeen.'

'Gaxeen? What's that?'

Makri puts down her tray, her meal unfinished. She is rarely an enthusiastic eater.

'Orcish. The Way of the Gaxeen. It translates as something like the "Spirit of the Insane Warrior". It's what you do when you find yourself faced with insurmountable odds. Or up against an opponent whom you can't beat with skill or craft. You go Gaxeen, as we used to say. A fury in which you do not fear for your life.'

I'm interested. Much of Makri's experience of Orcish ways is unknown to us in the west. A few months ago she helped me solve a case with her knowledge of Orcish religion and prior to that I didn't even know they had a religion.

'How long does it take to learn the Way of the Gaxeen?'

'Depends on the person, or the Orc. When I first started fighting I picked up skill with weapons easily enough, but one day my trainer said I hadn't enough spirit so he'd decided to execute me. He took away my swords and told the four gladiators standing nearby that whoever killed me would get a reward. And after I'd scaled the wall of the pit, slain a guard with my bare hands to get his sword, then massacred the four gladiators in a blind fury, my trainer clapped me on the back and said, "Well done, you have learned the Way of the

Gaxeen." I rather liked that old trainer. I had to kill him later, of course, when I made my escape.'

'Well, Makri, this is a fabulous gift for Isuas. When she starts slaughtering her playmates I imagine Lord Kalith will be beside himself with joy. How is she doing? If she can win one fight I might be up for some good winnings, which of course I'll share with you.'

Makri shakes her head.

'Don't bet on her. She's still hopeless. If her first opponent has two legs and two arms she won't last thirty seconds.'

'What if he's only got one arm and one leg?'

'She still won't win.'

Not wishing to let good food go to waste, I pick up Makri's tray and finish off what's left.

'I'm stuck in my investigation. I've managed to uncover some strange things but none of it is helping to clear Elith. You've heard about the dwa in the pool? That's what was polluting the water and giving the Elves bad dreams. And I'm sure that's what made you so stoned when we visited the Tree Palace. Someone has discovered that dwa mixed with the sacred water makes for a powerful drug that affects Elves. No doubt that's why all these young Elves have been acting so strangely, going around with glazed eyes, not working, breaking their word and so on. And though Kalith will never acknowledge it, I'm certain that the Elf who fell from the rigging did so while under the influence. Took his supply with him on the voyage.'

Makri nods. 'Makes sense. I can see why they'd all go for it. I felt great after I drank the water. Do you have any more?'

I frown. 'That's not quite the reaction I was looking for, Makri. You're supposed to be outraged that the foul substance dwa is now polluting the world of the Elves.'

'Oh well, that too. Yes, it's a shock. The Avulans will have to take swift action to prevent it spreading. Maybe we should hunt around, see if anyone else has some of the mixture and confiscate it?'

I glare at Makri. Back in Turai I have more than once suspected that she has been experimenting with dwa and I strongly disapprove.

'Never mind confiscating drugs. We already have a reputation as people of immoderate habits. Lord Kalith was fairly cutting on the subject, and that was before I beat him at niarit again. Now he's as miserable as a Niojan whore and will be down on us like a bad spell if he catches us doing anything disreputable.

'If Elith-ir-Methet would just tell me exactly what was going on between her and Gulas, I might be able to get to the bottom of the affair. I should look into who is bring-ing the dwa into Avula, but with so few contacts it could take me a long time to find out, and I'm short of time. I'll suggest to Jir-ar-Eth that he does some sorcerous scanning of the harbours. He might be able to pick up something. And I'd like to have someone examine Gorith-ar-Del's movements over the past few months. There's an Elf who's a strong suspect. He gave up his job and now he keeps hanging round the Hesuni Tree acting suspiciously.'

'Do you think whoever is dealing dwa is responsible for attacking us?' says Makri.

'Yes. Back in Turai it's the first thing I'd have suspected, but I just never expected it here.'

Makri wonders if Elith-ir-Methet is clamming up just

to avoid the disgrace of having a calanith relationship with a Tree Priest.

'Surely her being executed is more of a disgrace for the rest of the family?'

'Who knows? Taboos are funny things when you're outside them. I can't work out what they'd find most important. Every other Elf who's involved is running for cover. There's no chance of any co-operation there.'

Inspiration suddenly strikes.

'I know someone I might be able to put a little pressure on – Droo's boyfriend. Name of Lithias, I think. A poetic young Elf, last seen being tossed into a cell at the Tree Palace. From the way he was swaying around I'd say he was one rebellious youth who'd been dabbling with foreign substances. Perhaps Droo would persuade him to come clean about everything and that might give me some sort of lever over Elith.'

'Will Droo help you?'

'She might. She seemed to like me. Anyway, I'll tell her it's the best thing she can do for her boyfriend. That usually works, even when it isn't true.'

And so it proves the next day when we locate Droo at a treehouse not far from Camith's. She's not actually in the house; she's perched at the end of a slender branch high above the ground. Lithias's incarceration has plunged her into gloom and she has not moved from the spot for twenty-four hours. Her parents are so worried that they are actually glad to see Makri and me climbing up their dwelling place, although, as with most of the Avulans, they cannot prevent themselves from examining us with interest and some suspicion. Particularly Makri. Everyone still gapes at her, though less impolitely than when we first arrived. The mother is in tears, the father is raging, and they're cursing the fate that made their daughter fall in love with such a hopeless specimen as Lithias.

'Why couldn't she have fallen for a warrior?' wails her mother. 'Or the silversmith's son?'

'You aren't planning to jump, are you?' I call, from the safety of the treehouse.

'Maybe,' replies Droo.

'It's not that bad. Lithias hasn't done anything serious, Lord Kalith will let him go in a day or two. We're going there now. Come with us and we can sort things out.'

Droo looks up.

'You're really going to see him?'

'Yes. We have free access into the Palace, courtesy of Lady Yestar.'

Droo rises and hops nimbly along the branch. She ignores the admonitions from her parents and rushes inside the house, saying that she has to brush her hair before seeing Lithias.

'Lithias is a fool,' says her father. He turns to Makri. 'And your nose ring is disgusting.'

'Well, we'd better get going,' I say.

The Elf gives me a stern look. 'You are the Investigator? You look like you would have difficulty finding a large tree in a small field.'

This is one rude Elf. I start to understand why young Droo might not be that happy at home.

'I'd have let her stay on the branch,' he mutters as a parting shot, then departs into the house.

Droo reappears. Her short yellow hair is sticking up from her head. It's an odd style for an Elf.

'You know why Lithias was arrested? He tried to start

a fight with the blacksmith over a poem. How ridiculous. He's been like that for weeks. Just one irrational action after another.'

Droo studies Makri as we take the walkway towards the Tree Palace.

'Are your toenails really golden?'

'Of course not. I've painted them.'

Droo, unfamiliar with the concept of painted toenails, is impressed. 'Did it hurt getting your nose pierced?'

'Not really. But it was sore when the Orcs ripped it out during a fight.'

'I wanted to get my ears pierced, but my father wouldn't let me. It's calanith for Elves to pierce their bodies.'

I hasten to change the subject. Makri has an unfortunate habit of wondering out loud about getting rings put through her nipples and I never like to hear this sort of thing.

'How long has Lithias been acting strangely?'

'Months. Of course, he never did act entirely normally. That's why I like him. But recently he's just been out of control.'

'You know he's been taking dwa?'

Droo's face falls. 'I told him it was stupid.'

I ask the young poet if she knows whom he buys it from, but she says that she doesn't. Nor does she know who has been bringing it to the island.

'I stayed well away from the whole thing.'

I'm not sure if she's telling the truth, but I let it pass. Halfway to the Palace we come across an Elf I recognise. It's Shuthan-ir-Hemas, Avula's favourite juggler. She's lying on the wooden pathway, sleeping. Her juggling kit is strewn around her in disarray.

'Oh dear,' says Droo, who obviously recognises the symptoms. So do I. You can't walk around Twelve Seas without stumbling over addicts lying unconscious on every street corner, but I never thought I'd see it spreading like this among the young Elves.

We have some difficulty getting in to see Lithias and are denied access till Makri sends a message to Lady Yestar requesting permission as a favour to me. She smiles smugly.

'You'd be lost without me, Thraxas.'

'I can't think how I ever managed. Okay, let's question the errant poet.'

Lithias's cell is as clean and airy as was mine, but Lithias, unused to incarceration, is slumped in despair by the wall. When he sees Droo he leaps to his feet with a cry of joy and they embrace. I let it go on for a few seconds before getting down to business. I ask Droo to leave us alone. She departs unwillingly, promising Lithias that she'll wait for him.

'Lithias, I have some questions for you. Answer them, let me sort things out, and nothing much will happen to you. If you refuse to answer, Lord Kalith will be down on you like a bad spell. It's going to dawn on him soon how large a problem he has with dwa and I get the feeling he might just exile everyone who's touched it.'

Lithias hangs his head.

'I can't tell you anything,' he says.

'You have to. Otherwise you'll be banished from Avula and Droo's mother will marry her off to the silversmith's son.'

This gets to him. 'The silversmith's son? Has he been hanging around Droo again?'

'Like bees round honey. And if you ever want to get

out of this cell, you better talk to me. I want to know every-thing about the dwa in the sacred pool and I want to know everything you can tell me about Elith-ir-Methet, Gulas-ar-Thetos and his brother. Start at the beginning and don't stop unless I tell you to.'

Lithias begins to talk; what he has to say is very interest-ing indeed, and long overdue. It turns out that young Lithias has been filling himself up with happy juice for the past three months, since a friend of his, another young poet, told him that if he wanted to have an experi-ence that was worth writing a poem about he could show him how.

Lithias never wrote any poems. The drug made him too crazy to concentrate on poetry. 'It felt good at first. After a while I didn't like it so much, but I couldn't stop.'

He claims that only ten or so Elves were regular imbibers of the mixture of dwa and Hesuni water, but even so I'm surprised that such a thing could go on un-noticed right in the middle of the island. Lithias claims that they didn't actually have to go to the Hesuni Tree as the supplier would bring the mixture out to a clearing in the forest where he'd sell it to the Elves. Fairly cheaply, it seems, which would be standard behaviour at first. They'd soon find the price was on the way up.

'Who brought it to the island?'

Lithias doesn't know. He's frustratingly vague about the details and claims not even to know the identity of the Elf he bought it off.

'Would you recognise him again?'

Lithias shakes his head. 'He wore a cowl and stood in the shadows. I never saw his face. Everything was very secret.'

'It might have started off as a secret, but these things never stay that way. Earlier today I stepped over the unconscious figure of Avula's best-loved juggler and she wasn't making any attempt to hide what she'd been doing. How did Elith get involved? Was it through Gulas?'

Lithias doesn't know. He thinks that Elith was already taking dwa when he started.

'She was always hanging around the Hesuni Tree because she had a passion for Gulas. They were lovers before his father's death made him the Priest. He didn't want to be Priest, but he didn't have a choice. So they weren't meant to see each other any more, but I don't think they ever stopped. I used to hear some gossip about it. Lasas was never happy about it.'

'Lasas? His brother? Why not?'

'Because he was in love with Elith as well. It drove him crazy that she was in love with his brother. Didn't you know that?'

CHAPTER
SIXTEEN

Makri is waiting for me outside the cell.
'Learn anything?'

'Yes,' I reply. 'But nothing I like.'

Lady Yestar appears as we approach the rear entrance to the Palace. She dismisses her attendants and greets us in her amicable well-bred manner and asks me if I still have hopes of clearing Elith, to which I reply that I do. She looks at me in her farseeing manner.

'You do not,' she says.

'Well, I'm still going to try.'

Yestar turns to Makri. 'How is my daughter progressing?'

'Quite well.'

'I notice that she has been very tired when she returns home at night.'

'We've been practising hard.'

'I also notice that her clothes are torn, her eyes are red and she has been in need of the services of a healer.'

Makri shifts a little uncomfortably. 'We've been practising hard,' she repeats.

Lady Yestar nods. 'Please remember that Isuas is delicate. I do not really expect that she could ever win a fight. We will be grateful if you simply manage to strengthen her up a little.'

'Absolutely,' says Makri. 'That's precisely what I'm aiming for.'

Isuas trots out of the Palace. While not exactly the eager young Elf of a few days ago, she shows no sign of giving up and greets Makri brightly enough, and they depart.

'You might be pleased to learn,' Yestar tells me before I go, 'that both Deputy Consul Cicerius and Prince Dees-Akan expressed some satisfaction that you and Makri were in my favour. Of course, I have not explained exactly what Makri is doing for me.'

'I am pleased. It might get them off my back.'

Lady Yestar smiles as she digests this unfamiliar phrase. 'From their previous conversation, I'd say there had been every danger of them "getting on your back" in a, eh . . .'

'In a big way?'

'Exactly. I understand that there are many people you must stay on the right side of in Turai. Life would be difficult with both the Prince and the Deputy Consul against you, I imagine?'

'Very difficult, Lady Yestar. The Prince doesn't take to me at all. Fair enough, I don't take to him. I don't want to get on the wrong side of Cicerius though. He's been helpful to me in the past, if only because I've been helpful to him. I couldn't say I like him all that much, but for an important politician he's honest, and there's no denying he's as sharp as—'

I pause.

'Sharp as an Elf's ear?' says Yestar, filling in the blanks. She laughs. 'I have always enjoyed that Human expression.'

I reluctantly decline an offer of food and head back to the cells to interview Elith. One thing I dislike about life as an Investigator: there are times when you have to skimp on the foodstuffs.

My session with Elith-ir-Methet is short and depressing. She has accepted her fate. I tell her that this won't get her out of jail.

'I have no wish to be released.'

'Your father wants it, and I'm working for him. So let's get down to business. I know what's been going on. I talked to Lithias, an Elf you are no doubt familiar with from your days of intoxication. Don't protest, I know all about it. Is that why you've clammed up about everything? Because you didn't want your proud father to know you were one of the first Avulans to enjoy the effects of dwa? Congratulations on finding a way to get it to affect Elfkind by the way. Very ingenious. Whose idea was it to mix it with the Hesuni water?'

Elith has risen from her chair and now stands gazing out of the window.

'I can see you've a lot to feel bad about. That's a strong habit you've developed in a short space of time. I wondered why you broke your word to Lord Kalith about not leaving the Tree Palace. You just couldn't wait to get your next hit.'

Elith turns to face me, some anger in her eyes. 'That's not true. I needed to see Gulas. I needed to know if it was true that he had accused me of damaging the Hesuni Tree.'

'And once you found out that he had, you killed him?'

'Yes.'

'Why don't you tell me the full story? You can't prevent disgrace from touching your family, or that of Gulas.'

'Gulas had no part in the affair.'

'Affair being the correct word. Why didn't you tell me before that you were having a relationship with him?'

'Because it is calanith for the Tree Priest to marry anyone outside of his family. There would have been disgrace.'

'You think this doesn't count as a disgrace?'

'I would not expect you to understand,' says Elith witheringly.

'I won't give up on this, Elith. You see how far I've already got. I'm going to find out the whole truth and tell it to your father. I owe him that.'

Elith shrugs, the slightest movement of her shoulders signifying that she is beyond caring.

'I am tired of this, Investigator. You can do nothing to help me and I would far rather be left to my thoughts. If I tell you my story, will you leave me alone?'

'Yes.'

'Very well. I got involved in taking dwa through my cousin Eos. I was unhappy at the time, because Gulas had just been made Tree Priest and our relationship had to end. Gulas would have strongly disapproved had he known. At first it made me feel better, but later it sent me into madness. One day when I went for my supply I collapsed beside the Tree and when I woke it had been damaged. I could remember nothing about it, but by this time many Elves knew that I had been acting strangely. I was put in prison while the matter was investigated. And there I learned that the main witness against me was Gulas, Gulas who had been my lover of more than a year. I couldn't believe he would do that to me. I thought he would have supported me.

'He never even came to visit. His brother did, and was

kind to me. But I needed to see Gulas again. And I also admit I needed more dwa. As you can see, I am not worth defending. If they execute me it will be well deserved. I left the Palace. I took more of the drug, and then went to find my Gulas. He wasn't pleased to see me. He called me foul names and said that my behaviour was threatening his position as Tree Priest and that if he'd known what manner of things I was involved in he would never have become entangled with me. He said that no person who had defiled the water of the Hesuni Tree with a foreign drug was worthy of living. And then he told me that he had never loved me and was pleased that I was in prison. I was still insane from the dwa, so I picked up a knife that was lying on the ground and I stabbed him. That is the whole story. Everything that is alleged against me is true. The best thing for everyone will be my death.'

A tear forms in her eye but she brushes it away and refuses to cry.

I've plenty of questions left, but Elith absolutely refuses to continue. 'I have nothing more to say, and no matter how many times you return I shall have nothing more to say. Please leave.'

I leave. I descend to the ground beneath the palace. A choir is singing nearby. Two jugglers walk past, practising as they go. Parrots squawk merrily overhead. Three actors in white cloaks appear from the trees, declaiming with vigour. Some Elvish children race by, laughing and screaming with glee at the sight of all the preparations for the festival, due to start in just two days' time. On Avula everything is beautiful.

I'm in the worst mood I can ever remember. I stare at the Hesuni Tree and when I think of the story I'm going

to have to tell my friend Vas-ar-Methet I develop the
urge to attack it myself for getting his daughter into such
trouble. Trouble, it seems, from which I will not be able to
extricate her.

I walk along the path till I reach the paddock where
I left my horse. I offer the groom a small coin, but he
declines it with distaste. Too late, I remember that Makri
told me it was calanith on Avula to offer money for care
of a horse. It makes my mood even worse.

I ride on for a while till I reach the end of the outward
path and turn left to circle the island. Just before the
junction a horseman appears in front of me with a sword
in his hand. I watch dumbly as he approaches. After the
experiences with the masked Elves, I'm half expecting
him to vanish into thin air. He doesn't. He keeps on coming.
Though he's hooded I have the impression that my assailant is Human rather than Elvish. I draw my sword. Fighting on horseback is not my speciality, but I had enough
experience in the army not to do anything foolish. As my
attacker reaches me he tries to sweep me to the ground
with a great clumsy blow that I parry easily. As he slides
past I turn and cut him in the back of the neck. He slumps
from his saddle, dead.

I stare at the corpse, puzzled. The whole affair lasted
only a few seconds. I pull back his hood, study the man's
bronzed face, look through his pockets for some identi-
fication, but I can find nothing. Just a mysterious horseman who tried to kill me, and wasn't very good at it.
He looks like any common thug from any city in the
west.

I ride off, leaving the corpse where it lies. Someone
else can sort out the formalities. I'm not far from where

Makri is training Isuas. I dismount before the clearing
and advance softly. Makri is in the centre of the clearing
facing Isuas and if she hasn't actually got round to killing her yet it sounds like it might not be far away. Her
face is grim and her voice is venomous.

'You stinking little Elf cusux,' she sneers. 'This is where
it ends. You wanted to try out my Orc blade? Here—'
Makri takes it from the scabbard at her back and tosses it
to Isuas, who catches it by the hilt and stands awkwardly
with the evil-looking black metal blade pointed at the
ground.

'Now I'm going to kill you,' says Makri, drawing her
second sword.

'What?' stammers Isuas, and starts to tremble.

'You heard, brat. I'm going to kill you. You think I'm
here because I'm a friend of the Elves?'

Makri spits in Isuas's face. Isuas shudders like she's
been touched by a plague carrier.

'Think again, cusux,' sneers Makri. 'My allegiance is
to the Orcish Lands. I was sent to wreak havoc on their
enemies and everything I've done since that day has been
for the sole purpose of spreading destruction on the Elvish
Isles. You will be the first to die. After I've set your head
up on a spike I'm going to gut your mother like the Elvish
pig she is and then I'm going to burn the Palace.'

Makri, now wearing a hideous expression of rage and
loathing, leaps forward. Isuas jumps backwards to avoid
the murderous blow.

I watch with interest. I have no fear of Makri killing
Isuas – if she'd meant to do that, she would have connected with the stroke – but I'm impressed with her performance. Young Isuas, innocent of the ways of the

wicked world outside her island, firmly believes that her head is about to be cut off and takes action to prevent it. She appears to forget how to be clumsy or weak or awkward, and actually parries Makri's blow and counters it with an assault of her own.

Makri, without appearing to fake it, starts trading thrusts with her young opponent, all the while continuing to taunt her with the foulest of insults, which further enrage Isuas so that she finally screams out the ancestral battle cry of her family and hurls herself upon Makri with a rain of blows that, though not delivered all that skilfully, are not lacking in spirit.

Makri traps Isuas's blade with the hilt of her own and flips it away. She delivers a cruel kick into the young Elf's midriff. Isuas crumples on to the grass.

'Die, cusux,' roars Makri, raising her blade. Isuas, shaking off the effects of the kick, rolls out of the way, leaps to her feet, picks up a fallen branch and actually flings herself at Makri in an attempt to batter her senseless. Makri catches hold of the Elf's wrist, puts the point of her sword at Isuas's neck and stares at her coldly. Isuas, unable to move, stares defiantly back at her.

'Orc pig cusux,' she says, and spits in Makri's face.

Makri nods meditatively, and grabs Isuas by the throat. Again displaying her surprising strength, she hoists her into the air with one hand and pulls her forward so that their noses almost touch.

'That's a little better,' says Makri, calmly. She lets go of Isuas and turns away.

Isuas, still not understanding what's going on, swiftly gathers up the Orc sword and leaps at Makri's retreating figure, at which Makri, displaying the sort of skill and precision that sometimes startles even me, whirls round and deflects the blow with the metal band she wears round her wrist. She knocks the sword from Isuas's grasp and again lifts her off the ground.

'Good,' she says to the discomfited Elf. 'Never hesitate to stab your opponent in the back. You're learning. You've got five minutes to rest.'

She tosses Isuas into a nearby bush then picks up her Orcish blade. I advance into the clearing.

'Nice going, Makri. If we are fortunate she might get over her hysterics some time next year.'

Makri shrugs. 'She's all right. Good progress in fact, by her standards anyway. What are you doing here?'

'I was just attacked by a mysterious mounted swordsman. Human rather than Elf. I had to kill him. Anything happened here?'

Makri shakes her head.

'It sounds like you're getting close to something, Thraxas.'

'Seems like it. For all the good it will do.'

I tell Makri that after talking to Elith there just doesn't seem any way out for her.

'She did it. End of case.'

'What now?'

'I guess I'll keep ferreting around. Maybe if I can take details of what's been going on to Lord Kalith he might show some mercy. After all, Elith was under the influence of dwa when she killed Gulas, and under a lot of stress.'

I'm not sounding very convincing here. I need a beer. Or maybe some good news. 'You know we can get fifty to one on her making it past the first round of the tournament?'

'Who from? She isn't officially entered yet, it's meant to be a secret.'

I inform Makri that I have been making discreet enquiries of the Elvish betting fraternity. 'Don't worry, I couched my enquiry in the most cautious terms. So, is it worth a bet?'

Makri shakes her head. 'No. Not yet anyway.'

I'm disappointed.

'Has it occurred to you,' says Makri, 'that I'm actually taking this training seriously? I have a reputation to protect, not to mention a gladiators' code to live up to. And all you're interested in is gambling.'

'Who wouldn't be at fifty to one? I've got to make a profit somewhere; the juggling contest is too close to call.'

Makri promises to let me know if Isuas makes it to the point where she's worth backing. I remind her that Gulas's funeral is to be held this evening near the Hesuni Tree.

'I've never heard you mention the gladiators' code before.'

'There wasn't one,' admits Makri. 'I made it up. I was just trying to remind you that fighting involves more important things than betting.'

'Okay, I'll believe you. You're the philosophy student. If you get her up to scratch, how much do you want to bet?'

'Everything I have,' says Makri. 'You can't turn your nose up at odds of fifty to one. That would just be foolish.'

The slightest of sounds makes us turn towards the trees. A green-cloaked masked and hooded Elf steps out with a sword in his hands. I sigh. I'm getting fed up with this.

'Is he going to disappear?' says Makri.

'Who knows? If he can't fight any better than the last one he might as well.'

I saunter forward, sword in hand, and am instantly beaten back by one of the most skilful and lethal assaults I've ever encountered. I'm forced to give ground immediately and am frankly relieved when Makri hurls herself into the fray and distracts our assailant's attention by attacking him from the flank. He parries her blade and even though I'm not slow to join in, again I can't find an opening. We trade blows for a while and though the superior forces of myself and Makri drive him backwards we can't succeed in landing a telling stroke. I've rarely seen the like of this warrior. Our assailant keeps us both at bay till, realising that he has encountered rather more than he bargained for, he spins round and sprints for the trees. We watch him go.

'Who was that?' demands Makri.

'I've no idea.'

'He was certainly one hell of a swordsman. This is some Elvish paradise. Do they treat all their guests like this?'

She turns to Isuas, who is still wide-eyed after witnessing the fight.

'You see what happens when you get caught unawares?'

Makri is actually so impressed with the Elf's skill that she forgets to be annoyed about not vanquishing her adversary and looks forward to meeting him again. I'll be happy if I don't. I depart, heading home for food, refreshment, some serious thinking and a long nap before the funeral of Gulas-ar-Thetos, late Chief Tree Priest of Avula.

CHAPTER
SEVENTEEN

It suddenly strikes me as odd that there was a knife lying conveniently on the ground for Elith to stab Gulas with. Why? Knives are valuable items. Elves don't leave them lying around for no reason. I puzzle about it for a while without making anything of it, and file it away for later.

I eat at Camith's house, but more thoughts crowd in to disturb me. Why did Gulas suddenly go so cold on Elith? Was he really outraged at her behaviour? Maybe. He might have felt obliged to be thoroughly respectable once made Tree Priest. But that's not really the impression I have of him. More the passionate young lover, and only a reluctant priest.

And how come everyone around the Hesuni Tree suddenly got caught up in a dope scandal anyway? Who started it? Who benefits? Was there enough profit in it to make it worth the risk? I get round to thinking about the branch of the family who covet the position of Tree Priest. Might they have been trying to discredit Gulas-ar-Thetos? It can't look too good for the Tree Priest if all of a sudden Elves are dropping like flies because they've been soaking their drugs with the water that feeds the sacred Tree.

None of this is going to help Elith, but it serves as a

distraction. I want to be distracted because after the funeral I'm going to have to make a report to Vas-ar-Methet and I don't want to think about that.

I visit the Turanian Sorcerers Harmon Half-Elf and Lanius Suncatcher. It takes me a while to persuade them to do what I want.

'Working any sort of spell at a funeral is calanith,' objects Harmon.

'Everything on this damn island is calanith.'

Harmon Half-Elf points out with some justification that if the Elves have many taboos, they have far fewer written laws than we do, and are a more peaceful society.

'Calanith works well for them. It keeps the wheels ticking over without the need for too much heavy-handed authority.'

'Spare me the lecture. I need someone to check out Gulas's body and it's way beyond my sorcerous powers.'

They both look puzzled.

'Check the Tree Priest for dwa? Wasn't Gulas the clean-living one?'

'So they say. I just want to check.'

'Surely Lord Kalith's Sorcerers will already have done so?'

'Who knows? If there is a Sorcerer's report on the body, no one's making it available to me, even though I'm working for the chief suspect.'

Lanius Suncatcher raises his eyebrows. 'Don't you mean "person who admits the crime"?'

'Okay, she admits it. But there are extenuating circumstances. I won't see her executed.'

I remind Harmon Half-Elf that I saved his life during the city-wide riots last summer.

'Not only that, I've saved the skins of more than one Turanian Sorcerer. If it wasn't for me, Astrath Triple Moon would be languishing in a cell in the Abode of Justice. And who hushed things up when Gorsius Starfinder got drunk in that brothel in Kushni? Who was it that cleared Tirini Snake Smiter when she was accused of stealing the Queen's tiara? The Sorcerers Guild owes me plenty. If I was ever to report what I know about the dubious dealings of Turai's Sorcerers to the proper authorities, half of the Guild would be in jail before sundown and the other half would be high-tailing it out of town. And I can feel an attack of public-spiritedness coming on.'

My powers of persuasion win the day, though Lanius comments that if I ever do suffer from such an attack of public-spiritedness, I'd do well to make sure I never leave my house without my spell-protection charm.

'Because I seem to remember that not long after Senator Orosius accused Tirini Snake Smiter of theft, he found himself on the wrong end of a bad attack of the plague.'

Harmon and Lanius agree to do what they can as long as they're sure they can manage it without being detected. I thank them, help myself to a bottle of wine, and we set off for the funeral.

I'm certain that Lord Kalith would much rather not have been obliged to hold a state funeral for his murdered Tree Priest while his island was so busy with visitors. Needs must, however, and there are an impressive number of important guests at the affair, not only Elves from Ven and Corinthal but others from further afield, along with representatives from all the Human Lands who were invited as guests to the festival. A very impressive gathering. As the Ossuni custom is that burial must take place within five days of death, and the Human Lands are all several weeks' sail from here, it is a rare occurrence for Humans to witness such an event.

My two sorcerous companions go off to join the official Turanian party at the front, leaving me to hunt for Makri round the fringes. I find her at the edge of the crowd, talking to three young Elves. Makri appears interested, but hesitant. Her posture reminds me of the few previous occasions in Turai when she has encountered Elves, particularly handsome young Elves. Makri claims never to have had a lover and has been wondering recently if something should be done about this. Unfortunately she regards almost all men in Twelve Seas as scum and thinks that Elves might be a far better option. I've noticed signs of attraction on their part as well, although the Orcish blood in Makri's veins does present something of a problem for them.

Makri would probably have faced this dilemma already were it not for the fact that when we arrived we were pretty much in disgrace with Lord Kalith and no Elf was keen to talk to us. Since then she's been busy with Isuas. Now, however, with Makri being in favour with Lady Yestar, it seems like the young Elves are plucking up their courage. Some of them are now of the opinion that they really should be paying more attention to the exotic creature currently walking around Avula displaying a confident charm plus a figure rarely seen on an Elvish maiden.

The three young Elves who face her certainly seem to be doing a good job of forgetting calanith, not to mention any admonitions their parents might have given them about being careful with the sort of girl you talk to at funerals. Makri – dark-skinned, dark-haired, dark-eyed and underdressed – seems to be casting a powerful attraction over them.

I'd be pleased to see Makri having a little fun. The woman does far too much studying. It's unhealthy. So I'm intending to walk off and leave them to it, but when Makri catches sight of me she mutters an abrupt goodbye to the Elves and hurries over. I tell her she needn't have bothered.

'Should've stayed with your admirers.'

Makri looks doubtful. 'You think they were admiring me?'

'Of course. Hardly surprising, in that tunic. Didn't it cross your mind to dress formally for the funeral?'

'I painted my toenails black.'

'So which young Elf takes your fancy?'

Makri blushes, and suddenly becomes tongue-tied. Having spent her youth hacking up opponents in the arena, she missed out on any romance and the whole subject still makes her uncomfortable. She tells me that three of the Elves each seemed to be hinting that if she would like to see some of the more beautiful, not to say secluded, parts of Avula, they would be pleased to take her.

'What do you do if three Elves all want to take you somewhere?' she asks, quite seriously. 'Do I have to pick a favourite right away?'

'I wouldn't have thought so. We're going to be on Avula for a while yet. You can play the field.'

Makri considers this. 'Is that good advice? Do you know about these things?'

I shake my head. 'Not really. I never had a relationship where the woman didn't leave in disgust. Several of them actually tried to kill me. My wife swore she'd hire an Assassin. Fortunately she was exaggerating, though she did did smash eighteen bottles of my finest ale before she departed.'

Makri sees that I am a poor person to ask for this sort of counsel, and wonders about talking to Lady Yestar.

'Except I think Yestar might not be too pleased with me. I forgot that Isuas would have to attend the funeral and I bloodied her nose and blacked her eyes and I don't think there was enough time for the healer to fix things properly.'

We crane our necks to see over the crowd, but the Elves are tall and we can see little except for a sea of green cloaks and tunics and a lot of long blond hair. Light cloud has blown in from the sea and the day is dull and slightly chilly. The crowd is quiet, as befits the sad occasion.

'Do you think I'd look good with blonde hair?' asks Makri.

'I've no idea.'

'It looks good on the Elves.'

'Maybe. But only whores have blonde hair in Turai.'

'That's not true,' objects Makri. 'Senator Lodius's daughter has bright golden hair, I saw her at the chariot races.'

'True. Blonde hair is sometimes affected by our aristo-cratic females. But no one is going to mistake you for an aristocrat with your red skin and pointy ears.'

'You think I should buy a dress when we get home?'

'Makri, what is this? I don't know anything about hair and dresses. I have enough trouble remembering to button up my tunic in the morning. Weren't you going to take notes about the funeral for your Guild College?'

'I am. Mental notes. I just wondered if maybe I should get a dress. You notice how Lady Yestar has that blue eye make-up and she kind of fades it into grey at the edges? How does she do that?'

'How the hell would I know? Is this all connected to those young Elves? They seemed to like you fine the way you are.'

'Do you think so? I thought they might be laughing at me. I noticed when I was talking about rhetoric their eyes were sort of glazing over. I think I might have been boring them. And when I said I was champion gladiator I wondered if they might think I was boasting. It probably put them right off.'

I glower at Makri.

'Excuse me, I'm going to go and investigate something.'

'What?'

'Anything.'

'But I need some advice.'

'Pick a favourite and club him over the head.'

I walk off, keen to make an escape. Any observer might reasonably have assumed that Makri was a confident woman. Why a bit of Elvish attention should reduce her to a babbling idiot is beyond me, but I can't take any more of it. I drift around the edges of the crowd, not paying much attention to the funeral oration or the Elvish singing. I notice Gorith-ar-Del. Like me, he seems to be skulking round the fringes of the crowd.

Someone snags me as I pass. It's Harmon Half-Elf. He bends over to whisper in my ear, trying and failing to look inconspicuous. 'I did the testing spell,' he whispers. 'A difficult procedure, without letting anyone notice.'

'And?'

'The Tree Priest's body was full of dwa,' he says.

Lanius Suncatcher is right behind Harmon. The pair of them look pleased with themselves. For all their protestations, I'd say they enjoyed the opportunity to act surreptitiously. Sorcerers generally like a bit of intrigue.

It's always gratifying when a hunch pays off. Elith said that Gulas abused her cruelly for using dwa. Yet there he was, enjoying it himself.

'How much dwa had he taken?'

'Difficult to judge. Enough to put him to sleep, I'd say.'

Strange. He wasn't sleeping when Elith stuck a knife in him. And somehow I doubt he'd be able to ingest much dwa after that. It would be good to know if my number one suspect, Gorith-ar-Del, has been in recent contact with dwa. Now that Harmon has used his spell he won't be able to do it again till he relearns it, so I ask Lanius if he also loaded in a suitable spell. He tells me he did. I discreetly point out Gorith.

'Could you use it to find out if that Elf has been in contact?'

'My spell is for using on a corpse. You never said you wanted a live person tested.'

'Can't you improvise?'

As an Investigating Sorcerer at the Abode of Justice, Lanius often encounters dwa, and must have had to adapt his spells before. He agrees to give it a try, and sidles off. Gorith-ar-Del pays him no heed as he walks up behind him. The spell might lower the temperature around them slightly, but on a cold day like today Gorith might not notice. Lanius concentrates for a second or two, then heads back towards us.

'Been in contact,' he says. 'Definitely.'

It's a damning piece of evidence against Gorith. I'm delighted to finally have confirmation that he's been involved in this business.

After the funeral I wait around, wondering what to do. I should go and report to Vas-ar-Methet, but I can't face telling him that his daughter really is a murderer. I'm standing aimlessly in the clearing when Makri appears.

'I'm in trouble,' she says. 'Lord Kalith was as angry as a Troll with a toothache about his daughter appearing at the funeral looking like she'd just fallen out of a tree. Which, fortunately, is what she had the presence of mind to tell him had happened. She's been banished to her room and forbidden to leave the Palace.'

'At least you won't have to spend the rest of the day teaching Isuas to fight.'

Makri shakes her head. 'She's still coming. She sent me a message saying she'll meet me at the clearing in thirty minutes.'

'Is she going to exit via a window and shin down a tree?'

'Something like that.'

I congratulate Makri on improving the child's spirit in such a short time.

'Possibly the first ever Elf child imbued with the – what was the word for insane Orc warrior?'

'Gaxeen. Yes, she's learning all right. Too much Gaxeen in fact. Now I have to show her the Way of the Sarazu.'

'Sarazu?'

'The Way of the Contemplative Warrior. It's a kind of meditative trance for fighting. Very peaceful. You must be at one with the earth, the sky, the water and your opponent.'

'And then you kill him?'

'Sort of,' says Makri. 'Although in the Way of the Sarazu, time doesn't exactly flow in a straight line.'

I shake my head. It doesn't take much of this sort of thing to confuse me.

'I liked the Way of the Gaxeen better. Good luck with the kid.'

Makri isn't listening. She's staring intently at the Hesuni Tree. This goes on for quite a long time. Finally she shakes her head and looks puzzled.

'You know, I could swear the tree was communicating with me.'

'What did it say? Anything interesting?'

'I'm not sure. I'm only partially Elf. But I thought it was saying you should stay around here for a while.'

'It was a message for me?'

I'm not too surprised. On an Elvish island it was bound to happen sooner or later. Makri departs. I take her advice and stick around, slinking into the shadows, where I can watch unseen. At least it will delay having to see Vas. I have a feeling that something is about to happen, though whether that's my investigation or Makri's suggestion I'm not sure.

Darkness falls. I've finished my wine. I've been puzzling over the significance of Gulas taking dwa. Elith swore he didn't. Something moves in the trees behind me. I sit up and listen, then crawl forward, careful not to make a sound. By the time I've advanced twenty yards or so I can make out two voices though I can't see anyone.

I sense some dwa dealing going on here. Lord Kalith is even more hopeless about policing his island than I'd realised. He doesn't seem to be making any effort at all to stop it. I rise to my feet and command my illuminated staff to burst into light, which it does, quite spectacularly. Two hooded Elves and one bare-headed man look round in surprise and at the sight of me with my sword in my hand they flee. I'm about to pursue them when another Elf steps out of the shadows. I whirl round and put my sword point at his throat.

'Well, well, Gorith-ar-Del. Sorry to interrupt you about your business. Not that you've been very discreet about it. In Turai you'd have been in jail a long time ago.'

Gorith is speechless with anger.

'I imagine Lord Kalith will be pleased to find out what you've been up to.'

Rather to my surprise, Lord Kalith chooses this moment to step out of the bushes.

'Lord Kalith desperately wishes that you had never come near Avula,' he says, frigidly. 'Congratulations on scaring off the dwa dealers. And would you mind telling me why you have been continually interfering with my agent Gorith-ar-Del in the conduct of his investigations?'

CHAPTER
EIGHTEEN

I'm picking moodily at my food. Camith, used to my hearty appetites, enquires solicitously if there is anything wrong with the fare. I tell him no, the food is excellent.

'But it was a poor day, investigation-wise. Elith-ir-Methet is guilty of murder and I have shown myself to be an irredeemable idiot.'

My number one suspect in the case turned out to be Lord Kalith's special agent with responsibility for sorting out the dwa problem on Avula.

'A job rendered considerably more difficult by your interference,' as Lord Kalith pointed out to me. He further informed me that, far from ignoring events, he was well aware of the problems his island faced, and had been trying to deal with them discreetly.

'Gorith-ar-Del has more than once been on the verge of eradicating the dwa problem, aided by my extremely able Sorcerer Jir-ar-Eth. In this they have been severely hampered by you blundering about, alarming everyone. Had it not been for you we would now have whoever is behind the importing of dwa safely behind bars.'

I doubt this very much. I defend myself, but without too much spirit. Kalith might be using me as a scapegoat, but I can't deny I've made something of a blunder in pursuing Gorith-ar-Del and quite probably alerting the suspicions of the dwa dealers.

Makri arrives home late. She's sympathetic.

'He didn't even seem to believe we'd been attacked. When I described the masked Elves with spears he strongly implied that they were a thazis-induced hallucination. Seemed quite upset about it in fact. I don't think Kalith really knows who's behind it all, but whoever it is, I'm withdrawing from the affair. I can't do any more.'

After the painful interview with Kalith I had to tell Vas-ar-Methet that his daughter was guilty as charged. A tree desecrator and a murderer.

'I'll put the mitigating circumstances to Kalith before the trial. It might do some good.'

Vas thanked me for my efforts, but his eyes had a haunted look I never saw in them before.

'Are you really withdrawing?' asks Makri. 'You never do that. Even when your client is guilty. And you've found out some odd things.'

I raise my hands hopelessly to heaven.

'What have I found out? Almost nothing. The Tree Priest was full of dwa when he died. Enough to put a man to sleep. Seems strange, but maybe Tree Priests can take a lot of dwa. Elith swore he didn't use it, but she'd lie to protect his reputation. And Elith found a knife where no knife should have been, but what of that, really? Maybe someone dropped it. The rest – the Tree desecration, the Elves acting strangely – can all be accounted for by dwa and hopeless romance. I'm nowhere on this. I've let Vas down.'

I make a late visit to the drinking den of the armourers. I drink a lot of beer, but it fails to raise my spirits. The armourers are cheerful at the prospect of several days away from their forges but still pessimistic about Avula's chances in the dramatic competition.

'I saw the Corinthalians rehearsing the scene where Queen Leeuven leads an assault on the Enchanter's tree fortress and it was nothing short of sensational,' reports a shield-maker. 'It had everything. Music. Drama. Excitement. Beautiful costumes. And as for their Queen Leeuven . . .' The Elf makes a comically lustful face which makes everyone laugh. 'I can't see the Avulan company coming up with anything to match that.'

No one has actually seen the Avulans rehearsing. It is all being carried out in great secrecy.

'No doubt to hide the extreme incompetence of Sofius-ar-Eth's production. What ever induced Lord Kalith to appoint that old Sorcerer as director is beyond me.'

The Sorcerer seems to have even less support than before.

'He should've stuck to his trade. Okay, I admit he protected us from that tidal wave six years ago. He's good with the weather. And he made a cloak of protection for Lord Kalith so fine that no blade has ever penetrated it. No one's denying he's an excellent Sorcerer. But direct a play? Pah!'

There is still no clear favourite for the juggling competition, although Shuthan-ir-Hemas is commonly thought to be out of contention. Firees-ar-Key is still hot favourite to win the under-fifteens tournament. No one has heard about Makri training Isuas. This at least is a relief. I'm still hopeful that I might pick up a few winnings.

Perhaps tactfully, the subject of Elith-ir-Methet is avoided. Her guilt is now firmly established, but no one wants to talk about it. Not to me, and not with so many visitors on the island.

Droo, the young poet, makes a late appearance. She's more cheerful than the last time I saw her, and she tells me that Lord Kalith has released Lithias from prison with a warning that if he ever touches dwa again he'll be banished from the island. Droo is grateful to me for getting her in to see Lithias in his cell.

'If I can ever do you a favour, let me know.'

'I will.'

She goes off to talk and argue with her fellow poets on the hill. I leave soon afterwards, taking with me a quantity of beer. Enough to get me through tomorrow, I hope, because I've no investigating to do and I've lost my appetite for Elvish holidaying. I wish I was back in Turai, cold as a frozen pixie or not. If Elith is executed straight after the festival, I'll still be on Avula. The prospect of seeing my client hanged puts me into a mood of bleak depression and no amount of beer will chase it away.

Next day I find myself wandering aimlessly. Everywhere there are crowds of happy Elves. Bad things may have happened on Avula, but their nightmares have gone and there is a festival to be enjoyed. Whole families gather in the clearings to watch the jugglers practising or listen to the choirs. The temperature rises a few degrees and the sun shines on the island.

'I hate this place,' I say to Cicerius.

'I have found it to be congenial,' replies the Deputy Consul.

We're standing in the shadow of the Tree Palace.

'You don't have a client facing execution.'

Cicerius looks pained. Before his duties as Deputy Consul

started to take up all his time, he was famed as a lawyer. He's the finest orator in Turai but he has very rarely used his powers of speech to get a person condemned. Despite being a bastion of the traditional elements in the city, his role in the courts has almost always been that of defender. He no more likes to see a man, woman or Elf go to the scaffold than I do.

For the first time ever, Cicerius seems to be lost for words. We stare at the Hesuni Tree.

'You did your best,' he says, eventually.

The festival officially starts tomorrow. The juggling will take place around noon and will be followed by the tournament. Next day it's the turn of the choirs and then there are three days of plays. Which means that this is Isuas's last day of training. Having nothing better to do, I call in at the clearing to watch. Makri and Isuas are sitting cross-legged on the grass, facing each other, eyes shut. Each has a sword on her lap. They sit motionless for a long time. The Way of the Sarazu, I presume. At least it doesn't seem to involve Isuas being beaten half to death.

Suddenly Isuas makes a move, grabbing for her sword. Before her fingers can even close on the hilt Makri lifts her weapon and brings it down with great violence on her pupil's head. Blood spurts from Isuas's forehead and she slumps forward on to the grass. Makri, still cross-legged, reaches forward, grabs Isuas's hair and hauls her upright. She slaps the young Elf's face three or four times till eventually Isuas regains consciousness.

'Poor technique,' says Makri. 'Get back in position.'

'I'm bleeding,' moans Isuas, wiping her forehead.

'Stop talking,' says Makri. 'And start meditating.'

Isuas, still groggy, forces herself back into position. They both close their eyes. I make a mental note never to take meditation lessons from Makri, and leave them to it. I walk back to Camith's, where I spend the rest of the day sitting staring out of the window till the sun goes down over the trees and the moons appear in the sky. I don't feel any better. As miserable as a Niojan whore would be the appropriate expression, I imagine.

CHAPTER
NINETEEN

On the first day of the festival Elves from all over Avula stream towards the tournament field. Singers and lute players serenade the crowds. Isuas is due to fight in the afternoon and Makri confesses to feeling tense.

'If she lets me down I'll kill her.'

She still won't say whether or not we should bet on her pupil.

'Wait till I see what the other fighters are like.'

After packing a spare wooden sword in a bag for Isuas, she complains about not being able to bring a real blade, but it's calanith to take weapons to the festival.

'Who knows what might happen at the tournament? If some of these fifteen-year-olds get out of hand we'll regret not having swords with us.'

Makri is still wearing the floppy pointed hat she got from Isuas. Only Elvish children wear them, but Makri likes it. She's painted her toenails gold and is wearing a short green tunic borrowed from Camith. Through her nose she has a new gold ring with a small jewel in it, borrowed from Camith's wife. All in all, it's a notable get-up and even though the Elves are getting used to her it doesn't prevent them from staring as we pass.

Some stands have been set up for the convenience of important guests such as Prince Dees-Akan, but the great mass of the audience just perches on the grass round the clearing, which, dipping slightly towards the centre, acts as a natural amphitheatre. Makri is politely accosted by one of the Elves who showed such an interest in her at the funeral. I slip away and look for Voluth the shield-maker, who has promised to introduce me to the local bookmaker. Whilst searching I meet the young poet Droo, who beams at me in a friendly manner and tells me I'm just the man she's been looking for.

'I want to do you a favour, large Human,' she says.

I frown. I thought she'd got over the 'large Human' bit.

'Okay, I could do with a favour. What is it?'

'Last night at the clearing I heard you talking about making a bet.'

I start to get more interested. I had feared that the favour might turn out to be a poem in my honour. Droo informs me that while it is a surprise to her that betting goes on at the festival, she thinks she might be able to give me a hint.

'What do you mean, a hint?'

'On a winner.'

'You mean a tip?'

'That's right. A tip.' Droo beams. 'Do you gamble much in Turai?'

'All the time.'

'And you get drunk?'

'Every minute I'm not gambling.'

Droo looks wistful.

'I wish I could visit a Human city. It sounds like fun. You know my father won't even let me smoke thazis? It's not fair.'

'You were saying something about a tip?'

'That's right. You should bet on Shuthan-ir-Hemas to win the juggling.'

I make a face. That's not much of a tip.

'What about her dwa addiction?'

'That's the point,' says Droo, brightly. 'She hasn't had any dwa for three days. I know, because she's been staying at Lithias's house since her parents kicked her out of the family tree. She says she's determined to make a new start and has renounced dwa and she's been practising her juggling like mad, and really, last night I saw her give a sensational performance when no one else was around. And I heard the armourers say how no one will be betting on her because everyone thinks she'll be useless. So won't that mean you get good odds?' Droo looks doubtful. 'Unless I've got that wrong. I don't really understand gambling.'

'No, you've got it exactly right. The odds on her will be high. You're sure she's going to put on a good performance?'

Droo is sure. I'm still not certain, because it takes a lot longer than three days to kick a dwa habit. Still, if she's determined to do well, it might be worth a wager. I thank Droo, and hurry off to find Voluth. I've got a bag of gurans plus some Elvish currency. Makri has entrusted me to place bets for her.

Voluth introduces me to a bookmaker who's situated himself in the hollow of a large tree just far enough from the clearing to avoid giving offence to Lord Kalith and the Council of Elders. The bookmaker – an elderly Elf, and a very wise-looking one at that – is offering twenty to one on Shuthan, with few takers. It's a bit of a risk, but at these odds I take it.

With so many of Avula's lower-class Elves in attendance, there is more than one stall selling beer, so I pick up
several flagons and hunt for Makri. I find her on a slight
hillock, a good position to view the event. Her Elvish
admirer is not that pleased to find me barging in, but he's
not making much progress with Makri anyway. She's too
preoccupied with Isuas's fate.

I inform Makri that I've bet on Shuthan-ir-Hemas.

'Bit of a risk, isn't it?'

'Good tip from Droo the poet.'

Makri is less confident, but too busy thinking about
the tournament to give me a hard time. Personally, I'm
starting to feel more alive. Things in the case of Elith-ir-
Methet may be disastrous, but any time I get round to
gambling I find my problems just fading away.

Singers and tumblers are strolling through the crowd
as the jugglers take the field. As this competition serves
merely to introduce the festival, and is not considered
to be on the same artistic plane as the later dramatic
events, it gets underway with very little ceremony. Jugglers,
mainly young, march into the centre of the arena and do
their act while the audience cheers on their favourites.
I'm impressed with the performances. I've seen a lot of this
sort of thing in Turai, but the Elves seem to have taken
the art further. Usath, the juggler whom we saw practising earlier, has the crowd roaring as she keeps seven balls
looping through the air, an incredible performance in my
opinion, though Makri professes herself to be uninterested.

'Wake me up when something cultural happens,' she
says.

Despite her protestations Makri is all attention when
Shuthan-ir-Hemas takes the field. We have a hefty bet on

this young Elf, although the opinion of the crowd is still that Shuthan will certainly trip over her own feet and embarrass the whole island.

Shuthan does exactly the opposite. She comes on in her bright yellow costume with a determined air, hopping and tumbling for all she's worth and, despite a shaky start and a little trouble with her early rhythm, she goes on to give a performance that thrills the audience. Great cheers go up when she equals Usath's tally of seven balls in the air at once and when she adds an eighth and keeps it going for a full minute the crowd are up on their feet shouting their approval.

No one is shouting louder than me. I rush to pick up my winnings. An excellent start to the festival. And it is at this moment, while I am re-energised by a substantial win, that it suddenly becomes clear to me what has been going on with regard to Elith-ir-Methet and the shocking murder of the Tree Priest. Two Elves, complaining about some early gambling losses, are saying to each other that Shuthan's unexpectedly good juggling has cost them the cloaks off their backs. I get to thinking about cloaks and it strikes me that firstly I may well be able to save Elith's life, and secondly I am still number one chariot when it comes to investigating.

I hurry back to Makri with our winnings. She's about to meet up with Isuas and accompany her to the field of combat. I wish her good luck.

'I'd still like to know if Isuas is worth a bet.'

Makri motions for me to go along with her. When we near the centre of the field where the combatants are gathering, Makri halts and points out one of the fighters to a nearby Elf.

'That one. How does he rate?'

'One of the best,' the Elf informs her. 'The under-fifteens champion of Corinthal.'

Makri takes the wooden sword from her bag, strides up to the Corinthalian youth and without warning makes a cut at him. The Corinthalian, taken by surprise, still manages to parry the blow. Makri backs away, leaving the young Elf looking puzzled.

'Bet your cloak on Isuas,' says Makri.

'What?'

'If he's one of the favourites, then bet everything we have on Isuas.'

I can't see how Makri can possibly have made such a judgement after only one stroke, but I trust her when it comes to fighting. I retrace my steps to the bookmaker's, stopping on the way to tell Osath the cook that, in the opinion of her esteemed trainer, Isuas stands not only an excellent chance of winning her first bout but will do well in the rest of the tournament. The cook and his companions are sceptical.

'Well, that's what Makri says, and when it comes to single combat she's an excellent judge.'

By this time the entrants for the tournament have been announced. I'm too far away from the field to see Lord Kalith's face when he learns for the first time that his youngest daughter has made a late entry into the lists, but I can imagine his surprise. I can foresee some heated domestic arguments in the near future between him and Lady Yestar, but what is done is done, and family honour will not allow him to withdraw his daughter once the announcement has been made.

I arrive back at the clearing with a slip of paper in my

pocket acknowledging that I have a large wager on Isuas at the excellent odds of five hundred to one to win the tournament outright, with another bet on her winning her first fight. Normally, for an event like this I'd have a large-scale plan of campaign worked out and I'd be betting on several of the contestants to cover myself, but I haven't really had time to organise such a strategy, nor the opportunity to study every entrant's form. I'll just have to cope with any emergencies as we go along.

There are sixty-four entrants, eight of them female. It's a straight knockout competition, so to win the tournament a fighter will have to defeat six opponents. The first bout is already under way. I watch with interest as the two young contestants engage rather tentatively with their wooden swords. The fighters are meant to hold back slightly and not deliver blows that might severely damage their opponent. An experienced Elf judges each fight. The first fighter to inflict what would be lethal damage, were a real weapon being used, is declared the winner. The spectacle takes place right in front of Lord Kalith and Lady Yestar, and I can tell from Kalith's face that he was not pleased to learn of his daughter's entry. Around me the crowd are still talking of little else, and the common opinion is that their ruler has lost his senses in inflicting such an ordeal on his notoriously weak daughter.

The first bout comes to an end when the fighter from Ven delivers a neat cut to the throat of the Avulan and the judge waves a small red flag indicating that the affair is over. The winner departs to generous applause. For all their fondness for poetry and trees, Elves are keen swordsmen, and appreciate any display of martial skills.

Makri and Isuas are sitting on the grass at the front. I use my body weight to force my way through till I'm close enough to lend assistance if necessary. Makri, lone bearer of Orcish blood in a huge crowd of Elves, might possibly find herself in some trouble if anything goes badly wrong. Isuas looks nervous but doesn't have long to wait. Her opponent is a fellow Avulan, a tall lad of fourteen who advances with a grin on his face that implies that he knows he has easy passage into the next round. He has a wooden sword in one hand and a wooden dagger in the other. From the way he holds them I can tell that he's thinking that while he had better not seriously damage the daughter of Lord Kalith, he isn't going to have to try too hard to defeat her. The crowd crane their necks in anticipation, but as it turns out there is little to see. Isuas's opponent makes a lazy attack and Isuas quickly and confidently parries the blow and runs her sword up his arm to his neck. The lad looks surprised, the judge holds up his red flag, and the fight is over. Isuas trots back to Makri an easy winner with the crowd wondering if Isuas just got lucky or whether her opponent let her win.

'Daughter of Lord Kalith or not,' says the Elf next to me, 'she won't get it so easy in the next round.'

I collect up my winnings, place another bet on Isuas for the next round, then cut through the crowd in the direction of Lady Yestar. I have some trouble reaching her and am obliged to elbow a few attendants out of the way. Yestar smiles as I arrive.

'An excellent victory. Who would have thought Makri could do so much in such a short time?'

Beside us Kalith is being congratulated by the Turanian

Ambassador. He acknowledges the compliment but he sounds like an Elf Lord who's suffered a severe shock. I lower my voice to a whisper.

'Lady Yestar, I need a favour. It concerns Elith-ir-Methet. And whoever is in charge of Lord Kalith's wardrobe . . .'

Lady Yestar leans forward, and listens to what I have to say.

The sixty-four entrants are whittled down to thirty-two. I see quite a lot of good fighters, and several excellent ones. Each island has sent their junior champions and the combat is of a very high standard. Best by far is Firees-ar-Key, the son of Yulis-ar-Key, finest warrior on Avula. Firees is large for his age and wouldn't look out of place on the battlefield. His first opponent is swept away in seconds and the crowd bays in appreciation. Firees is the firm favourite and is being offered at odds of just two to one, by no means a generous price in a competition of this nature.

The second round gets under way. Firees skilfully dispatches one of the favourites from Ven and another bright hope from Avula is defeated in a long struggle by a girl from Corinthal. The sun shines down on the arena and the watching Elves burst into applause each time they see a skilful manoeuvre. Makri sits quietly with Isuas, offering a few words of encouragement. Soon it's her turn again and there is some collective intaking of breath from the crowd when it is seen that her next opponent is Vardis, a youth of striking size from Ven who carries a wooden sword that appears to have been made from the branch of a particularly large tree. He towers over Isuas and looks like an Elf who does not intend to

show any mercy to his opponent, daughter of a Lord or
not.

He leaps at Isuas and beats her back with a series of
heavy blows. Isuas gives ground, retreating step after
step till it seems like she must soon run out of room.
However, as Vardis thrusts forward with a stroke that
would gut an ox, Isuas calmly takes the sword on the
edge of her dagger and uses Vardis's momentum to turn
him round, an advanced technique of which Makri is a
master. Vardis finds himself looking in the wrong direction
and Isuas wastes no time in stamping viciously on the
back of his leg, which brings him down on one knee. She
smashes her forearm into the back of his neck, sending
him slumping to the ground, and then runs her sword
over his back in a motion that, if performed with a real
weapon, would let daylight into his vital organs.

There is pandemonium in the crowd. The Avulans
cheer with delight and the Venians complain about the
brutal manner in which Isuas has won the fight. Nothing
she did was against the rules, however, and the judge
declares her the winner. Lord Kalith's mouth is hanging
open in shock. Beside him Lady Yestar has a broad smile,
and applauds along with the other dignitaries.

As the second round continues I consider what else
needs to be done, and go in search of Gorith-ar-Del. I find
him close to the bookmaker's.

'Making a bet?' I enquire politely.

'No.'

'You should. I've picked up a bundle. I'm starting to
enjoy life on Avula. And I'm soon going to enjoy it more.
After the tournament, I'm going to unmask the killer of
Gulas-ar-Thetos.'

'The killer is already known,' says Gorith.

'Wrong. The killer is not known. But if you want to be one of the first to know, stick close to me.'

Gorith tells me sharply that if I have any information regarding crime on Avula I should inform Lord Kalith immediately.

'It can wait till after the tournament. Makri's student is putting up a fine performance, don't you think?'

I return to the wise old Elf in charge of the book to relieve him of a little more cash. Osath is there, and he's mighty pleased with me. Despite Isuas's good showing so far, few other Elves are backing her and we still mange to get twenty to one on the third round. No one else can really believe that Isuas can possibly make any further progress.

Isuas, however, is making an excellent attempt. With Makri keeping her calm between bouts, she dispatches her next two opponents in a skilful if somewhat brutal manner. The trainer of a Corinthalian fighter actually complains in public to Lord Kalith after Isuas leaves him rolling round in agony with a series of wicked blows to the shins and ankles, followed by a sword pommel full in the face. The fighter from Corinthal has to be carried from the field and there are some fairly aghast expressions on the faces of the onlookers, the Corinthalian supporters howling their disapproval. Makri is unperturbed. Anything not actually illegal is fine in her eyes. The Avulans don't seem to mind either. They may be astonished at the sight of gentle young Isuas dealing out destruction on all sides, but they're with her all the way.

Isuas progresses without too much difficulty through

her next fight and is now in the final. I am reliably informed by those close to me that there has never been such excitement here before. It's unprecedented for a rank outsider like Isuas to make such a showing. As the final bout between Isuas and Firees-ar-Key approaches, the crowd is in a state of extreme animation. The only person still sitting is Lord Kalith, who remains motionless, unable to believe that the Orc woman has trained his daughter to fight like this in just over a week.

Firees himself has shown excellent form. In the semifinal he faced a youth from Ven who was favourite with many of the crowd and a fighter of unusual skill. The adroitness that Firees showed in overcoming him leaves the majority of Elves still certain that he must be the winner. The bookmaker has Firees as favourite at eight to eleven but is now only offering five to four on Isuas. I've already picked up plenty on Kalith's daughter and I back her again in the final, but I also bet against her to cover myself, which is the prudent thing to do in the circumstances.

Right now I'm about as happy as an Elf in a tree. In fact I'm happier than most of the Elves in the trees. Successful gambling and a solution to the mystery, all in one day. I shouldn't have succumbed to depression, really, but I don't blame myself. If you put a man in a strange land, deprive him of beer and give his client a really hard time, you can't expect him to remain cheerful in all circumstances.

The fighters walk out. The crowd bellows in anticipation. Lady Yestar has long ago abandoned all aristocratic reserve and is up on her feet cheering. The Council of Elders show every sign of equally enjoying the event.

I'd say that Kalith's daughter's performance can only raise his status with his subjects. Even our Turanian Prince, not well disposed towards Makri, cheers as Isuas, thin, puny but determined, raises her sword against the formidable Firees-ar-Key.

Both fighters make a cautious start. Having got this far, neither wishes to make a foolish mistake early on. Makri, who up till now has remained impassively on the sidelines, finally gives in to the tension and rises to her feet to yell encouragement to her pupil. Beside her is a man who, from the family resemblance, I take to be Yulis-ar-Key himself, the mighty warrior.

The fight quickly heats up, with Firees having slightly the best of it. He gradually forces Isuas back, always searching for an opening. Isuas defends stoutly, but at no time does she have the opportunity to attack. After several minutes of fighting I can see that if it goes on like this, Isuas will tire long before her stronger opponent.

Misfortune strikes. Isuas drops her dagger when she mistimes a parry and suddenly finds herself at a disadvantage. Firees senses victory and moves in with renewed vigour. He forces Isuas back to the edge of the crowd, but just as it seems that he must soon overwhelm her, something seems to go off inside the younger Elf and she abruptly mounts one of the most furious attacks ever seen on the tournament field. She flies at Firees with a fury that whips the crowd into a frenzy, a frenzy that becomes even greater when she lands a stroke on Firees's sword hilt, which causes him to drop his guard for a fraction of a second. In one fluid movement Isuas kicks him in the ribs, sending him flying backwards, and she takes the opportunity to quickly retrieve her dagger from the grass. The fighters again hurl themselves at each other. It seems to me that the fight has in fact got rather out of hand, though neither the judge nor the audience seems to mind.

The fighters tire, but neither of them loses spirit. No longer moving so freely, they stand facing each other, thrusting and parrying. Isuas looks close to exhaustion. Under a furious barrage of blows her legs start to give way. Firees rains blow after blow down on her till Isuas is on her knees. Finally Firees brings his sword down in a tremendous cut that shatters Isuas's sword. He tries to follow up, but Isuas twists her body to avoid the strike, leaps to her feet and sprints towards the stands. Firees, momentarily puzzled at her flight, sets off in pursuit.

The crowd, thinking that Isuas is fleeing the field, cheer and clap in anticipation of Firees's victory, but Isuas is not leaving. Rather she reaches the stands, grabs an elderly member of the Council of Elders by his tunic and hauls him off his chair. She then picks up the chair, whirls round and lands a crushing blow on the head of the advancing Firees-ar-Key. The chair splinters into tiny pieces. Firees is stunned. His arms drop to his sides.

'Die, cusux!' roars Isuas, then kicks him in the groin, stamps on his knee, and manages to chop him in the throat and claw his eyes as he falls unconscious to the ground.

For a second or two the only noise to be head is Makri whooping in triumph from the sidelines. Then chaos erupts in the crowd. Isuas has set new standards in foul play. She's destroyed her opponent by the use of practically every illegal tactic in the book, and she's roundly condemned for her tactics. On the other hand, no one can deny that she showed a lot of spirit.

Firees's father is outraged. He rushes on to the field and in his haste to reach his son he bats Isuas out of the way. Makri cries in protest and races after him. I'm already on my way, fearing the worst, but the next thing anyone knows Makri and Yulis are facing up to each other, wooden swords in hands, and trading blows. Fortunately the Elves in attendance bring it to a swift halt, rushing on to the field to drag them apart.

I keep close to Makri, who throws off the Elves who try to hold her, and pushes her way through to Isuas. When she reaches the young Elf she picks her up and hugs her.

'Well done,' she says.

Isuas looks happier than I've ever seen her. Neither she nor Makri seems at all concerned that she will be disqualified, and Firees proclaimed the winner.

'Who cares?' says Makri. 'He's unconscious and Isuas is still on her feet.'

Makri turns to me.

'You remember the Elf who attacked us in the clearing? It was him, the father, Yulis-ar-Key.'

'Are you sure?'

'Of course. As soon as we traded blows again I recognised his style.'

Lady Yestar appears, smiling broadly. She sweeps Isuas up in her arms and congratulates her.

'I'll see you both at the reception at the Palace,' she says to us, before taking Isuas off to have her cuts and bruises treated by a healer.

The whole day has been so exciting that it only now

strikes me that Isuas's disqualification has cost me a great deal of money.

'A shame,' agrees Makri. 'But it had to be done. Did we win anything?'

'Sure. I bet on her for the previous five fights. We won plenty. I'm back on top form. When we get to the Tree Palace, I'm going to unmask a murderer.

CHAPTER
TWENTY

Lord Kalith hosts a post-tournament reception at the Tree Palace. As the attendants open the doors for us, Makri receives plenty of congratulations for her success with Isuas. I'm not really surprised. Isuas might have been disqualified, but the Elves can tell a good fighter when they see one. When the next Orc War happens along, no one will care about fighting fairly.

The Palace is full of dignitaries. I see Lord Lisith-ar-Moh, who previously encountered Makri in Turai, congratulating Kalith.

'It was clever of you to hire her to train your daughter.'

'Indeed,' replies Kalith weakly.

Lady Yestar seeks us out.

'How is he taking it?' I ask, indicating her husband.

'Still getting used to it. The incident with the chair was a terrible shock. And no Elvish father likes to hear his daughter using Orcish oaths. But he is pleased, really. He used to worry terribly about Isuas's weakness.'

'He won't have to do that any more.'

Lady Yestar knows I'm not here to make polite conversation. I ask her if she can arrange for me to speak privately with Lord Kalith. A few minutes later Makri and I find ourselves ushered through a door on to a secluded balcony that overlooks the pools by the Hesuni Tree.

'What is it that is so important?'

'Elith-ir-Methet is innocent.'

Kalith's eyes gleam with annoyance. 'I have told you already—'

I interrupt him, rudely. 'You can hear it first or you can hear it after I tell everyone else. Either way is fine with me.'

'Very well, Investigator.'

'Elith became addicted to dwa. It made her crazy, as you know. But she didn't damage the Tree and she didn't kill Gulas. Both crimes were committed by Lasas, Gulas's brother. He damaged the tree to discredit Gulas because he was insanely jealous of his brother's relationship with Elith. He loved her too, unfortunately. When you threw Elith in prison, Lasas spread it around that it was Gulas who accused her, which wasn't true. Lasas had done the accusing after he found Elith conveniently unconscious at the scene of the crime. I don't know if that was just lucky for Lasas, or if he saw to it that she had plenty of dwa at just the right moment. Either way, he harmed the Tree and made sure she took the blame. But that wasn't the worst. He encouraged Elith to leave her confinement and confront Gulas, but Gulas was dead by the time she got there. Lasas drugged him and stabbed him. If you want proof, I've two Sorcerers who will testify that the priest was so full of dwa before he died he couldn't have stood up, let alone talked.'

'This is insane,' protests Kalith.

'Not at all. I'm giving you a precise account of what happened, which I would have been able to do much earlier had you not obstructed me at every turn. When Elith arrived at the Hesuni Tree, Gulas was already dead in the bushes. Lasas then did something very cunning. He put on a hooded cloak and pretended to be Gulas, which wasn't too difficult, given that Elith was again full of dwa, and only barely in touch with reality. He tormented her till she couldn't take it any more. She picked up the knife that Lasas had left for her and lashed out at him. I don't know if her stroke would have been lethal or not, but it didn't matter. Lasas had taken the precaution of stealing one of your excellent cloaks of protection from the Tree Palace. A cloak that will turn any blade. And, as proof of that, I've already checked with your wardrobe attendant. He confirms that one of the protection cloaks that Sofius-ar-Eth made for you is missing. Lasas then crawled off into the bushes, hid the cloak, and pretended to arrive at the scene of the crime along with everyone else. Including Elves who had seen Elith stab Gulas, or so they thought.

'Which makes Elith innocent of all crimes. I admit she might be held to have attempted to murder someone, but that someone was dead long before she got there. Lasas, however, is about as guilty as an Elf can get. He damaged the Tree to discredit his brother and then he killed his brother through rage and jealousy and tried to pin the crime on the woman who had spurned him. I suggest you lock him up as soon as possible.'

Lord Kalith is doubtful.

'I believe it to be true,' says Gorith-ar-Del, stepping forward. 'At the very least, we should subject Lasas-ar-Thetos to some stringent interrogation and have our Sorcerers investigate him in the greatest detail.'

'Are you telling me that my new Tree Priest is the one behind all my recent troubles? Did he initiate the importing of dwa on to Avula?'

'Interestingly enough, he didn't,' I reply. 'While he was busy trying to discredit his brother, the rival branch of the Tree Priest's family was trying to discredit them both. They brought it in to start a scandal around the Hesuni Tree. I imagine they hoped that once it was known that Gulas couldn't prevent the sacred Tree from being besmirched and abused, their claim to the Priesthood would be taken more seriously.'

'Do you have any proof of this allegation?'

'Not exactly. But ever since I started digging into the affair I've been under attack from various persons. Some of them were Human, probably sailors who've called here on the pretext of trade. but one of them was a very fine Elvish swordsman. Best swordsman on Avula in fact. Yulis-ar-Key. He was masked, but Makri recognises his style.'

Makri, quiet up till this moment, confirms this. Kalith considers my words.

'Yulis is head of the branch of the family who contest the Tree Priesthood,' I point out. 'I think you'll find it all adds up.'

'Have them brought to me—' commands Kalith, but that's as far as he gets. No one has noticed the appearance of Yulis-ar-Key on the balcony. We soon notice that, while we are all without weapons, Yulis has somehow managed to procure two fine swords, which he brandishes menacingly.

'I will not be subjected to sorcerous examination like a common criminal,' he snarls.

'Why not?' I retort. 'It would be entirely fitting.'

Yulis rushes at us. Things look bad till Makri steps into his path. Yulis brings each sword down at her. Almost quicker than the eye can see, Makri raises her arms, deflecting each blade with her metal wristbands. She then steps in and butts Yulis with her head. Yulis howls and drops his swords. As he goes down he grabs Makri by the leg and they crash through the thin fence at the edge of the balcony. They plunge over the edge into the pool, far below.

We stare over the edge. Elves are already running from all directions towards the water.

'She can't swim,' I yell. There are some tense moments before Makri is hauled out out by her rescuers. Moments later, Yulis struggles out of the pool and is immediately apprehended.

Lord Kalith looks down at the scene below. He frowns, and utters an Elvish oath.

'Did she have to fall right into the sacred pool?' he says. 'I just had it ritually cleansed.'

Two days later I'm lounging on the grass in the large clearing, feeling satisfied. The plays have commenced. As I expected, I'm finding them a little highbrow for my tastes but I've a plentiful supply of beer and a fine reputation as an Investigator. Number one chariot, and no one can deny it. Elith is out of jail. It couldn't be said that her name is exactly cleared. After all, she did go wild under the influence of dwa, and she did make an attempt on the life of an Elf she believed to be Gulas. But there are plenty of mitigating circumstances. Besides, whatever she might have meant to do, she didn't actually kill any-one, and is innocent in the eyes of the law. Vas-ar-Methet has taken her home and has high hopes of rehabilitating her with his healing powers and the love of his family.

Yulis and Lasas are in prison. Both branches of the priestly family are now in disgrace. Lord Kalith will have some serious thinking to do before he makes a new appointment, but it can wait till after the festival, when the island is empty of visitors. Cicerius has expressed his satisfaction at the services I've performed on the island, and Kalith is too fair-minded not to be grateful.

Makri is now something of an Avulan hero, and not only for her amazing results with Isuas. The story of how she defeated the finest swordsman on the island without the aid of a weapon has been the talk of the festival. Isuas wishes to learn how to head-butt her opponents, and Droo has already composed several poems about the affair. She has also composed one about my investigating triumph, which she brought to my house.

'Droo likes you,' says Makri. 'Strange, I never saw you as a father figure to disaffected young Elves.'

'Very funny. Is anything ever going to happen in this play?'

I'm bored with the drama. The Avulan version of the tale of Queen Leeuven is not stirring. Makri tells me that I'm missing the finer artistic points, but I long for something exciting to happen. I'm starting to agree with the Elves who regarded Sofius-ar-Eth as a poor choice of director.

'I'm puzzled about something,' says Makri, sipping beer. 'Who were those masked Elves who kept chasing us round?'

'I don't know. I'm puzzled myself. Part of the gang, I suppose, though they don't seem to fit in.'

In front of us, Queen Leeuven is rallying her army. Suddenly, from nowhere, a huge crowd of spear-wielding villains appear on stage, march around for a few seconds, then disappear again. The crowd gasps. The masked Elves appear again and there is some frantic dramatic fighting as Queen Leeuven's supporters battle with the spearmen, who magically vanish, only to reappear at the other side of the stage.

The crowd go wild, clapping and cheering at this new dramatic innovation.

'Right,' says Makri.

'Indeed. They were part of the play.'

'That must be why Kalith appointed a Sorcerer as his director.'

'He was trying to beef up the production.'

We stare at proceedings. I'm feeling a little foolish. All the time I thought they were after us they were just rehearsing for the festival.

'It's low culture,' objects Makri. 'Cheap stage effects detract from the drama.'

'I like it. But when I get back to Turai, I'm leaving this bit out of the story.'

THRAXAS

Martin Scott

In the magical city of Turai, murder, mayhem and ruthless criminal brotherhoods are rife. The only people more corrupt than the politicians are the Royal Family. And the weather is awful.

It's down these mean, muddy streets that Thraxas, ex-soldier, failed Sorcerer and epic drinker, ekes out a living as a Private Investigator.

But when Princess Du-Akai, third in line to the throne, asks him to investigate a very delicate matter, it seems that his luck is about to change. And it does. A few hours later, he's in jail accused of murder.

Thraxas is a new star of comic fantasy. A man of extraordinary courage, legendary strength and nerves of steel he isn't, but his unique charm and very well-hidden talents are destined to make him one of the best-loved characters in fantasy fiction.

THRAXAS AND THE
WARRIOR MONKS

Martin Scott

It's summer in the magical city of Turai and it's hotter
than Orcish hell. All that Thraxas, third-rate sorcerer,
second-rate private investigator and first-rate layabout,
is looking for is a bit of peace and quiet. But when one
of his clients is arrested in his office for murder,
even Thraxas has to act.

It should be a simple enough case. So why do rival
bands of warrior monks keep turning up? And how did
a life-size bronze statue of Saint Quatinius disappear
into thin air? And what's all this got to do with the
dolphins and their lost healing stone?

Before long, Thraxas and his friends find themselves at
the heart of another incredible case of sorcerous
skullduggery and magical mayhem.

Orbit titles available by post:

☐ Thraxas	Martin Scott	£5.99
☐ Thraxas and the Warrior Monks	Martin Scott	£5.99
☐ Thraxas at the Races	Martin Scott	£5.99
☐ Thraxas and the Sorcerers	Martin Scott	£5.99

The prices shown above are correct at time of going to press. However, the publishers reserve the right to increase prices on covers from those previously advertised, without further notice.

orbit

ORBIT BOOKS
Cash Sales Department, P.O. Box 11, Falmouth, Cornwall, TR10 9EN
Tel: +44 (0) 1326 569777, Fax: +44 (0) 1326 569555
Email: books@barni.avel.co.uk

POST AND PACKING:
Payments can be made as follows: cheque, postal order (payable to Orbit Books) or by credit cards. Do not send cash or currency.

U.K. Orders under £10	£1.50
U.K. Orders over £10	**FREE OF CHARGE**
E.C. & Overseas	25% of order value

Name (Block letters) ....

Address ....

....

Post/zip code: ....

☐ Please keep me in touch with future Orbit publications

☐ I enclose my remittance £ .

☐ I wish to pay by Visa/Access/Mastercard/Eurocard

Card Expiry Date
